City of Vultures

a&b

City of Vultures

(A Johnny Ace Mystery)

RON ELLIS

This edition first published in Great Britain in 2004 by
Allison & Busby Limited
Bon Marché Centre
241-251 Ferndale Road
London SW9 8BJ
http://www.allisonandbusby.com

A catalogue record for this book is available from
the British Library.

10 9 8 7 6 5 4 3 2 1

ISBN 0 7490 8361 1

Printed and bound in Great Britain by
Creative Print + Design, Ebbw Vale

It was the summer of 2003 and Liverpool had hit the jackpot. European City of Culture 2008. Five years to go but the party had already begun.

Rows of warehouses, that in the Sixties had housed discos and nightclubs echoing to the sounds of Merseybeat bands, were being razed to the ground to be replaced by endless blocks of luxury apartments. Property prices were said to have risen twenty per cent within two weeks of the announcement.

Britain's richest man, Gerald Grosvenor, Duke of Westminster, was planning a giant £700m shopping complex to outshine Manchester's Trafford Centre, stretching from the city centre to the Pier Head.

Will Alsop's controversial modern building 'The Cloud', had won the contest to be the Fourth Grace to be built alongside the Liver Buildings, The Port of Liverpool and the Cunard Building, on the most famous coastline in Europe. One critic described it as 'a wigwam designed on speed' whilst another likened it to a bouncy castle. Some people just don't appreciate Post Modernist irony.

On the Kings Dock beside the Mersey, people packed into the giant Summer Pops marquee, night after long sultry night, to see international stars like James Brown, Paul McCartney, The Beach Boys and, the hottest ticket in town, Bolton comedian Peter Kay.

And, after years in the wilderness, Everton seemed to be on their way back to the top of English football under manager David Moyes. With teenage prodigy Wayne Rooney in the side, England's finest prospect since Dixie Dean, skies were no longer grey over Goodison Park.

One man didn't share in the celebrations. His name was Stewart Davis and he was a vagrant.

He slept in doorways at night in areas that were not yet

part of the city's resurgence, run-down streets like Breck Road, Hawthorn Road and Kensington, which once bustled with life but now boasted shuttered shops, derelict pubs, vandalised cars and persistent graffiti.

An unemployed teenager, on his way home from the Lomax at three in the morning, found Davis slumped in a doorway in Picton Road opposite the old Green Lane tram sheds.

His head was lying several yards away in the gutter.

When the police eventually arrived, they searched his pockets in an effort to establish his identity but all they found was a crumpled business card bearing the inscription 'Johnny Ace Investigations'.

Which was when they came looking for me.

I'd been back in Liverpool just a couple of months from my extended sojourn on the Costa Blanca. Things had changed while I'd been away. Most importantly, my old partner, Jim Burroughs, had retired and I'd taken on a new assistant in the agency.

Jim had not only handled most of the paperwork and manned the office but also, being an ex-DI in Merseyside Police, he'd kept his contacts in the Force, which had come in very useful on the investigation side. Now, though, most of his old colleagues had either moved on or retired themselves.

I'd advertised the job in the *Echo* without knowing quite the sort of person I wanted and I was surprised at the number of replies I received. I guess the idea of working in a detective agency carries a certain aura of glamour to some people. If only they knew.

Most of the applicants were in 'security', which usually means they work the doors on the clubs. A few were ex-cops, some were school-leavers who were just as likely to have approached Radio City wanting to be DJ's, and several were desperate redundant 50-year-olds yet to see the fruits of the government's promised policy on anti-ageism.

Not many were from women.

I picked out four of the most promising letters and arranged for the people to come in for an interview at the end of the week. The first in line was a Cameron Morgan, a 25-year-old psychology graduate whose CV boasted he was proficient in IT skills and held a black belt in judo.

Seemed reasonable qualifications for a guy wanting to become the next Philip Marlowe. Maybe 25 was a bit young but at least he wouldn't be on the waiting list for a Stannah Stair Lift.

Friday came and I was in the office sorting through the

post as I waited for him to arrive when I heard the tap of stilettos on the stairs. Roly, on his usual blanket beneath the desk, gave a low growl.

The door opened and in stepped a girl in designer flares and an alarmingly small bandana top. She had flaming red hair hanging to her shoulders, which contrasted with her coffee coloured skin, and she would still have been six feet tall without the heels. A Calvin Klein thong displayed its label above her jeans as she turned to close the door behind her.

I didn't reckon her as a prospective client. For a start, she didn't look the victim type.

'Hi,' she said. 'Are you Johnny Ace?'

I nodded. More likely, I figured, she was selling advertising. Either that or she'd mistaken the place for a model agency.

'I've come about the job. I'm Cameron Morgan.'

My fault of course. I should have guessed Cameron could be a woman's name. Think Cameron Diaz. Mind you, anything can be a woman's name nowadays, even a football club. Ask Bill Clinton.

'You didn't mention in your letter that you were a girl.'

'I didn't mention I was a Buddhist either. Would it have made a difference?

I said I guessed it wouldn't. In these ridiculous times of political correctness, of course, you can't object to anything. Not when the government can talk of banning smoking in the home and the Lib-Dems want to forbid you for smacking your own children, even George Orwell wouldn't believe how far things have gone.

She took a chair without asking, sat down facing me and smiled confidently. 'What does the job involve then?'

I tried to explain but it wasn't easy. 'Checking databases, searching for people, chasing up debts, dealing with callers at the office, sending out invoices, maybe some driving...'

'Anything dangerous?'

I thought of the times Jim Burroughs and I had been attacked, shot at or nearly run down in the course of duty not to mention the odd close-up glimpses of the graveyard.

'No, nothing like that. At least, not often.'

'I don't mind. I like a good scrap now and then.' She leaned down to stroke Roly who had leaned across to sniff at her feet. 'A lurcher isn't he?'

'Part deerhound, part lurcher. I got landed with him on a case a while back and he's been around ever since.'

'I thought detectives had bloodhounds.'

'No, most detectives I know have lurchers.'

'Who else works here?'

'Just me.'

I also have a property business, several flats around the city that I rent out but most of that is handled by my manager, Geoffrey Molloy, from an office in Aigburth.

'Sounds boss to me. When do you want me to start?'

'Hang on a minute, I have other people to see.'

But there was no competition. Of the other three applicants due that day, only two turned up. One was a bovine creature who worked for Group Four and acted like he's been hit too many times without his protective helmet on. The other was a pot-bellied man who said he was only forty-six but judging by the way he was panting after climbing the one flight of stairs up to my office, he looked like a regular in the Pensioners Portions queue at the nearest Beefeater.

Cameron started the following week. Since I got back, I'd converted the outer office into a reception area and I installed her in there with her own PC leaving Roly and myself in the inner sanctum.

We'd worked out a pay structure similar to the one I had with Jim Burroughs. A fifty-fifty split of the profits.

'Does that make me an equal partner?' she asked.

'No, it makes me the boss and I give the orders but as you put in an equal amount of time, you get half the money'

'Sweet.'

I didn't mention that, at quiet periods, she'd probably earn more welding X-type Jaguars down at Halewood.

'What do I call you for short?' I asked. Cameron was a bit of a mouthful and Cami had connotations of an Ann Summers catalogue.

'Try Ronni without the 'e'.'

'Ronni it is.'

'What do I call you? Guv'nor?'

I shuddered. 'Certainly not. Johnny will do fine.'

'I listen to your show sometimes,' she told me as she settled down to sort out the backlog of paperwork. As I'd been away a long time, over a year, things had rather piled up. 'You play some really random records.'

I host an hour's phone-in show every night on local radio between six and seven. I mostly play records that I actually like instead of somebody else's computer playlist, records you rarely hear on radio. Really, I'd been lucky to get the show back after my long absence but my replacement, Shady Spencer, hadn't been an overwhelming success in the slot. All you could expect really from someone who thinks Fame Academy is a female road worker from Inverness.

'I have some really strange listeners,' I replied.

'Who's the weird guy they used to have on? The one with the James Last hang-up. He was gross.'

'You mean Shady Spencer?'

'That's the one. All he played was records for flintstones.'

'Who?'

'Flintstones. You know, old people.'

This girl's vocabulary needed a dictionary to itself. Conversing with her was almost as bad as trying to make Americans understand English. And vice versa.

'Not many DJ's play an Elmore James record after Atomic Kitten like you do,' she continued. 'That's really cool.'

'Atomic Kitten are today's Shangri-las,' I explained, surprised she'd ever heard of the long-dead Chicago blues man, 'it's just the backings that have changed. Imagine *Whole Again* with *Moonlight Sonata* playing in the background.'

'Or Destiny's Child's *Independent Woman* over *Air on a G-String?*'

I guessed Cameron was going to be fun to work with, despite the potential language problem. Her appreciation of music went beyond Jim Burroughs' limited knowledge of early R'n'B, gained from the days when he first played bass with The Chocolate Lavatory back in the Sixties.

Jim still does occasional charity gigs for the Merseycats. The band reformed a few years ago with the same line-up of forty years ago albeit with less hair, larger stomachs not to mention a few replacement body parts. They also play much the same material but those halcyon days of Merseybeat are now as much part of the past as Flappers, Bessie Smith and the Charleston. The Roaring Twenties? The Swinging Sixties? They're history.

'You're right. So what are the cases we're working on at the moment?'

'None. I've been over in Spain these last few months. I was running the agency with an ex-cop called Jim Burroughs but he retired while I was away so I'm just starting the business up again.

'How do we get new clients?'

'I've put an ad in the *Echo*, bought some space in Yellow Pages and put the word around some of Jim's old pals in the Force in case they have something they can pass on to us. Word will soon get around town that I'm back in business. Liverpool is like a big village.'

The village grapevine didn't take long. The very next day,

Cameron buzzed through to the office.

'There's a zany out here to see you. Says his name is Lucky Learoyd.' She sounded uncertain. 'I think he's in dame gear,' she added in a barely concealed whisper, 'you know, pantomime, fancy dress.'

It was a name I hadn't heard for a while. Lucky Learoyd was a vocalist who had never made the big time but who earned a passable living playing the cruise ships, the odd summer season in a faded English resort and the many social clubs and hotels around Merseyside.

Our paths had crossed occasionally over the years. In the late Seventies, when I was just finishing my earlier career as drummer for The Cruzads, Lucky was starting out and we'd been on the same bill a couple of times. He'd always been renowned for his flamboyant attire.

'He's an entertainer,' I pointed out. 'It's his job to be noticed. Show him in.'

Lucky strode in buoyantly. He was dressed in a curious lime green suit that looked a size too large for his thin frame and clashed dramatically with a yellow tie and orange shirt. His Adams apple protruded above the tie.

'You've branched out, Johnny. Nice to see you're doing well. Couldn't happen to a nicer fellow.' He paused for breath long enough to shake my hand.

'You're still singing on the circuit then?' I said.

'Certainly am, Johnny, and doing better than ever.'

It was a familiar story. Lucky went in for the big ballad style, which has always been popular in the clubs, probably because the audience know most of the words and like to sing along.

'I'll tell you why I'm doing well. When I'm performing, they're listening to themselves not to me which can be a good thing if I'm having an off night.'

Recently, though, he'd found a way to double his fee.

'I used to do three or four PJ Proby numbers in the act,' he told me, 'and they always went down well, so I decided I'd do a full set of his hits, wear a fake pony tail and tight velvet trousers and go out as a tribute act.'

'Don't tell me, you split your pants every night?'

'You've got it. What would we do without Velcro, eh?'

'So what do you call yourself? PJ Probably?' There had once been a TV documentary of that name.

'No, nothing so fancy. They bill me the way they do all the others, you know, "LUCKY LEAROYD IS" in tiny print then "PJ PROBY" in bloody great capitals. This is the best thing I ever did, Johnny. I've hit paydirt at last I do practically the same act as before but get twice the money for it.'

The tribute act is something I'll never understand. If I like Dolly Parton, I want to see Dolly Parton, not some pneumatic, siliconed Oldham housewife trying to imitate her. Similarly, as Robbie Williams is still alive, why pay to see someone else sing his songs when I can see the man himself?

It never used to happen in the days when Woolworths put out cut-price copies of hits sung by unknown artists on their Embassy label. Not one of them ever made the charts. The public were wiser then. Now, of course, some of those records are worth a fortune especially as we know that people like Elton John and Gary Glitter were just two of the 'unknowns' that appeared on Embassy under various guises.

I suppose the answer is money. You can't afford the real *Mona Lisa* in your living room so you buy a framed print instead. So what? Same picture. "Lucky who?" Doesn't matter. Same songs.

Yet tribute bands are enormously popular everywhere, even in Las Vegas, so who am I to judge? And I had to admit that Lucky had found a gap in the market. There are dozens of Rod Stewart and Tom Jones look-alikes about, and a million Elvis clones, but I'd never heard of anyone impersonating

Proby.

The Texan had been a major star in the Sixties, with a distinctive style that was easy to parody. Furthermore, the old boy was still touring today on the oldies circuit, which kept his name in the public eye.

'Who does your backing tapes?'

'Fellow who has a studio behind this greasy spoon in Garston called Monty's Caff and he's good. He has this keyboard that duplicates every sound imaginable on it, choirs, orchestras, the lot. You couldn't tell it wasn't the Philharmonic bloody Orchestra playing on some of the tracks he does.'

'I know Monty's. They do a great bacon sandwich.'

'And, of course, I don't have to pay a band to back me either and I've got my own CD that I sell on gigs. In fact, Johnny, I was going to ask you if you'd play a couple of numbers from it on your show sometime.'

Technology has certainly done wonders in the last few years for musicians like Lucky. Making a CD costs peanuts and you can run off as many copies as you want at home on your PC, not to mention print labels and sleeves, just as good as the product the majors put out that would pass muster in any record shop. Every group and singer can now be his or her own record company.

It's the distribution that lets them down.

'I'll certainly listen to it,' I said cautiously.

'I'm doing a video next, to send out to agents instead of doing those bloody auditions and showcases. I tell you, Johnny, I may be coming up forty but I'll make the big time yet.'

Coming up fifty would be more like it, I thought, but we people in show business are allowed some latitude and the Grecian 2000 looked like it was doing its job well, not to mention the botox. 'So what are you doing here then, Lucky?'

His face fell. 'I'm in a bit of trouble and someone told me you'd started up as a sort of detective.' I winced at the description. The ads couldn't be having the desired effect. 'Have a look at this.' He pulled a sheet of paper from his jacket pocket and handed it to me.

The message written in red thick felt tip pen, in block capitals, was stark and to the point. KEEP OUT OF LIVERPOOL OR WE WILL KILL YOU.

'I haven't an enemy in the world,' he assured me.

'You could be wrong there, Lucky,' I said, reading the note a second time without being able to find a different interpretation. 'I'd hardly call this a fan letter.'

'No, I mean it. I can't think of anything I've done to upset anyone. I've not shagged anyone's wife, never cheated anyone out of money...'

'What about rival acts, jealous of your success?'

'Bollocks. Nobody's going to kill for that. There's enough work around for God's sake.'

Of course, people have killed crippled pensioners in their own homes for twenty pence or less but I thought it better not to appraise Lucky of the fact.

'I might be doing well,' he continued, 'but I'm hardly in the Des O'Connor league.'

Hardly in the PJ Proby league either and despite being a quarter of a century younger than the American, he never would be.

'How did you receive this?'

'It was pushed through my letterbox during the night. I noticed it on the hall floor the next morning.'

'And is this the only letter you've had?'

'Yes but then I had a phone call. Last night. That's why I've come to you today, Johnny. I'm a bit scared.'

'What did they say?'

'Same thing. It was a someone with a deep voice. They said

"Remember. Keep out of Liverpool if you want to live". Then they rang off. I dialled 1471 but it was a payphone. I took the number.'

He'd written it at the bottom of the note. 'That's somewhere in the Toxteth area,' I said. Do you know anyone there?'

He thought. 'A few people but no one I'm frightened of. Look Johnny, I'm not asking you to solve this mystery for me. I just want a bodyguard. I want protection.'

'I can understand that, Lucky, but you need to find out who's behind this. You can't have a minder following you around forever. Where are you playing this weekend?'

'I'm on the Old Swan Social Club on Saturday. Why don't you come down and see the show? We can have a pint afterwards and it'll give you time to think about it in the meantime and maybe come up with some ideas?'

'I might just do that,' I promised. 'But I've got a better idea. What time do you finish there?'

'It's got to be before midnight.'

'Fine. We'll go down to the Masquerade when you've done, and see Tommy McKale. He'll be a better person than me to help you if you just want muscle and, with a bit of luck, you might get a gig out of it as well.'

The McKale Brothers owned the Masquerade Club near the Pier Head and any gangster in Liverpool who hadn't worked for them wasn't worth his place in the starting line-up. Before I left for Spain, Tommy had started up a security business with his brother Denis so I figured they'd be ideal people to guard Lucky.

'OK, Johnny. I'll give it a try. Can't do any harm meeting the man.'

'Why would they want you out of Liverpool particularly, that's what seems strange? Do you do many gigs here?'

'This one on Saturday is the first round here for six

months.'

'Any more coming off?'

'I might be doing the Olympia next month but it's not confirmed. But there's nothing special about those gigs to warrant this.'

'I'll give it some thought,' I promised him. 'In the meantime, take extra care and I'll call for you at the Old Swan on Saturday.'

'Come early and catch the act.'

It was only Tuesday. Lucky Learoyd had five days on his own to try and stay alive. I figured the odds were just about in his favour but, then, I was never much of a gambler.

I didn't get the chance for further discussions with Lucky because at the moment I was seeing him out, two policemen walked through the door demanding to see me and I first became aware of the death of Stewart Davis.

✳ ✳ ✳

Chapter Two

'Are you sure you don't recognise him, Mr Ace?'

The older of the two detectives pushed the photograph in front of me for the third time. It showed an unshaven man in his late thirties, his face grey, gaunt and waxen, his hair matted and his eyes sightless. Just shows what a night in a mortuary drawer does for you.

'Quite sure.'

'Then how come we found one of your business cards in his pocket?'

'I haven't the faintest idea but I didn't put it there.'

The detective was a short, stocky man, aged thirty-nine at most. He wore a dark green anorak and denims and a pair of those large bifocal glasses that I thought went out with Dennis Taylor the erstwhile snooker king until I noticed Bill Wyman wears them when he tours with The Rhythm Kings. Twenty years ago, before they started recruiting half blind midgets in a desperate attempt to keep staff levels up, he'd never have got into the Force but nowadays, as Cole Porter might have observed, anything goes.

His sidekick looked older. He had a drinker's nose, bulbous and bloodshot, which I put down to long hours on the Vice Squad.

The younger man gave a long sigh. He'd introduced himself as DI Sam Reubens, working out of Copperas Hill station, and he seemed a decent enough guy once he'd accepted I was telling him the truth. His companion was Sergeant Jeff Monk.

'I was hoping he was one of your clients and you could identify him. It's the only lead we have to go on so far.'

'You don't know who he is?'

'Not yet. We're checking missing persons, dental records, clothing, the usual sources, and, of course, we've circulated his photograph to the media.'

'What about DNA?'

'We're still in the queue. As you will no doubt know, we can only get a positive DNA match if the person has a record. The waiting list for testing is close on a month and, as we're not checking a suspect here, I can't get it through as urgent.'

'You say he was living rough. How did he die?'

Reubens shuddered. 'Not nice. He was stabbed in the heart and then beheaded after death. Incidentally, we haven't made the last bit of information available to the press,' he added hastily.

I agreed. 'Probably for the best'. Copycat killings were all too common and Merseyside Police had enough crime to contend with without people roaming the streets playing John the Baptist games.

'We've been through the missing persons file and, God knows, there's enough of them.'

'And none that fit the description?'

'No. As far as we know he's just another of the great unwashed.'

'But somebody must have missed him. You've tried the usual hostels I take it?'

'And the benefits office and the Pier Head winos.'

'Nothing?'

'Nothing.'

I looked again at the photo. 'Well, he's never been near my office, I can assure you.'

'Where were you last night between the hours of midnight and three am?'

'That's when he was killed?'

'Somewhere round then.'

'I was at home in bed.'

'On your own?'

'No, my girlfriend was with me. I got in about quarter to

eight from doing my radio show and I didn't go out again.'

'Your girlfriend lives with you?'

'Yes.'

This wasn't exactly true. It was I who lived with her. At least, most of the time. I'd renovated this house in Sefton Park for Maria and Victoria, our daughter, but I still kept on my flat in the Waterloo Dock. I'd never been able to adapt fully to family life but, then, everybody needs some space don't they?

There was a silence while he weighed up my alibi. I wasn't too concerned that I might be a suspect but I was curious about the connection. Had the murdered tramp really been coming to see me or had he merely picked up one of my cards by chance, possibly from somebody's trashcan?

'Think about it.' said Reubens, at last, 'There's a tie-in with you somewhere. If anything comes to mind, give me a shout.'

I didn't expect I'd be much help to him. I wasn't on first name terms with any dossers, alive or dead. But I promised to think about it like he suggested and they left, reasonably satisfied.

Before I had time to give the matter any further consideration, Cameron buzzed through again.

'They're like buses,' she said.

'What are?'

'Clients. Don't see one for ages then two of them turn up in the same day.'

'You mean there's someone else to see me?'

'Mr Mohair 2003. Says his name is Oliver Clarke.'

I'd known Ollie from way back in the Sixties when he'd sold old bangers from an bomb site in Walton; most of them the sort of cars that had starting handles and managed 60mph flat out with a following wind. I'd bought a couple of Commer vans from him for the band, which transported us to exotic venues like New Brighton Tower Ballroom and The Klic Klic Club in

Southport. Since then, he'd moved his operation gradually more upmarket and now he owned a garage somewhere out towards the Dingle. If we met in town, we'd have a drink together and run through old times.

'I wonder what he wants. You'd better send him in.'

'OK. They didn't arrest you then?'

'What?'

'The bluelamps? They burst in here as if you were hiding The Yorkshire Ripper in a cupboard.'

'Don't worry about that. It means nothing. It's just a walk they practice to make them feel important. All policemen do it.'

'Right. I'll send the gentleman in.'

Ollie strode purposefully into the office, shook my hand and clasped his other arm round my shoulder.

He was a big man with a thick head of white hair and matching goatee beard and had an air of earnest sincerity like an American evangelist on a Save the Sinners mission. No wonder he sold so many cars.

'Nice to see you, Johnny,'

'And you, Ollie.'

He was even sporting one of those shiny mohair suits that salesmen used to wear in the Eighties along with sheepskin coats and two tone shoes. I could see what Cameron meant.

He settled himself down in the leather armchair on the other side of my desk and let out a big sigh. 'Cares of the world,' he explained.

'What's the problem? I take it you haven't come to sell me some wheels?'

'Vandals, Johnny, that's the problem.' Roly crawled over and licked his calf leather brogues. 'Still got the mutt then.'

'Part of the furniture. He doubles as a shoe shine boy.'

Ollie managed a weak smile.

I didn't get it. Vandals were an ongoing problem everywhere nowadays. You hardly saw a shop window that wasn't shuttered up at nights. I said as much to Ollie.

'This isn't your normal spur-of-the-moment, having-a-lark stuff; smashed windscreens and sugar in the petrol tank. This is more subtle. Interior light bulbs removed, seat belts slit, brake pipes cut. The sort of thing that you don't know about till the punter brings the car back and gives you a bad name.'

'If the punter isn't dead when the brakes fail.'

'Exactly. Imagine the compensation.' Oliver always looked for the money angle first 'But it's the trouble these people are taking. They have to break into the garage, unlock the cars and then have some knowledge of the mechanics.'

'What do the police say?'

'Waste of time. Say it's just kids. They're too busy counting the money they make from all the speed cameras. I want this investigated properly, which is why I've come to you, my son.'

'What about other businesses round about? Have they had similar trouble?'

'Not that I know of.'

'Someone got a grudge?'

'There've always been people with grudges but nothing like this.'

I thought of Lucky Learoyd. 'No threats or anything like that?'

'No. And not a writ in sight before you ask.'

'How long since the trouble started?'

He thought. 'About two months. Look, why don't you come over in the morning, take a look around?'

'OK Ollie. Is about ten OK?'

He said it was.

'I'm going for some lunch,' I told Cameron when Ollie had gone. I took Roly with me and walked across to Richie's in Paradise Street for a mug of tea and a toasted teacake with cheese. Billy Butler and Alec Young from Radio Merseyside were in. Alec reached down to pat Roly. A mistake. The dog took the opportunity to crane his neck under Alec's arm and eat his bacon sandwich.

'He's a hunting dog,' I explained to the startled broadcaster. 'They do that.'

I wondered how long Richie's would be there if the proposed developments came to fruition. Come to that, would Paradise Street still be there? Certainly, the Moat House was earmarked for demolition. The city was changing beyond recognition from the Sixties. Someone was going to make a lot of money selling new street maps. At least the trams were scheduled to be coming back.

I felt like an afternoon away from the office and figured I could leave Cameron on her own there to familiarise herself with everything.

I'd not seen Jim Burroughs since my return from Spain, although we'd spoken several times on the phone. It seemed a good time to pay him a visit and keep him up to speed with events.

Jim and his wife Rosemary had moved to a retirement bungalow in West Kirby. Rosemary had always set her heart on returning to the place she grew up in but I couldn't see Jim being happy stuck out there. He'd always been a city person.

Jim was pleased to see me although Rosemary was less than delighted to encounter Roly, who'd come along for the ride, and she ushered him straight out into the tiny back garden with a lawn the size of a trampoline.

'How's it going then?' Jim asked.

I told him about my new partner and he looked concerned. 'Don't make the mistake of shagging her, Johnny,' he warned. 'I know what you're like.'

'You must be joking. I've got enough on my plate. Besides, she's thirty years younger than me. I don't kid myself she'd

fancy me in a million years. Anyway, she's not my type, Jim.
Too in your face. But she'll do well in the agency. She's sharp
and she can look after herself and she's got a black belt in judo
no less.'

'You're back on the job proper again then?'

'We certainly are. We've got a couple of cases on the go
already.' I told him about Lucky Learoyd and Ollie Clarke.

'I know Clarke. He's been dealing in cars for years.'

'Nothing on him?'

'No. He always seemed straight enough.' Jim grinned. 'As
straight as any car dealers are.'

'What about Lucky Learoyd?'

'Don't know the man. There was a Victor Learoyd years
ago.'

'What did he do?'

Jim stroked his chin. 'Can't remember. Just the name rang
a bell. It's not one you come across very often."

Rosemary came through carrying a tray of tea and scones.
Jim would have preferred Newcastle Brown but I didn't think
he'd be getting much of that in his retirement haven, with
Rosemary keeping a careful eye on his diet since his heart
scare. I was surprised she still let him turn out with The
Chocolate Lavatory. What Jim needed was a nubile young
lover to liven him up. She would probably be the death of him,
of course, but at least he'd die happy.

'Do you get to town much these days? I asked him.

'No. Don't go out much at all really. Safeways down the
road on a Saturday afternoon is about as exciting as it gets.'

'Could be worse, Jim. You could be at Goodison Park.'

'Wait, I tell a lie. I do go across the water sometimes, on a
Thursday night to the jam nights at the Marconi Club.'

'The Merseycats ones? Any good?'

'Not bad.'

'What about the band? Are you still doing a bit with

them?'

'The odd gig, Johnny, that's all. Funnily enough, we're doing a charity night at the Bamalama a week tomorrow. Why don't you come down?'

'I might just do that, so long as you don't ask me to drum.'

We chatted a little while longer. Jim had changed in the year since I'd last seen him. I felt he'd aged considerably. The old sharpness had gone and he didn't seem as interested as he used to be in events in the outside world. That's what retirement does to you. Keep going till you drop, that's always been my motto.

I stayed another half hour then thanked Rosemary for the tea, collected Roly and left. I didn't think I'd be going back there again for a while.

I touched base with Cameron on the mobile. There were no messages so I went to the radio station to do the show after which I drove straight back to Waterloo Dock to my flat. I'd moved a lot of my stuff like my hi-fi and computer over to Maria's in Sefton Park but I still kept the recording equipment and my piano up there and tonight I wanted to put down a couple of new tracks.

It had been years since I left the Cruzads but, even back in the Seventies, I'd been realistic enough to know that we'd never get a hit record. Merseybeat had passed us by and we were too old by the time punk came round. But I still liked to dabble on my own, writing songs and putting them onto a CD.

Maria accepted that I spent the odd night at my flat when I was doing my music and it went without saying that I always slept there alone.

It was after midnight when I finished recording and turned in but I was up again at eight. It was another sunny day so I decided to forego the car and take a stroll up to Oliver Clarke's showroom. I reckoned the exercise would do the dog good. It wouldn't hurt me either.

All along Duke St, old warehouses that had once been home to nightspots like the Knightsbridge and Adams Club were being either renovated and turned into luxury flats, or knocked down in favour of brand new apartment blocks. At one time, streets like Cornwallis Street had been no-go areas but not any more. To complement the makeover, the media had got in on the act and whole area had been renamed Ropewalks. Glossy magazines declared city living was the new vogue and prices skyrocketed.

I hadn't been slow to get into the action myself. I'd recently put a deposit down on a couple of flats in Liberty Place. My idea was to rent them out for four years then sell them in 2007 before the bubble burst. This was a departure for me as my other flats were in converted Victorian mansions round the L8 and L17 areas, prime student areas. However, the market was becoming saturated with purpose built student accommodation so I'd decided to target young professionals instead...

Ollie's place was a little further away, on the edge of Chinatown. The area had become somewhat run down. Parts of Park Lane where Dingle meets Toxteth were being renovated but all around the Oliver Clarke Motor Showrooms was the smell of urban decay.

Roly stopped by a nearby patch of wasteland to relieve himself. I watched a car being jacked onto a ramp in the garage adjoining the glass fronted showroom. Ollie was standing beside it but when he saw me watching he came over to greet me.

'You're early, Johnny. Come inside. Can I get you a coffee?'

'Tea?' I enquired but then I realised it was from a machine and settled for the hot chocolate as the best option.

I followed him into his office carrying the two steaming polystyrene cups and placed them down on his desk.

'I've set aside a couple of the vehicles to show you that

they've been messed about with. We can look at them while the drinks are cooling.'

He led me to a parking lot beside the garage where a green Nissan Primera and a silver Rover 75 were parked.

'This is the one where they tampered with the brakes.' He indicated the Rover. 'Just a second, I need to check something.' He went into the garage. I wandered across to the Rover but I never got the chance to examine it. Suddenly, there was a tremendous crash followed by a terrifying scream.

'Oh my God, the ramp!'

A Ford Mondeo that had been on the ramp was now on the ground. Two legs were protruding from the side and three mechanics were frantically trying to lift the car. Another was at the controls of the lifting gear but it was all too late. There was nothing they could do.

The broken, crushed body of Ollie's chief mechanic lay at the bottom of the ramp.

* * *

Chapter Three

The three other lads in the garage stood looking at the body almost in disbelief. One of them turned away to vomit on the floor; another broke out crying whilst the third knelt down and held the dead man's head as if he might bring him back to life. None of them looked older than twenty.

Ollie was white with shock. 'That was a narrow escape.' I looked at him quizzically. 'I was under that car myself just before you came. I'd been checking the shock absorbers.' His voice was shaky. 'Christ, what a mess. You realise, Johnny, that was meant for me.'

'Who was he?'

'Graham Wharton. He's been with me for eight years. Best mechanic I ever had. Oh God, who's going to tell his family?

The ambulance was on the spot within twenty minutes, ten minutes after the police had arrived. The two officers in the patrol car were sceptical when Ollie suggested that Wharton's death might not have been an accident.

The younger constable looked uneasy. 'In what way, not an accident?'

'Your lot know all about the trouble I've been having here. Not that you've been too bothered to do anything about it. But now we're talking murder.'

'Why should anyone want to kill Mr Wharton?'

'Not him, me. They wanted to get at me. Probably hoped I'd be under that ramp. Why don't you get on your radio and tell Detective Inspector Reubens to get down here. He was the one dealing with it.'

DI Reubens name obviously counted for something because once the officer had contacted the station and mentioned his name, the whole shooting match swung into action.

Ollie and I had retreated to his office by the time Sam Reubens arrived. He saw me, blinked, then glanced down at

Roly who had made himself comfortable under the table. 'Does that dog follow you everywhere.'

'He's my minder. He's on the payroll.'

'Is this a coincidence, you being here? Two suspicious deaths in three days and you're involved in both of them.'

'Pure coincidence,' I said. 'I didn't know the man.'

'That's what you said about the last one.'

'This one hasn't got my card in his pocket.'

'You mean you've looked?'

Ollie broke in. 'Johnny was having a quiet drink with me when this happened.'

'Is that a recreational drink or is Mr Ace here in his capacity as a private investigator?'

'Look, I've been having trouble with vandals here for weeks now and you didn't seem particularly interested. I'd just asked Johnny to come and have a look round.'

Reubens turned to me. 'And what did you find?'

'He hadn't had time to find anything,' broke in Ollie. 'He'd only just got here when the ramp collapsed.'

'And what makes you think it wasn't an accident?'

Ollie sighed. 'All my equipment is checked regularly. Nothing like this has ever happened before. It seems to me that it's just the latest in a long line of attacks except this one has had horrendous consequences.'

'Has anybody that you know of got any reason to want to kill Mr Wharton?'

'Not that I know of, he's a quiet sort of bloke. Keeps himself to himself. Likes a couple of pints at night then home to the wife and the soaps.'

'Any children?'

'Three but they're grown up and left home, but hang on, you're looking at the wrong man here. It's me, I tell you, that was meant to be under that ramp.'

'Have you got enemies then, Mr Clarke?'

'I must have, mustn't I? Surely it's obvious after what's been happening here these last few weeks?'

'So who do you think they are?'

'You asked me that last time and I'll tell you now what I told you then. I don't know. If I knew, I'd deal with them.'

Ollie had grown up in a rough part of Everton. I was sure he could call on a few choice people to help him if there was any trouble going.

At that moment, the forensic team arrived and the area round the garage was sealed off as a Scene Of Crime area.

'I'll want to question all the men working in the garage,' instructed Reubens. 'And nothing to be touched. The Health and Safety people should be here shortly.'

A pathologist arrived to examine the body in situ before it was taken away in the ambulance.

'I don't think there's anything I can do at the moment,' I told Ollie.

'No. Right, Johnny. I'm going to have to ring his Missus up aren't I?' Oh shit.'

'Better coming from you, Ollie. He's worked for you a long time?'

'Over eight years. A good man was Graham.' He walked to the door with me. 'I still want you to look into all this, Johnny. I can't see the police getting anywhere.'

'Leave it a few days, Ollie. Give them a chance at least.'

'Why, that's what I want to know. Why?'

'You're sure you haven't upset anyone, sold them a dodgy motor...'

'My motors aren't dodgy, Johnny, you should know that.'

'Gangs? Protection?'

He shook his head. 'Nothing like that. I'd soon see them off if they tried it on with me.'

'What about rival firms? Someone wanting to muscle in on the business?'

'Can't see it. All the folk I know have their own place. Why should they want mine? It's hardly a prime location for selling cars.'

'Then why are you here?'

'Because I can't afford the rates in town, that's why.'

I looked across towards Paradise Street and the distant River Mersey. I could spot a dozen cranes where new apartment blocks were going up. A good time to buy shares in construction companies.

'Well, think about it,' I said. The same words Sam Reubens had said to me the previous day when he was referring to the identity of the dead tramp. I'd had precious little time to wonder who he might be.

But, come the next morning, I didn't need to speculate any longer.

* * *

Chapter Four

The Daily Post had the story plastered across the front page. I'd walked across to the Royal Liver Building from my flat for breakfast in The Diner and I picked up the paper from the kiosk.

The headline hit me. 'Murdered tramp is a city financier'.

There was very little more to the story other than the fact that police confirmed that the man found stabbed in an Old Swan doorway earlier in the week had been identified as 33-year-old Stewart Davis.

A colleague from his office had recognised the photo on the television newsreel.

Investigating officer, DI Sam Reubens, confirmed that the police had still no clue as to the identity of the killer, the motive for his death or the reason why he was living rough when he was on a £50k a year salary as an executive with a respected city financial institution called Oates International.

His wife said she hadn't seen him for two weeks prior to his death. She was said to be 'very distressed'. They had no children. She'd just returned from holiday with her sister in the Algarve. Davis had taken a fortnight's leave from work, ostensibly to fit a new kitchen in their expensive Crosby home in Blundellsands ready to greet her when she returned home.

The report didn't say whether the new dishwasher was installed yet.

Stewart Davis's name didn't connect with me in any way and I still had no idea why he'd had my card in his pocket.

I turned to the sports paper. In his preview of the Blues' forthcoming season, the reporter described how a Formby pigeon fancier and ex-international footballer who turned out occasionally for Everton might be in the squad for Saturday. I wasn't sure how Duncan Ferguson would take this description of him.

I was on my second cup of tea when my mobile rang. It was Cameron and there was an acerbic edge to her voice. .

'Are you coming into work today. Its quarter past nine.'

'Is it?'

'Only a lady's been asking for you. Says it's very urgent. She's rung twice already.'

'What's her name?'

'Jeanne McGhee. She says it's about that ragbag that was murdered.'

I sat up straight. 'Have you got her number?'

She had. I wrote it down. 'Well done, Ronni. I'll ring her immediately.'

It was a Southport number. She answered at the second ring.

'Johnny Ace,' I said. 'You wanted to speak to me.'

'Thank you for ringing so promptly.' She sounded young and nervous but the accent was cut-glass.

'I'm told it was urgent.'

'Yes, it is rather. Can you come round to my apartment now?' She gave me an address in Birkdale. Stockbroker country. 'I'm close to the Royal Birkdale Golf Course.'

'Can you tell me what it's about?'

'I'd rather not. Not on the phone. But if you want to know who I am, I worked with Stewart Davis.'

'I'll be there in half an hour.'

It was more like three quarters. I forget that to travel anywhere in this country it takes twice as long as it used to, even ten years ago. The sooner the Tardis becomes reality the better. I rang Cameron and told her I wouldn't be in the office till after lunch.

It was only a short walk to my flat where the RAV4 was parked. I put Roly in the back and took the dock road heading for Southport.

Jeanne McGhee's apartment occupied the top two floors of a newly built block set in landscaped gardens with an attractive water feature. The entrance was on a lower level round the back. I drove round and parked in the driveway behind a new black Honda Accord.

I pressed the Entryphone and announced myself. Miss McGhee's voice told me to come in and take the elevator to the second floor. I did so and she was waiting to greet me when the doors opened.

I saw a striking looking woman dressed in a dark business suit and white blouse with her auburn hair pinned up into a bob.

'Mr Ace?' she said. 'Do come in.' She still sounded young but not so breathless anymore. I put her age around thirty.

I followed her into a large front lounge where a living-flame gas fire burned in an ornate white marble fireplace. The floor was a light wood laminate covered in places by three Persian rugs.

'Take a seat.' She indicated a large white leather sofa. 'Would you care for some coffee?'

I explained I had just finished breakfast so she closed the door and joined me at the opposite end of the sofa.

'I'm so glad I managed to get hold of you in time,' she said, 'before the police.'

'But why, exactly?' I asked. 'I must tell you, Miss McGhee, that I don't understand how I have come to be involved in Mr Davis's death. I never knew the man and, in fact, I never even knew his name until I read it this morning in the paper.'

'That's probably true,' she said.

I told her about my visit from the police. 'Apparently, he had my business card in his pocket when he died.'

'I know.'

'You know?'

'Stewart knew he was in danger and he'd picked your card

up from somewhere. He was going to ring you on the day he was murdered but, unfortunately, someone got to him first'

'You mean he was in touch with you when he was living rough?'

'Yes. He was hiding from some people...'

'Hang on. Have you told the police all this?'

'Not yet. They were at the office yesterday but I was away on a course and missed them. But I'm told they want to interview me today, which is why I asked you to come here this morning, to tell you my side of events first As you will hear, there are obviously things I do not want the police to know.' And she related her story.

Stewart Davis, it appeared, was not just an employee. He was actually one of the three founders and sat on the board of Oates International. She herself was his personal assistant. The company's main business was locating land and properties for investors and setting up the finance for them to purchase.

Originally, the company had been based in London but they had moved their operations to Liverpool when the city was designated as the 2008 European City of Culture and the area suddenly became ripe for redevelopment.

'They realised that prices on Merseyside were going to skyrocket and they moved here lock, stock and barrel.

'Whereabouts are they based?'

'We have a suite of offices in Victoria Street.'

Nothing wrong so far, in fact Oates International seemed to have come up with a first rate business idea. Not only did they make the commission for finding the property, they then doubled their money for arranging the finance.

'More than that,' said Jeanne when I said as much to her. 'Often we buy the land ourselves and sell it on to the client.'

'At a vast profit, of course?'

'More than the commission would be, certainly.'

'Ah. And what about the finance? Don't tell me, you lend them the money yourselves at punitive rates?'

'We do have a bank subsidiary, yes, but the rates have to be competitive otherwise the clients would go elsewhere.'

'But, as you say, it beats working on pure commission.'

'Of course, but there's nothing wrong with that. Why has profit become such a dirty word these days? I thought the Thatcher revolution had converted people to the entrepreneurial society.'

'Profit isn't a dirty word if it's honest but, judging by what's happened to your Mr Davis, maybe his transactions may merit closer scrutiny.'

She reached for a packet of cigarettes on the coffee table and held it out to me. I shook my head. It seems to be young women who are the big smokers nowadays. Perhaps they have a death wish? She lit one for herself and blew the smoke into the air like Lauren Bacall before replying.

'Maybe not but that isn't the main thing.'

'What is?'

'Liverpool is soon going to be awash with money, mark my words.'

I couldn't argue with that. All the major hotel groups had already moved in, Coutts Bank was due to open any day and it seemed that almost every other street corner boasted a building site and a giant crane.

She continued. 'Which is when the mobs come on the scene.'

'Which mobs are these?'

'Take your pick. Eastern European gangs, the IRA, drug barons, the Triads, anyone with money to launder.'

'Where does Stewart Davis fit in?'

'Stewart was negotiating a big deal on some land between Dingle and Toxteth. He had a buyer lined up but someone was putting pressure on him to ditch the deal and sell it to them instead.'

'Didn't the other partners know of this?'

Jeanne McGhee hesitated. 'Sort of.' Her tone was evasive.

'How do you mean, "sort of"?'

'I suppose it doesn't matter if I tell you now, now's he's dead.' Her eyes filled with tears as she said the words and it didn't take a genius to realise that there was more to the relationship than just boss and PA.

Nonetheless, I tried to ask the question discreetly. 'How close exactly were you to Stewart?'

Her lips tightened. 'We were seeing each other, I guess you realised that?' When I didn't answer, she added. 'He was married.'

'I know. I believe the paper said his wife was away when it happened.'

'She'd gone on holiday with her sister. That's one reason I don't want to go to the police. Ruth doesn't know about Stewart and me and it's better she doesn't find out now. Why ruin her memories of him?'

'Very solicitous of you,' I commented, but the sarcasm was wasted on her. 'You said there were other reasons?'

She hesitated yet again and made a play of stubbing her half-smoked cigarette into the silver ashtray.

'He was getting a back-hander from the people he was selling the land to. His partners didn't know about it but if the other people bought it, he'd lose that.'

'Sounds like a nice guy, your Stewart. Cheats on his wife and swindles his partners. Can't be too surprising he ends up wide-eyed and headless.'

'You don't know the circumstances,' she snapped. 'Everyone in the property game is on the make.'

'So that makes it all right?'

'I didn't say that. Look, are you going to help me or not?'

'In what way can I help you? Stewart's dead isn't he, so end of story.'

'Not quite.'

'Oh?'

'Whoever killed Stewart may be after me next.'

'Why you?'

She sighed. 'Because Stewart had arranged for the people who were buying the land to pay the money into my bank account.'

'Don't tell me; they'd already made a down payment?'

She nodded. 'On the promise of the deal.'

'And they'll want their money back?'

'Yes.'

'So give it to them and you're in the clear.'

'It's not as easy as that. Stewart got me to withdraw the money out of my account the day he died. That was the last time I saw him. He told me he was using it to finance another deal.'

'And where did that money go?'

'I don't know. I took it to him that morning and it was later that same night that he was killed. Needless to say, the money wasn't on him when he was found.'

So the question was, had his killers taken the money or had Davis already spent it and, if so, what on?

'How did you contact him during his fortnight on the road?'

'It wasn't a fortnight. He'd only been on the road for four or five days. He was staying here with me when his wife went away but on his way home one night, he was attacked by two men so he went into hiding. He was hoping to keep out of the way until the deal went through.'

'But they got to him first?'

She closed her eyes and silently nodded.

'So how did he keep in touch with you?'

'He rang me from phone boxes every evening. Look, I

really don't know what he did with the money but I don't think these people will believe me.'

I wasn't sure I believed her myself, and I was pretty sure Davis's buyers would be sceptical, but I felt I ought to offer her some reassurance. 'If they think you know where the money is, they won't want to kill you or they'll never get the money at all.'

More likely, I thought, they'd kidnap her, force her to find out where the money was, tell them, and then kill her to prevent her talking. But she'd probably worked that one out for herself. Jeanne McGhee was no fool.

The real issue, of course, was still the land. I asked her who was going to get it now that Stewart was dead.

'I don't know. As far as I know, nothing has been signed.'

I pondered. 'If Stewart had assured these people the deal was going through, why would they want to kill him?'

'Because they'd heard that another party was interested in the land. They told him that if they didn't get it, he'd be a dead man. I can only suppose that, for whatever reason, they thought they'd lost the deal and killing him was their revenge.'

'When did they first learn about the other prospective buyers in the offing?'

'A fortnight ago. Just before Stewart's wife went away. He was frightened to stay alone at his own house in case they knew where he lived so that's why he came to me.'

A good excuse for a spot of extra-maritals it might have been but it didn't work out so well for him on the protection angle.

'All he had to do was give them their deposit back if he couldn't persuade his partners to go ahead and cut the deal with them.'

'That wasn't an option. They wanted the land.' She shuddered. 'They made that plain.'

'I take it the so-called deposit represented his unofficial cut?'

'Yes.'

'What about the other people who were after the land? Who were they?'

'Russians. They'd approached the other partners with a bigger offer. If the Russians knew that Stewart was trying to scupper their chances, they'd have had no hesitation in killing him.'

'A dangerous game your lover was playing. Piggy in the middle with a butcher wielding an axe at either end.'

'There's more. Yesterday I had a phone call at the office. A man's voice. He said, 'We want the deposit back and the land. Get it for us or you'll be next.' She reached out and held my arm. 'I'm frightened what they might do. I need a bodyguard.'

You and Lucky Learoyd too, I thought. Forget detection. Why didn't I just call myself Minders Inc., hire out a bunch of heavies and sit back and rake in the cash?

'OK,' I said. 'It'll cost you.'

'I'll put it on expenses. The firm can pay.'

I named a price double what I would have charged her if she'd been paying herself. It seemed everyone else was taking a hefty slice of this cake along the way so I didn't see why I shouldn't have my share.

She accepted without argument. 'I'll write you a cheque.' She walked across to a walnut davenport in the corner, took out a pen and chequebook.

'I'll need names of the various parties.'

'Come to the office tomorrow morning and I'll give them to you.'

'Won't the partners think it odd?'

'They've got a meeting with their bankers in Manchester. Besides, I have my own office.' She signed the cheque and handed it to me. 'What happens if you fail?'

'You don't get your money back,' I said, 'but you'll be buried in a top of the range coffin.'

* * *

It was after twelve when I finally reached the office. 'If there are no messages or visitors,' I told Cameron, 'I'll buy you lunch and bring you up to date on the cases so far.'

She was wearing a red top, short enough to expose a large stretch of bare midriff above a pair of denim flares with multi-coloured threads up the side. Today's belly button jewel was a ruby, presumably to match her top. She didn't look much like a private eye.

We went to the Bluecoat. The food's good, although you do have to wait in line, but at least there isn't the bother of waiting for a waiter to bring the bill half an hour after you've finished the meal. I decided on the mushroom and chive quiche with three salads whilst Cameron went for the Broccoli soup with granary roll.

'So we're talking three cases on the books already and we've not been out of the stalls a week yet.' Cameron was clearly impressed. I hoped she'd be as impressed when it came to the clear-up rate. As things stood at the moment, I was just as puzzled as all of the clients.

'The Jeanne McGhee thing interests me,' she said. 'I'd like to meet her. Something very shady going on there, apart from the murder.'

'On the next table, a couple of dark-suited lads who looked like fledgling shop managers couldn't take their eyes off Cameron. They looked in their late teens and probably spoke in a similar tongue to her. No wonder there was a generation gap.

But that's really a police job,' I pointed out. 'All she wants from me is protection. The Fraud Squad will deal with the boardroom skulduggery and DI Reubens is already working on Davis's murder.'

But I didn't really believe that. Stewart Davis had had my

card in his pocket when he was killed which, in a strange way, made me regard him almost as a client. Therefore, like it or not, I considered myself involved. And now his mistress had hired me to protect her so that was it. Game, shot and match. It was my case.

'Won't he expect you to pass on all the info you got from that Miss McGhee?'

'If he asks for it, I'll tell him.' She saw my expression and knew not to pursue that line. Instead, she asked, 'What about your friend Lucky Learoyd? What does he do again?'

'He's a vocalist. He does a P J Proby tribute act.'

'P J who? Never heard of him.'

Few people under forty had. 'Before your time, Ronni. He was the biggest star in England in 1965 when he split his pants at the Croydon Empire. The press pilloried him and his career went down the pan. Now, that's what most people remember him for. Split trousers.'

'Wicked. So what's Lucky's problem?'

'Another one with death threats.'

'So that case is just about protection as well?'

'Pretty much. I'm putting him in touch with Tommy McKale,' and I filled her in with details of the colourful careers of Tommy and his brother Denis.

'Which just leaves Mohair the Motor Maestro, what was his name again?'

'Oliver Clarke. We're supposedly dealing with vandals here but I think there's more to it than that. My guess is that someone wants him out of there for whatever reason.'

'The premises, you mean?'

'Yes.'

'So why ice his mechanic?'

'I'm not sure they meant to. It could have been just another "warning".'

'A pretty extreme one. The man's brown bread.'

'They might not have meant that to happen. Wharton could just have been unlucky. In the wrong place at the wrong time. Think about it, Ronni, they wouldn't necessarily have known that anyone was going to be under the ramp when it crashed down.'

'From what you say, Ollie was under the ramp just before it happened though.' She was a sharp girl.

'That's what he pointed out himself. He said he only came out to meet me so it's certainly possible it was meant for him but, if that were the case, it suggests that one of his own men would have to be involved.'

'Why?'

'To make sure it was him underneath when it crashed. A stranger wouldn't have been able to stick around the garage unnoticed long enough to get the timing right.'

'I suppose so.'

'Of course, it could just as easily have been a genuine accident. The ramp might have malfunctioned in some way.' But neither of us really believed that.

'So what's the game plan?'

'I'm leaving Ollie for the moment. The police will be crawling all round the garage. And we don't know for certain that this accident is linked to the other business.'

'And Lucky?'

'He can wait till Saturday when I see Tommy McKale which means I can concentrate on the dead tramp. Or Stewart Davis as we should now call him. Tomorrow I'm going over to Oates International to see Jeanne McGhee. I need to find out more names.'

'And today?'

'You're going back to the office. I've got a few calls to make. If you need me for anything urgent, you can get me on my mobile and if DI Reubens calls, you don't know where I am.'

I wasn't trying to obstruct the police but I knew from experience they didn't like outsiders like me muscling in on what they regarded as their territory, especially if I'd been hired by someone involved in one of their cases.

I took a few minutes out to look at the bargains at the Bluecoat bookshop before driving out to Aigburth to see Geoffrey and check on my property deals.

'How are things progressing at Liberty Place?' I asked him.

'Not ready for completion till September, that's the latest'

I wasn't worried. The real profit would be in the capital gain not the rent and I didn't have to pay the balance till completion.

'Pat Lake from Livingstone Drive phoned,' he added. 'She's having trouble with her central heating boiler and her old mother's feeling the cold. I sent Gary, the new plumber, round.'

'Fine. If he can't fix it, get her a couple of blankets from Oxfam and a hot water bottle.'

Geoffrey looked puzzled for a moment. He was never quite sure when I was joking. After twenty years of aggro running the whole show myself, I delegated virtually everything to Geoffrey nowadays whilst I concentrated on the detective agency. Tenant troubles I could do without.

'How's the private eye work going, boss? Need any strong-arm stuff?'

Geoffrey had leant a hand in that direction from time to time; on occasions when I'd needed some reliable assistance. I thought about Lucky Learoyd and told him there might be a very good chance I might be able to use him if Tommy McKale wasn't able to help in the bodyguard stakes.

'Changing the subject, Geoff, have you heard anything about any dodgy property deals around town lately?'

"More than normal, you mean? Where do you want me to start? The city's suddenly full of prospective Donald Trumps.

They're like piranhas with a scent of blood in their nostrils.'

At one time, Geoffrey would have read *Builder* magazine and *Loaded*; now it was *Move*, *Estate Agents Gazette* and *Property World*.

'What do you know about Oates International?'

'One of the new outfits in town. They came over from London a few weeks ago.' It tied in with what Jeanne McGhee had told me. 'They do land deals mostly but they have put plans in for a couple of developments themselves.'

'Whereabouts?'

'Not sure, boss, but I could find out.'

'Do that, Geoff, and get back to me. How's Badger by the way? I haven't seen him for ages.' My tenant Neville Mountbatten, nicknamed Badger on account of his peculiar hair colour, lives in the same house as Pat Lake, has a masters degree and thrives handsomely on his wits.

'That's because you've been in Spain. Same as ever. Badger doesn't change except he's driving a Lexus these days.'

'God, he must be getting old. He'll be getting a Rover 75 next and after that it's a hearse.'

'You're wrong there, boss. The Lexus is the new BMW, the gangsta motor. They call it the Rapper's Special.'

I looked at my watch. It was two thirty and I'd promised Maria I'd pick up Victoria from nursery school in Aigburth at quarter to three.

'Must be off, Geoff, I'm late for Vikki again. Don't forget Oates. Give me a ring as soon as you've got something.'

I made the school with a minute to spare. There were still four or five other children in her classroom waiting to be picked up. Vikki saw me and came running to be picked up and swung round. She had Maria's dark hair and wore it long, hanging over the shoulders of her maroon school blazer.

'How's she been?' I asked the teacher, a plump, jolly girl in her early twenties who once told me she was a regular listener to my show. Her name was Carolyn.

'Fine. She's drawn a picture for you,' and she handed me a piece of paper daubed with a conglomeration of primary colours showing no recognisable pattern or subject.

'Very good,' I told her. Who was I to argue? I'd been to the Tate Gallery on the Albert Dock and it didn't look too much different to some of the work exhibited there.

'I think she belongs to the primitive school,' smiled Carolyn.

'Don't knock it,' I said. 'Van Gogh would have given his left ear to paint like that.'

Maria was due back from work at five thirty, which gave me half an hour to get to the station to start the show.

Victoria was used to having me around now. I don't know how Maria explained her daddy's months of absence but I know I was probably lucky to be there at all.

About a year ago, I'd gone over to the Costa Blanca on a case and ended up staying out there for several months, I told Maria I needed a break, which I did, but the real problem was Hilary.

I'd known Hilary from way back in the Seventies and we'd been what I guess you'd call 'loving friends' ever since. Maria had accepted this when I first met her but when Victoria came along she was, understandably, not too happy. Carrying on seeing them both was becoming increasingly difficult, especially as Maria was putting pressure on me to move into the new house with her. Which is when I went to Spain.

When I came back, Maria told me she still wanted us to live together as a family and would I move into the new house with them? I was glad to do so as I'd missed both her and my daughter. I wanted us all to be together. But...

The deal was, of course, that I didn't see Hilary anymore and I'd every intention of keeping to it. Hilary knew the score and she never made any demands on me. She had a busy social life of her own. I'd spoken to her when I returned from Spain and we'd kept in touch by phone. We both accepted that there might be times when we needed each other's company in which case we would meet up together. But that was as far as it would go and so far it hadn't happened yet. If Maria still suspected I might ever see Hilary, she said nothing.

I'd made Vikki a drink and myself a cup of tea when Maria returned from her job at the library.

'You're early?' I said, kissing her as she walked into the hall.

'Traffic wasn't so bad.' Vikki ran out from the lounge where she'd been watching Teletubbies and threw herself into her mother's arms. 'How's she been?'

'Fine. She's going to be an artist'. I showed her Vikki's painting and she studied it carefully.

'Mmm. A bit like Paul McCartney's stuff at the Walker.'

'A pity she can't sing like him instead.' I gathered together some CD's for the show as half the stuff I play never appears on the station computer. 'There's some tea in the pot, I've only just made it.'

'Thanks. What time will you be back?'

'About seven thirty if I'm not delayed.'

'I'll get the meal for eight to be on the safe side. I'm doing duck in cranberry sauce with parsnips. It was on *Ready Steady Cook* last week.'

'I'll pick up a bottle of Merlot on the way home.'

Ken, my producer, was already in the studio waiting for me.

'Cutting it fine aren't you?' he grumbled, making a point of looking at his watch. I noticed he'd taken to wearing cardigans at work, probably to affect an air of casual competence. Unfortunately, the garments looked like the sort of things dogs sleep on and he always bought dull colours like puce, mushroom and stone giving him the look of a poor man's Gyles Brandreth.

'Nothing startling today I hope,' he went on. 'Your remark

about footballers' wages yesterday upset some people over in Sports. They rely on those players for quotes and stories and you go and upset them by suggesting they get bonus payments for results instead of wages.'

'I stand by all I said. If Dwight Yorke was paid by the number of goals he scored last season, he'd be eligible for housing benefit. No wonder people are turning to non-league football.'

'You do like living on the edge, don't you?' In more ways than one, I thought. 'I want a nice pleasant show,' he continued.'

'I promise to be as bland as Shady Spencer,' I lied. If he wanted a nice pleasant show, he'd picked the wrong presenter. I wondered what Ken would be like when he reached forty, as he was already seventy in his head.

I started off by playing a couple of Sex Pistols tracks to remind people how bland music had become since shows like *Pop Idol* had taken all the anger and rebellion out of what was supposed to be young people's music.

"Barbara from Prescot" rang in to protest about the possible demolition of Quiggins to make way for the proposed new shopping plaza.

Quiggins is an old building in the city centre, Liverpool's version of Manchester's Afflecks Palace, which houses numerous individual businesses in shops and stalls on three floors selling designer clothes, gifts and gadgets, jewellery, CD's, antiques, etc. All the street people and young trendies go to Quiggins because it represents the cutting edge of fashion but, despite a vigorous protest campaign, I didn't give it much chance of surviving against the relentless wave of multinationalism and globalisation that was sweeping the Western world.

'It's Quiggins v. McWorld,' I told Barbara, 'and, sad to say, there'll be only one winner.'

Behind the screen, Ken was flapping his arms at me like a demented porpoise.

'Don't say that, Johnny' said Barbara. 'David beat Goliath, remember.'

'Oh yes. And one day Everton might beat Manchester United. I'll believe it when it happens.'

'They've got a petition going,' Barbara said. 'Don't forget to sign it next time you go in and tell the listeners to do the same.'

'You've already told them, love.'

Before the show was over, I took a few more calls on the subject, all on Barbara's side, and I was on my way to the car park when Ken shouted me back. 'Urgent phone call for you.'

I followed him back to the studio. He was muttering about me upsetting the city fathers on the eve of the City of Culture. I ignored him and picked up the phone. It was Cameron.

'You're working late,' I said.

She sounded agitated. 'I'm glad I managed to catch you in time. It's your warbling chum, Lucky Learoyd. He's in Walton Hospital. He's been shot.'

* * *

Chapter Six

Lucky was still alive.

Cameron was waiting for me at the hospital entrance and was able to tell me what had happened. He'd been fortunate. The car had slowed down as he walked along Granby Street, a side window opened and a man leaned out and fired twice at just the moment that Lucky tripped over an uneven paving stone. One bullet hit him in the shoulder and the other missed him completely. As he fell to the ground, the car drove off.

'Lucky by name,' I said as we joined him in the Casualty waiting room but Lucky didn't think so.

'They'll get me next time,' he complained. 'I told you I needed a bodyguard.'

Lucky was perched precariously on a cracked plastic seat next to a screaming child and an elderly man with an arm bandage which was turning redder by the second as blood seeped through. The man's face was grey. Lucky himself seemed less badly damaged.

'The bleeding's pretty well stopped,' he said, 'but I think the bullet's still in there.'

'What did the police say?'

'I never called them.'

This seemed curious but I kept the thought to myself for the moment.

'Did nobody witness this shooting?'

'Nobody witnesses anything in Granby Street,' said Lucky. 'Not if they want to live.'

A thought struck me. Granby Street was on the Jenkinson's manor, one of the city's most notorious families.

'You've not upset the Jenkinsons by any chance have you, Lucky?

Cameron looked puzzled. 'Who are the Jenkinsons?'

'Liverpool low-life. Most people run a mile when you mention their name. They're not people you'd want to cross. There must be three generations of them out there now, each one more violent than the last'

If Lucky Learoyd had crossed the Jenkinsons, he had every reason to be afraid.

The question startled him but he gave a hollow laugh. 'Don't be silly, Johnny. Why would I have anything to do with them?'

'Just a thought that's all.' I wasn't convinced by his denial but it was something that could keep. 'So how did you get to the hospital? Ambulance?'

'I brought him,' said Cameron.

Lucky confirmed this. 'I rang your office on my mobile.'

'Surely the doctors got in touch with the police when they realised you had a bullet inside you.'

'The doctors haven't seen him yet,' complained Cameron. 'And we've been here an hour.'

That seemed par for the course for an NHS A & E Dept.

'No need to call the police,' said Lucky.

'They'll be here soon enough when they see what's happened to you. Did you get the car number?'

I wasn't hopeful but I thought I ought to ask him and he didn't disappoint me. Neither did he know the make of the vehicle although he thought the colour might have been green.

'Is there a reason you don't want the police involved?' I said suspiciously. Something didn't add up here. 'You know who they were don't you? Was it the Jenkinsons?'

Lucky looked sheepish, bit his lip and said nothing.

'Look here, Lucky. I'm pissed off with this. You get death threats in the post and on the phone. Someone takes a shot at you and you tell me you don't think you've upset anyone. Well, I don't fucking believe you so you either tell me what this is all about or you can find yourself another sucker to watch your back.'

Before he had chance to reply, a nurse with a clipboard walked up. 'Mr Learoyd?'

'That's me.' Lucky looked relieved to see her.

'Would you come with me please,' and she escorted him through to a doctor's cubicle.

'What do you think it's all about?' Cameron asked me.

'I don't know but it's obviously more serious than we thought. Those weren't idle threats. I do believe someone did try to kill the silly fool but why? What could someone like Lucky have done to them to warrant this treatment?   His singing isn't all that bad.'

'Has he always been a warbler?'

'That's all I've ever known him as and I'm going back twenty years. Mind you, I only know him from the clubs.'

'But it's hardly likely to be anything from his former life if it's that long ago. Is he full-time on the stage or has he got a day job?'

I've no idea. Maybe it's something you could follow up, Ronni.'

Lucky eventually emerged from the cubicle looking crestfallen. 'I was right,' he said. 'The bullet's still in there. They're keeping me in and they're going to operate in the morning.'

That was good news. At least he'd be in no danger confined to a hospital bed for a few days. I could turn my attention to my other two cases.

The nurse stayed by his side waiting to take him to a ward.

'I'll be round tomorrow with the grapes then.' I could see there was no chance of any further questioning tonight.

'Thanks for ringing me,' I told Cameron as we walked out to the hospital car park. 'You did well.'

'I wonder why he came to us in the first place if he won't let us help him?'

'I don't know. Something very odd about the whole thing but right now, I don't care. I'm going to be bollocked for being late home as it is.'

Indeed, Maria wasn't too happy when I walked in three hours late for my meal, although I had rung to warn her.

'The last two nights you didn't come home at all and tonight you stroll in when I'm ready to go to bed.'

I explained to her about Lucky and the shooting, which calmed her down a little, and she brought out my warmed-up duck in congealed cranberry sauce.

'Vikki and I had ours at eight, we didn't know how long you'd be.'

It was fair comment and I didn't argue. I ate my meal and, by midnight, we were both in bed. After two nights at the flat on my own, I was glad to feel Maria's warm body next to mine.

Next morning, I was at the offices of Oates International at nine prompt. I wanted to get to Jeanne McGhee before the police got round to see her and advised her not to talk to me.

The foyer was impressive. Black and silver walls were lined with giant framed photographs of impressive looking properties.

Jeanne was already at her desk when the receptionist showed me into her office. She wore a black striped trouser suit with a pale blue high-necked jumper and matching shoes and earrings.

'Bring us a pot of tea through would you, Simon.'

'Yes ma'am.'

It was a nice show of authority but it didn't impress me.

'You're early,' she said.

'You wanted protecting. I thought I'd better start right away. You haven't opened your mail yet?'

'I don't open the mail, Simon does that...' She stopped and her hand moved involuntarily to her mouth. 'Oh, you mean there might be a letter bomb in there?'

'It's been known,' I said. I thought it would be extremely unlikely but the best way to make sure she helped me was to remind her how frightened she was. 'Make sure Simon there examines each package carefully and anything suspicious he leaves alone.'

'I will.'

'Now then, the names you were going to give me.'

'I have them right here.' She reached into a drawer in her desk and pulled out a thick box file, which she opened. 'The people who were originally buying the land, the ones who paid Stewart the deposit...'

'The backhander, you mean?'

She shrugged. 'Whatever.'

'Into your bank account.' I laboured the point.

'Yes, into my bank account. Their outfit is known as Leprechaun Developments. Stewart dealt with a man called O'Toole, Michael O'Toole I think it was, and a Gene Flynn. They're both Irish. Their head office is in Dublin but they've opened a branch in Old Hall Street in Liverpool near the Albany.'

It was much as Geoffrey had said. I wrote the details down in my notebook together with their address and phone number.

'Right. That's the first party. What about the others that you say the partners wanted to sell to.'

'The Russians, I call them.' She gave a grim smile. 'I don't know their individual names but they go under the name of St Petersburg Properties and their letter heading shows a Moscow address. Here.'

She handed me an A4 sheet bearing a crest of a domed building and the name and address of the company printed in Gothic script. The signature at the bottom was illegible and there was no name beneath it. I read the letter. It served to introduce the reader to St Petersburg Properties and to ask whether Oates International would be in a position to purchase any land on Merseyside on their behalf and on what terms.'

She waited while I entered the details in my book.

'I take it your people wrote back?' I said.

'We sent them a list of land and properties currently on the market on which we could make an offer for them.'

'Some of which Oates International owned?'

'One or two.' She didn't offer any more details. I felt they could wait until later.

'And they picked the same property that Leprechaun thought they were buying?'

'It's land, not property.'

'When you say you wrote to them, do you mean you wrote to them in Moscow?' I pointed to the address on the notepaper.'

'No. They had a P.O. Box number on a compliments slip.'

'And they replied?'

'If I remember rightly, they rang and spoke to one of the partners and, later, someone from the company came over.'

'What was his name?'

'I don't know. I wasn't told.'

'So what's the position now? Remind me. Does Oates International still own it or has it been sold?

'I told you yesterday, as far as I know, we still own it.'

'And this is the land you mentioned yesterday? Between Toxteth and the Dingle?'

'Yes. I'll show it you on the plan.' She went over to a filing cabinet and flicked through the folders. 'That's odd. It isn't here. One of the partners must have borrowed it. I'll have to locate it and print you a photocopy.'

I wasn't surprised it was missing but told her I'd be grateful to receive a copy whenever she had the chance. 'It sounded like a fair size plot,' I said. 'What plans did Leprechaun have for it?'

'Redevelopment, the same as the Russians.'

'What sort of redevelopment?'

'I don't know exactly but I presume upmarket apartments, maybe houses.'

'Hardly the area for it is it?

Toxteth was where the 1980's riots had been and parts of the area were still no-go areas with gangland shootings fuelled by drug barons whilst Dingle, which led down to the docks, had always been an industrial area with low cost housing for the workers.

'That's the time to get in these areas, at the start of gentrification. That's when you can make a killing.'

'True.' After all, hadn't I just bought flats in Liberty Place so I knew the logic of it but, as a Scouser who was around in the Sixties, I found the idea of luxury apartments in the Dingle hard to visualise.'

'You've only got to look about you. Many of the big Victorian merchants' houses in Princes Drive have been totally refurbished and restored to their former glory. Ten years ago they were like rabbit warrens of squalid bed-sitters, full of drop-outs and druggies.'

'Not all of them,' I protested. I owned a house in Princes Drive myself, which I'd converted into self-contained flats and none of my tenants were drop-outs or druggies.

'Maybe not, but enough of them to make it a slum area. And what about the changes in Upper Parliament Street?'

There, I had to admit, she had a point. Although earlier councils had scandalously allowed some of the grand Georgian terraces to be demolished, most of the remainder had been smartly renovated. Furthermore, the University had expanded far beyond the original campus boundary and a host of new buildings had completely altered the landscape with more blocks appearing every month.

'OK, I take your point, Jeanne. I know the land is valuable. Does this mean your people will now hold an auction or is it to be best bids in sealed envelopes?'

'I don't know what they're going to do. All I know is that Gene Flynn and Michael O'Toole are not going to give up easily.'

'Who do you think killed Stewart?'

For the first time, the cool efficiency she had displayed faltered. 'I don't know.'

The way I saw it, there were three contenders up for it. The Paddys, because they'd thought they were losing both the deal and the cash they'd paid out and didn't look like getting back; the Ruskies, either to stop Davis selling to the Paddys or to punish him because they thought he had; or his own partners because they found out he was creaming off some of the profits for himself.

If I'd been a gambling man I'd have plumped for the boys from the Emerald City but, then, as I'd once backed Crisp to beat Red Rum in the Grand National, you wouldn't set any store by that.

'Do any of the other three partners know you were having an affair with Davis?'

'No. We were very discreet. A divorce would have ruined Stewart financially.'

I gave her a serious look. 'The police will want to know all this, Jeanne. It's a high profile case for them, a city financier murdered. Not your usual run of the mill crime in Liverpool.'

It seemed to me that crime in the city tended to fall into four main categories: - domestic killings ("wife fatally stabs husband as revenge for shagging her mother"); gangland executions ("drug dealer shot dead in crowded pub by masked man as innocent families with young children look on in horror"); muggings gone wrong ("blind bedridden war-hero pensioner dies of heart attack after teenage burglar steals 10p from his bedside table") and hit and run joy riders ("14 year old ploughs into bus-stop in stolen car during police chase killing pregnant mother and her two year old crippled son").

'I suppose not.'

'So do you really still want to hire me? I haven't cashed your cheque yet.'

She looked me in the eye. 'I'm in danger, don't you see?'

'Maybe, maybe not. Maybe they're just idle threats. Either way, the police will offer you protection if you tell them you've been threatened.'

But Jeanne had as much confidence in the police as guardian angels as Ollie did.

'They might offer it but we all know what really happens with their Witness Protection Programmes. Sure, they give you a new identity and move you to another part of the country but you're always looking over your shoulder and you can't hide forever. One day, someone will recognise you and that will be it. Your picture and details all over the Internet.' She paused for breath. 'Anyway, I haven't seen the police yet. They came here yesterday and spoke to all the partners but I rang in sick.'

'All right,' I said. 'You've convinced me. I'll give it a go. You never know, I might find out who killed Stewart as a bonus.'

I said it mainly in jest. If I'd known the danger I was getting myself into, I might not have said it at all. In fact, I might have steered well clear of Jeanne McGhee and her company altogether.

But I didn't know and, from then onwards, it was Trouble with a capital T all the way.

* * *

Chapter Seven

Cameron was ensconced in the office when I arrived.

'Any news?' I asked her.

'Ollie Clarke called. I told him you'd be in at eleven so he's coming over.'

I checked my watch. It was quarter to eleven already.

'How's Lucky? Have we heard from the hospital?'

'No. He was due to have his operation this morning.'

'What about his family, Ronni? They've never been mentioned in all this. I presume someone's contacted them. I don't even know whether he was married or not but he's bound to have someone. An ageing mother perhaps, wondering where her son has got to.'

'He was having an operation so the hospital would have had to ask him who his next of kin was. It's not like he was unconscious or anything.'

'I suppose so. Anyway, see what you can find out.'

'I'll do that. In the meantime, how did you get on with Miss McGhee?'

'She gave me the names of the companies trying to buy the land. What I'm waiting for now is the inside information on the people she works for, this Oates International. Geoffrey is sorting that out for me.'

'Anything I can do?' she asked.

'You could get in touch with Companies House and find out what you can about Leprechaun Developments and St Petersburg Properties.'

'They're the ones after the land?'

'That's right. I have the names of the guys supposedly running the operations but it won't do any harm to check them out in more detail.'

'Ride on.'

I went through to my desk and Roly took his place on his

blanket beneath it. It made a change for him from sitting in the car, I suppose. They say dogs like to keep to a regular routine, something Roly has never known since I acquired him. He never knows where he's going to sleep from one night to the next but he always seems to be pleasantly acquiescent wherever he ends up. Much like his owner really.

Ollie Clark turned up dead on time.

'Any sign of an arrest?' I asked him.

He sank heavily into a chair. 'I don't think they take me seriously. That Inspector chap hasn't said so but I get the impression they're regarding Graham's death purely as an accident.'

'And what about the vandalism? Don't they regard it as relevant?'

'No, it would seem not. Separate issue altogether. No connection.'

'But you don't believe that?'

Ollie bristled. 'No I don't but what can I do about it?'

'Wait a minute; you're saying you think Graham's death was deliberate? Someone meant to kill him.'

'No. I'm saying the ramp was interfered with and it was unfortunate for Graham that he was underneath it at the time.'

'Exactly,' I said. 'So, strictly speaking, it was an accident then, but not in the way they mean. The ramp could well have been deliberately vandalised but the accident part of it was in the timing.'

'What it boils down to in fact, is that Graham was simply in the wrong place at the wrong time?'

We paused whilst we considered the implications.

'Forensic are still down at the garage,' Ollie added. 'Measuring and fingerprinting and God knows what, not to mention the Health and Safety people.'

'Has DI Reubens interviewed all the staff?'

'He has. Me and all, and I believe he's coming to see you next.'

'There's been no further trouble I take it, Ollie?'

He looked at me sharply. 'Christ Almighty, Johnny. Isn't this enough to be going on with. Maybe when whoever it is sees what's happened to Graham, they'll give up their game.'

'It's possible.'

But unlikely, I thought. If Ollie was right and someone wanted him out of there badly, well nothing had changed. They'd still want him out. But maybe they'd try other, and more sinister, methods. Only time would tell but I saw no point in alarming him even further.

'I'll put a few feelers out, Ollie, and see what I come up with.'

We left it at that. Cameron came though after Ollie had departed.'

'Anything on the property companies?'

'Not yet,' she said, 'give me time. You wanted the 411 on Lucky Learoyd.'

'What have you got?'

'Nothing yet but I found out he works quite a bit for an agent called Hymie Stein.'

Hymie Stein was well known in the show business world. He'd always had a good reputation for reliability and, from what I'd heard, over the years his agency seemed to have developed into quite a successful business.

'Steen,' I corrected her. 'He likes to be called Steen not Stein. In fact he's insistent about it. His office is in Stanley Road near the old Rotunda. I'll think I'll drive over there after lunch and pay him a visit.'

I went across to the Grapes in Mathew Street for a cider and a Sandwich. Over forty years had passed since The Beatles drank there with Bob Wooler, the Cavern DJ, after the lunchtime sessions at 'the best of cellars'. Now Bob Wooler himself has had a book written about him.

I figured Hymie Stein should be back from his lunch by two thirty and it was twenty past when I drove away from the city along what is still called Scotland Road but now looks more like a Los Angeles freeway than the Scottie Road that old Scousers remember.

Beyond the Rotunda, many of the shops in Stanley Road had not fared well, like small independent businesses everywhere, and several had the metal shutters permanently down. The front of Hymie Stein's premises looked in better shape than those of his neighbours on either side, both of which were badly in need of a lick of paint.

Stein's office had been freshly decorated in a bright primrose yellow with an illuminated neon sign above the door bearing the inscription Wunderland Entertainments. The place gave every indication of a thriving concern, even if the sign writer couldn't spell. At least he hadn't put an unwanted apostrophe in.

I noticed the sign also included the words, "Established 1965". Hymie had started out in the wake of the Merseybeat boom and prospered through the golden age of cabaret and theatre clubs in the Seventies.

Strangely, we'd never worked for him as The Cruzads but that didn't seem to have hindered his progress.

I parked a few yards down the road and walked back. A buzzer sounded when I opened the door, which alerted the receptionist who looked up from her desk behind a protective glass grill.

'Is Mr Stein in?'

'Who shall I say it is?'

'Johnny Ace.'

'Just a moment'.

She picked up the phone and rang through to an extension. I studied the photos on the wall behind me, most of them of unknown club acts. All the prints looked professional and up to date, in ten by eight colour.

I recognised Lucky Learoyd, complete with his ponytail, sporting velvet trousers with a rip down the left inner thigh. He was displayed between Ricki Amazon and his Amazing Drinking Parrot and Zina Lambourghini — The New Madonna. I wondered why we needed a new Madonna when we were still saddled with the old one.

'Mr Stein will see you now if you'd like to go through.' She indicated a door to the left. I opened it and found Hymie Stein sitting behind a large old oak desk facing the door. I put him in his late fifties, Jewish, short but well groomed and smoking a small cigar. He wore a carnation in the buttonhole of his navy blue suit. Suit by Hugo Boss, cigar by Danneman.

'Mr Ace, do sit down. To what do I owe this pleasure? I am familiar with your radio programme of course. Would you care for a coffee?'

'I'd prefer tea.'

'No problem.' He picked up the phone and sent his request to the secretary.

'You're not thinking of taking to the boards are you?'

I assured him I wasn't.

'Pity. With your exposure on the local airwaves, I could get you a good fee.'

'Doing what? I gave up the juggling act, I couldn't afford to keep replacing the teacups.'

He smiled indulgently. 'Personal appearances at various events, conducting charity auctions, opening supermarkets, compéring shows. Lots of opportunities and all very lucrative engagements.'

'I don't think so, Mr Stein but thanks for the offer. I actually came to see you in my other capacity.' I handed him a Johnny Ace Investigations business card, similar to the one found in the pocket of the decapitated Stewart Davis. 'It concerns one of your acts. Lucky Learoyd?'

'I do book Lucky out from time to time,' he admitted. 'Has he done something he shouldn't?'

'Yes. He shouldn't have allowed himself to be shot whilst walking through Toxteth.'

Hymie Stein's face paled. 'When did this happen?'

'Last night.'

He immediately consulted his computer screen. 'He's supposed to be working for me on Sunday night in Accrington.'

No "how is poor Lucky"? People like Hymie Stein didn't get rich worrying about anyone but themselves.

'He's advertised to play in Old Swan tomorrow but I don't think he'll be appearing there either.'

'Have they got the killer?'

'Oh, he's not dead, Mr Stein. The bullet lodged in his shoulder but, no, they haven't caught the gunman.'

'How terrible.' He stubbed out his cigar and made a note in a foolscap diary. 'I'll have to bring in a replacement act.'

'Is Lucky much in demand?'

'He's quite popular, yes. There must be a million Elvis impersonators out there but not many people doing P J Proby and he is good, no doubt about that.'

'Does he have a day job?'

'I've no idea. I don't believe he's mentioned it if he has.'

'Would he earn enough from his singing to live on?'

'He can command £200 a night and he has no musicians to pay as he uses backing tracks like most of them do nowadays. Lucky's were top quality mind you; I'll give him that. As for the number of bookings, I'd guess he'd expect to be out at least two nights a week.'

'Twenty grand a year. Not bad for a couple of nights' work.'

'At least two nights. It might be more although there isn't that much midweek work nowadays with a lot of the old social clubs closing down.'

'Do you know any reason why anyone would want to harm him?' I asked.

'None at all. He's always struck me as an affable, cheery sort of man. Pays his commission regularly, doesn't try to book himself back into venues like some acts try to do.'

'Has he worked for you a long time?'

'About five years, since he first started with the Proby act. That was when he came to me.'

'What can you tell me about his personal life?'

Stein looked at me suspiciously. 'In what respect?'

'I don't mean anything untoward,' I reassured him. 'Although I've known Lucky for years, I don't know very much about him. Where he lives, for instance, or whether or not he's married.

'He lives over the water in Hoylake.'

I hadn't even known that. I made a point of noting down the address Hymie gave me.

Stein continued. 'As for being married, he did have a wife but she ran off with some young tearaway a year or so ago. From what I can gather, the divorce was pretty acrimonious. Lucky was very distressed.'

'In what way?'

'He didn't want her to go. Followed her around begging her to come back but she didn't. He was in a state; didn't work for ages.'

'Is the wife living with this guy now?'

'I've no idea but I would imagine so.'

'You don't know his name by any chance?'

Hymie Stein thought for a minute then, 'Yes. I think he was called Jenkinson. Jason Jenkinson.

✲ ✲ ✲

Chapter Eight

'So you reckon these Jenkinsons are the people we've got to watch?' asked Cameron. 'Your pal Lucky goes crawling after his ex-wife till, in the end, the Jenkinson clan decide to finish him?'

It was late afternoon and I was back in the office.

'Perhaps they didn't mean to kill him, just to give him a warning.'

'Some warning. A bullet in the head.'

'In his shoulder actually,'

'So, the guy was a bad marksman.'

You're forgetting the death threats,' I reminded her.

'You're right. They meant to kill.'

'This is one case that'll be taken out of our hands then. There'll be a policeman at his bedside and Lucky will tell him about the Jenkinsons and they'll be arrested before you can say "Somewhere".'

'There's a place for us,' warbled Cameron, in a fair imitation of the Texas troubadour.

'Thinking about it though, it doesn't add up. Why didn't he just tell us that it was the Jenkinsons who were after him in the first place.'

'Well, the divorce was two years ago. Surely he's come to terms with it by now?'

'You'd think so. In which case, there really is someone else out there threatening to kill him.'

Cameron agreed. 'That's just what struck me.'

'I give up,' I said. 'I'll go and see him in the hospital tomorrow and find out exactly what's going on.' Everton's first match at the season was away at Highbury so I had the afternoon free. 'Any joy with Oates International?' If I was getting nowhere with the other cases, I might as well give Jeanne McGhee my best shot.

'Your Mr Molloy rang earlier with the information. It's all here.' She handed me a sheet of paper filled with names, addresses and dates. 'These are the directors.'

I studied the names. Geoffrey had done well. There appeared to be three people involved in running the operation, Jeffrey Taggart, Patrick Dixon and Stewart Davis.

'They started out in 2001 in Old Street in London,' said Cameron. 'Moved up here in June.'

'Just after the City of Culture announcement.'

'A week after to be precise.'

It confirmed what Jeanne McGhee had told me. 'They probably had premises lined up in all the short listed cities and jumped in the moment the announcement was made.'

'Could be. Mr Molloy did say something else. He said they kept dubious company, whatever that means.'

'Anything from ties with the Mafia to illegal bill posting I should imagine.' But it was interesting to note that Davis's partners might not be above a bit of fiddling themselves.

'I wonder how long Leprechaun Developments have been in existence.'

'I checked on them myself. The company was formed in 1999 in Dublin and opened a Liverpool office in...'

'Don't tell me. June this year.'

Cameron smiled. 'July actually.'

'And the Russians? St Petersburg Properties?'

'No information at all on them.'

'Except that letter heading with an address in Moscow although they had a P.O. box number as well.' I realised I'd forgotten to get hold of that compliments slip. 'Yet one of their people came over here, Jeanne McGhee told me.'

'Did she tell you his name?'

'She wasn't told. The partners were the ones dealing with him.'

'So who does she think she is in danger from?'

'It's got to be Leprechaun Developments, the Irish contingent, hasn't it? They must have made the phone call because they mentioned the deposit. It was Jeanne's bank account the money disappeared from and they'd want it back. The Russians wouldn't have known about that.'

'Unless it was the Russians who killed Davis and he told them about the deposit before he died.'

'I suppose that's a possibility,' I conceded.

We were interrupted by an unexpected visitor. Maria came through the door, carrying Victoria in her arms.

'I'm so glad I caught you,' she said. 'I've just had a call from the library. Someone's gone off ill; they want me to go in until eight.'

Maria works part time at the Picton Library. She used to be full time in charge of a department but a couple of years ago she took up craftwork as a hobby and it caught on. Now she supplies a few local shops with greetings cards and jewellery. There's not much money in it, and sometimes it seems like every other person you meet is doing something similar, but she finds it fulfilling which is what really matters.

'Maria, you've not met Cameron, yet. Ronni, meet Maria and this is our daughter, Vikki.'

Maria put Vikki down so she could shake Cameron's hand. I noticed Cameron hardly glanced at Vikki. Obviously not child friendly. At the same time, Maria's handshake could be described at best as perfunctory. The two eyed each other like hungry lions in a jungle weighing up the options on one dead hyena.

Vikki clutched a dirty and worn grey teddy bear to her cheek and glared defiantly at Cameron.

I took her hand and sat her on my knee. 'So you want me to have Vikki? She'll have to come to the radio station with me.'

'That's OK, but make sure you don't let her lose Real

Teddy.'

Real Teddy was so called because, when Vikki was two, Maria had replaced her frayed and shabby teddy with a brand new one, identical in every way. But Vikki had not been fooled. 'That's not my real teddy,' she complained. 'That's More Teddy. I don't want More Teddy, I want Real Teddy.'

So the threadbare teddy was rescued from the bin, put in a washing machine, which unfortunately removed the last remnants of its fur, and restored to its rightful place on her pillow,

I assured Maria that both of them would be safe in my custody although I wondered how Ken would react when we all turned up at the radio station.

Maria smiled sweetly at my new partner. 'Nice to meet you, Cameron. She turned to me. 'Don't forget you'll have to feed her,' she instructed. She handed me a large shopping bag. 'All the stuff you'll need is in there.'

I took the bag from her. 'I'll see you about half eight then. Should I get a takeaway?'

'I'll bring something. You just get Vikki to bed.'

'So that's your partner?' said Cameron after Maria had left. 'An attractive lady.' She made it sound like an insult.

I've always described Maria as being like Cher but that was before the singer went blonde and acquired replacement body parts. Maria is slim with jet black hair and all her bits are her own.

'She is.'

Cameron quickly went back into her office, probably frightened she'd be given crèche duties. I settled Vikki in the corner with a scribbling pad and crayons that Maria had left in the bag. Roly crawled off his blanket and sat next to her, eyeing the crayons hungrily.

I rang Geoffrey at the Aigburth Road office. 'You know you mentioned doing a bit of bodyguard stuff yesterday?'

'Yes?' He sounded eager.

'Well, I've got a young lady who needs looking after. She's been threatened over the phone.'

'Jealous wife is it? Or a spurned boyfriend?'

'Neither. She's a business woman. Someone's fucked up on a deal and she's getting the blame.'

'What are they likely to do?' Some of the excitement had gone out of his voice and he sounded a little unsure.

'I don't know but if you read in the paper yesterday about the man found stabbed in Picton Road last night, that was her boyfriend.'

There was a silence. I didn't feel I'd sold the idea to Geoffrey as well as I might.

'Hasn't she told the police? Shouldn't they be guarding her?'

'Possibly they will be by now but just in case.'

Who knew what D I Reubens would do when he got to the bottom of Jeanne McGhee's story, as he undoubtedly would.

'She lives in Southport. I just thought if you were to pick her up from work in town, perhaps take her out for a meal and escort her to her door, she'd be safe for another night. Not an unpleasant task.'

Had Geoffrey been a ladies man, he'd have jumped at it but he was not. Nearing forty, he still lived with his mother in Aintree. Nothing gay about Geoffrey, you understand, just one of life's bachelors in the old meaning of the word. They seem to be a dying breed these days, like old men who wear cavalry twills instead of Nike track suits and grannies who knit. He'd probably turn up with a bunch of roses.

'OK, boss. I'll do that for you.'

'Here's where you pick her up.' I gave him the address of Oates International's office and then I rang Jeanne herself at work to explain who Geoffrey was and what was happening.

'The police have been here this afternoon,' she said.

'Detective Inspector Reubens was it?'

'That was the one who did all the talking.'

'He's handling the case,' I told her. 'What did you tell him?'

'Nothing. Just what a terrible shock it was and how I'd no idea why it should have happened. I emphasised that Stewart was a happy family man and good at his job.'

She sounded convincing enough to me but I knew the truth.

'They seemed very interested in the recent deals Stewart had been working on but nothing came up about the other business.' She spoke guardedly and I hoped her office phones weren't bugged. 'They were here ages. They took statements from the partners.'

'Exactly what you'd expect. I wouldn't worry about it.'

It was what I would have done in their place. As it was, knowing about Davis's dodgy deals, I had to approach the case from a different angle, working on the assumption that Jeanne was in danger.

However, with Geoffrey looking after Jeanne and Lucky in hospital, I figured I had everything under control, at least for one night.

Ken surprised me when I arrived at the radio station with Vikki. Instead of the horror or disapproval I expected from him, he positively fawned over her.

'You start the show, I'll take her for something to eat.'

Maybe the plum yoghurt from the station canteen wasn't the best choice for a three year old, as most of it went on her face, but Vikki seemed happy with her new Uncle Ken. I played *Baby Sittin'* by Bobby Angelo and The Tuxedos, one of the best ever, yet sadly unknown, British rock'n'roll records and Buzz Clifford's *Baby Sittin' Boogie*. Vikki always enjoyed the gurgling bits in that. I dedicated both songs to Ken who grimaced at me through the glass partition.

Roly, I left in the RAV4. I didn't think Ken could handle both child and dog at the same time.

It was seven thirty when we arrived back home at Sefton Park. There was a message from Cameron waiting for me on the Answerphone.

'Johnny. Ring me on my mobile when you get back. It's Lucky. He's gone AWOL.'

It wasn't what I wanted to hear.

I rang her straight away and got the full story. Lucky had had the operation as planned. The bullet had been successfully removed from his shoulder and he was wheeled back to the ward. But when they took his tea round some time later, his bed was empty.

Lucky had hired me to protect him. He'd survived one attack. Would I find him in time before whoever had shot him came back to finish the job?

'Do you know where he lives?' asked Cameron.

'In Hoylake. But I can't go yet. Maria isn't back to stay with Vikki.'

'Give me the address. I'll go.'

This took me by surprise.

'We are partners aren't we?'

'Yes but…'

'But nothing. I'm actually still in the office as we speak so I can be through the tunnel in five minutes.'

'OK but be careful. I don't want you shot.'

'Don't worry. Neither do I.'

She rang off. Hardly had I put the phone down before it rang again.

'Is that you, boss?'

I recognised Geoffrey's voice and I immediately knew it was bad news. 'Is something wrong?'

'It's Miss McGhee. She'd already left work when I got there. They told me she'd gone early. I'm outside her flat now in Birkdale, I thought I'd better come straight here but there's nobody in. it's all in darkness. There's no sign of her.'

'Are you sure you're at the right address?' But I knew Geoffrey didn't make mistakes like that.

He described the building and mentioned the cascade in the front garden. It was the right place all right.

Two people to guard and both missing. A hundred per cent cock-up rate. It almost made me wish I'd stayed in Spain. At least I'd had a cheque from Jeanne McGhee. I made a mental note to tell Cameron to bill all clients in advance in future.

It wasn't looking good. What were the chances Lucky Learoyd and Jeanne McGhee would still be alive by morning?

* * *

Chapter Nine

Maria came home an hour later by which time I'd managed to coax Vikki into bed.

'I've brought an Indian,' she said, producing a myriad of trays from a brown carrier bag. 'Vegetable biryani, chicken tikka dhansak, pashwari Nan bread, popodoms and chutney with prawn purée and onion bhajis for starters.

I told her what had happened.

'Oh no,' she said, then, 'It must be coincidence surely, them both disappearing at the same time. There's no connection between the two cases is there?'

'None at all. Just bad luck that I got landed with both of them at the same time.'

'What do you think's happened?'

'Lucky will probably be found dead at the side of a road somewhere, mown down by a hit and run driver in a green car that didn't stop. As for the girl, I don't know about her. Ronni should have rung by now.'

After what had happened to Stewart Davis, it was Jeanne I was most worried about.

'Try her mobile.'

'I have. It's switched off.'

'That's silly of her.'

I helped Maria set out the food, opened a bottle of White Zinfandel and we started our meal. We were down to the last glass of wine before the phone finally rang. I jumped up to answer it.

'Johnny? It's Ronni.'

'Thank God, I wondered what had happened to you. Your phone was off.'

'I was stuck in the tunnel. There was a breakdown, some lorry with a flat tyre. Took ages to move it because it jack-knifed across two lanes.'

'So where are you now?'

'Outside Lucky's house. Johnny, you want to see this place. It's a mansion.'

'What?'

'It's huge. In its own grounds, detached, wrought iron electric gates, stone lions on the gateposts, pillars round the front door, ten foot high wall all round. Are you sure you've given me the right address? This looks more like a property tycoon's place.'

Or a footballer's, I thought. 'You must have the wrong place, Ronni.' I took out my notebook and repeated the address

''Yes, this is the house all right.'

'And there's no sign of Lucky?'

'It's all in darkness. The gates are locked. I've buzzed the Entryphone but there's no reply.'

I couldn't see her scaling a ten foot wall. Besides, a house like that would probably have a pack of Rottweilers stationed in a nearby kennel ready to repel intruders.

'What about neighbours? Anyone you could ask?'

'Almost a bus ride to the next house on either side. Not the sort of road people walk along.'

'Just hang on there a minute. I've got his phone number here, I'll try ringing it and get straight back to you.'

'You could have done that to begin with,' pointed out Maria.

'If I'd thought of it.'

'Your Spanish holiday must have dulled your faculties.'

Maria was wont to make regular sarcastic remarks about my elongated trip. I couldn't blame her but that didn't make it any easier to put up with them.

I dialled Lucky's number. The phone rang four times before an answerphone picked up and I was treated to the strains of 'Somewhere' before Lucky's voice cut in. 'Hi, this is

Lucky Learoyd who IS PJ Proby. You want to book me? Then leave a number and I'll get right back to you. Have a nice day.' The music faded followed by an abrupt beep.

'Lucky,' I said. 'This is Johnny Ace. It's nine o'clock Friday night. Ring me the minute you get in.'

I rang Cameron back. 'An answerphone. I left a message for him to get in touch the minute he gets back.'

'I'll hang on here then. He's got to come through the front gates. I can't see there's any back way in.'

Maria looked at me. 'What's all that about?'

'Lucky Learoyd. It turns out he lives in a mansion.'

'I thought he was just a two-bit crooner.'

'Exactly. So did I.'

So how had Lucky managed to accumulate such wealth? And how come the estranged Mrs Learoyd hadn't got her hands on it? As a caller on the show said last week, a woman nowadays can have it away with half the men in the street, run off to live with the milkman and still cop for the family house, half the marital assets and a big chunk of the husband's salary and pension. And that's before the Child Support Agency moves in.

'Perhaps he won the Lottery,' suggested Maria.

'No. He'd have made sure his name was in the papers if he had. The publicity would have done wonders for his date book.'

'Then what?'

'I don't know but I don't like it. Something smells.'

The whole business of Lucky hiring me to protect him seemed odd at the time but after he was shot, I was more inclined to believe his claims to be in fear of his life. However, knowing now about his house, I just wasn't sure again. There were too many things unexplained.

On the other hand, of course, he was still missing so he could quite easily be dead. Maybe the Jenkinsons had got to him already?

We sat and watched a *Dalziel and Pascoe* re-run on BBC1. The characters now bore little resemblance to the books with Pascoe divorced and merely a stooge to Warren Clarke's caricature of his fat boss. I hoped Reg Hill had been suitably compensated.

I found it hard to concentrate on the plot as all the time I was waiting for a phone to ring but it remained silent.

We watched the news followed by Graham Norton and I realised why I was glad I'd bought a DAB radio as an attractive alternative to the television, if only to listen to BBC7.

At midnight, I rang Cameron again.

'Good job it's not winter,' she said, 'sitting out here for four hours.'

'No sign of him then?'

'Not a whisper.'

'Then I think you might as well get home now, Ronni. No sense in hanging around all night. Thanks for going.'

'All part of the job description.'

'I'll see you in the office on Monday.' I hung up.

'That just leaves Geoffrey and Miss McGhee,' said Maria.

'Geoff said he'd ring when she turned up.'

'Did he try her at her office?'

'Yes. An Answerphone there too.'

'So he's sitting waiting for her in that old banger of his in Birkdale?' Geoffrey's latest vehicle was a ten-year-old bright red Volvo estate; large enough to accommodate half the Russian Ballet troupe and with more scrapes on it than a coke addict's nostrils.

'That's about it. I told him to give it until midnight and, if she hasn't turned up by then, to go home.'

'That's all you can do.'

'That's all any of us can do until tomorrow.'

Maria took my arm and squeezed it coquettishly. 'In that

case, darling, let's go to bed before we get tired.'

I needed no persuading.

Geoffrey did finally ring but not until the next morning when we were in the middle of breakfast

'I gave it till midnight like you said, boss but she never showed.'

'No other callers?'

'Not one.'

'Right. Thanks anyway, Geoff.'

'Just let me know when you need me again.'

I said I would. But that rather depended on whether Jeanne McGhee was still alive and, at the moment, the odds were not looking too good.

'So what are you doing today?' Maria asked.

'I was going to see Lucky Learoyd in hospital.'

'You can't if he's not there.'

'That's true.'

'Then why don't we all go out for the day? We could have a drive to Blackpool and take Vikki to the funfair. We can take Roly to Kaye's for the day.' Kaye was Maria's sister. She lived with her husband Alex in Formby near the red squirrels.

My mind was still on the cases but I knew there was nothing I could do immediately. I wanted to look into Oates International's property deals but it was weekend and everywhere would be shut. I could only wait for Jeanne and Lucky to turn up. As for Oliver Clarke, that situation could well have come to an end after the tragedy of Graham Wharton.

'Why not,' I conceded whilst secretly wishing Everton had been playing at home. It seemed an odd way to start a new season with no match to go to.

It was a warm, sunny day. Too hot for driving. Even with air conditioning, the sun's rays through the car windows get pretty hot but opening the windows invites neuralgia.

I was glad to reach our destination. The bracing air was

welcome as we stepped out into the central car park in the shadow of the Tower. Blackpool was packed, as might be expected of the country's leading resort in August.

In many ways, the town had changed little since its heyday after the War. Although the amusement arcades and rides boasted the cutting edge of technology, the fortune tellers' booths, tacky gift shops, streets of terraced boarding houses, and the old-fashioned trams did not look much different from the photographs of the 1930's.

Vikki was very excited about going to the seaside. Luckily, the tide was out so she was able to play on the sands, albeit a lot less golden than the old adverts suggested. I bought her a bucket and spade and Maria and I sat in the sunshine on deck chairs watching her build sand castles.

After a while, she came running over. She'd spotted a chain of animals being led onto the beach.

'Can I go on one of those donkeys, Daddy?'

She chose an old grey creature with a wispy mane and hardly any tail. It hobbled a few hundred yards towards the Pier then trotted back. Vikki was ecstatic and I feared I could be in for a long and expensive stint at riding schools before too long.

'I'm hungry,' she announced eventually. It was coming up to one o'clock.

'I know where they do great fish and chips,' I told her. 'It's called the Bispham Kitchen on the road to Fleetwood and we can go there on a tram.'

Vikki was excited, as she'd never seen a tram before. If all went to plan, she'd see a lot more shortly in Liverpool but I tended to believe these things when they happened.

As the vehicle rumbled along the tramlines, we could see the scaffolding being erected ready for the famous Blackpool Illuminations. 'We must bring her in October,' Maria said. 'She'd love to see the Lights.'

The fish and chips were followed by rice pudding with jam after which we took another tram, this time a double-decker, back along the Promenade, right down to the Pleasure Beach. Here Vikki ate candyfloss, rode with us on the miniature railway and the Ghost Train and, with her Mum's help, won a small furry tiger rolling the balls on the Arabian Derby.

It was all very 1950s but I'd read Nick Oldham's books and I knew that, behind the fun and innocence of Golden Mile, Blackpool was as crime ridden as any British city.   I was also well aware that, if the town did succeed in becoming Britain's answer to Las Vegas, very little of the current Blackpool would remain.

'It's been a lovely day,' said Maria, as we made our way back to the car park. 'We ought to do this more often.'

I agreed and looked at my watch. It was coming up to five o'clock. We reached the car just in time to hear the football results on Five Live.

Arsenal had beaten Everton by one goal to nil.

'Never mind,' sympathised Maria. 'It's only one game and everyone loses to Arsenal don't they?'

'Pretty well, yes.' It didn't make it any better. We set off along the M55.

'Why don't we stop for something to eat on the way home? We could find a little country pub.'

'Good idea'.   I came off the motorway and took the Kirkham road towards Preston then snaked off down one of the side roads.'

Driving out along the narrow lanes, we had to stop for a herd of cows crossing the road. I turned off the engine and sat back.

'It's nice to see you relaxed,' smiled Maria. 'At one time you'd have gone mad being held up like this. Remember when you used to race to the next junction to beat the train at the level crossing gates?'

'I still do but cows defeat me.' I watched the last of the Friesians to straggle its way to the byre and started the engine.

'Catforth,' said Maria, reading the signpost as we moved on. 'There might be a village pub here.'

There was. It was a long white building called The Running Pump and it was perfect; home cooked food, a glamorous barmaid and packed with local drinkers.

Unfortunately, my relaxation didn't last long. We'd hardly finished our meal when my mobile rang.

'Oh shit. This could be trouble.'

'You should have turned it off,' Maria said.

'Can't do that. Twenty four hours on call in this job.'

'So which of them is dead? Lucky Learoyd or Jeanne McGhee?'

'We'll soon find out.' I pressed the keyboard and answered reluctantly. 'Johnny Ace.'

'Johnny, It's Oliver Clarke. I've been trying to get you all day. Someone's burnt my showrooms down.'

* * *

Ollie Clarke was not exaggerating. Bits of jagged glass hanging in the window frames were blackened and, in what was once the showroom, the charred remains of four vehicles were still smoking. It looked like a bomb had hit it and I told Ollie so.

'You're not far wrong,' he grimaced. 'Petrol bombs. We couldn't have been closed for more than half an hour either.'

We were standing outside the ruins of his premises watching firemen were sifting through the rubble and debris, pools of water everywhere. Two fire engines, lights blazing, stood nearby next to a police van.

I'd picked up Roly from Maria's sister's and dropped him off at home, along with Maria and Vikki, before coming out to see the damage.

'Nobody hurt?' I asked.

'Luckily no. Nobody there. And the flames never touched the garage. The fire brigade got here in time.'

The significance of this didn't escape me. 'At least they can't say you tried to destroy any evidence.'

Ollie jerked round. 'What do you mean, You're not saying they think I did this?'

'First thing they think of,' I told him. 'Is it an insurance claim? Or maybe he's getting rid of something he doesn't want people to see.'

'Christ, half my bleeding business has gone up in smoke.'

'At least, like you say, the garage is untouched so all that valuable repair equipment is safe. And I presume you're insured for fire damage?'

'Oh yes, no problem there except with the catalogue of damage I've had recently, my premiums are going to rocket and they've gone up enough as it is.'

I sympathised with him. Many small businesses were going to the wall since the American style litigation culture caught on over here. They can't afford to pay premiums which have tripled to meet escalating claims from a public who feel a scratched knee from a trip over a cracked payment is worth a couple of grand. Forget about the old-fashioned notion of 'look where you're going'. Nobody seems to accept responsibility for themselves anymore.

'What do the police say?'

'They're waiting for forensic results and the fire chief's report before they'll confirm anything officially but any fool can see that it's arson.'

'You reckon it's the same people?'

'That have done the other things? Yes, of course.'

'They must want you out pretty badly.'

'At the moment I feel like walking away from it all but I wouldn't give them the satisfaction.'

Two uniformed policemen came over and spoke to Ollie. 'We'd like to take a statement, sir. Would you care to follow us down to the station?'

'Where's DI Reubens. I told you, he's the one who should be dealing with this.'

'He's out on another case, I'm afraid. But I'm sure he'll be in touch with you as soon as he can. In the meantime...'

'OK, I'm coming.' He turned to me. 'I'll see you at your office on Monday morning, Johnny. We've got to thrash out a new strategy.'

In view of recent events, I thought Group 4 might be his best bet but I said I'd be there.

I strolled up to one of the firemen whom I recognised as a former footballer with Southport in their Northern Premier days.

'You reckon it's arson then?'

'No danger, mate. Can't you smell the petrol?'

'It's a bad do. His mechanic was killed by a falling ramp yesterday.'

'Doesn't have much luck, does he? Remind me not to buy a car from him.'

I wandered back to the RAV4. It was ten o'clock. This was the night Lucky Learoyd was supposed to be on at the Old Swan Social Club. Maybe the concert secretary had heard from him explaining why he wasn't turning up. It seemed worth the short drive to go and have a word with him in case Lucky had been in touch.

The car park was full but I got a spec not too far down the road and strolled over to the club.

Before I reached the door, I stopped in amazement. I could hear the strains of the opening bars of 'American Trilogy'. This was PJ Proby's encore number. I couldn't believe that Lucky had actually turned up to do the gig and yet...

I went inside and there he was, sitting on a stool in the middle of the small stage beneath a bright spotlight, wearing his white sequinned jumpsuit and holding the microphone away from his mouth with his other hand cupped to his ear á la Proby.

The only thing different about him was a sling over his left arm.

I turned to the man on the door and asked him what time Lucky had arrived at the club and received my second surprise of the evening.

'He's been here all afternoon, rehearsing.'

So where had he spent last night?

I went to the bar to buy a cider and waited for Lucky to come off stage. As the song reached its climax, he stood to attention next to the American Stars and Stripes, which he'd draped over the back of his chair. The words 'The eyes of Texas are upon you' sung in a soaring tenor which moved up a whole octave sent shivers down my spine. He sounded uncannily like the real thing.

The song ended and Lucky stepped down from the stage to

tumultuous applause and made his way to the small dressing room at the back. I followed him there. He looked surprised to see me.

'Johnny. What are you doing here?'

'We had a date, remember? We were going to see Tommy McKale at the Masquerade Club after this gig, to sort out your protection. Seems to me you don't need nurse-maiding the way you ran out of the hospital.'

He took off his jacket carefully, placing the sling on the dresser in the corner, and wiped the sweat off his face with a towel.

'Yeah, sorry about that, Johnny. I was in a bit of a panic. This bloke came along the ward wearing a white coat but he didn't look like a doctor and I suddenly thought he might be one of the men in the car what was after me so I legged it pretty smartish.'

I didn't believe him for a moment. That's what becomes of being a landlord. You hear so many sob stories and lies, you get cynical.

'So where did you go when you left the hospital?'

'I went home didn't I?'

'No.'

'What do you mean, no?'

'You didn't go home because my partner waited outside your front gate until well after midnight. We were supposed to be guarding you, remember. So try another excuse.'

'Nothing sinister about it. It was after one when I got home. I went to see this bloke in town about a gig.'

'Name and address, please.' I took out my notebook expectantly.

'Christ, you sound like the law. Lighten up, Johnny.'

'Who was the man offering you this gig, Lucky?' I asked him in a firm, quiet voice but he didn't answer. I was getting angry. 'Look here, you're the one who hired me, not the other

way round. So, you either cut the bullshit and tell me what's
going on or I walk away from here with the £200 that you're
being paid for tonight's show. That's my fee.'

Lucky clutched his injured shoulder and winced. Playing
for time while he thought up a good answer.

'Shouldn't be here really,' he said, 'not so soon after my
operation but I didn't want to let anyone down.'

'Very noble of you.'

He stood there for a moment making up his mind until
finally he said, 'Look, I'll come to the Masquerade with you,
Johnny. We can sort it all out there. OK? Just let me get my
gear together.'

'Right. How did you get down here?' I couldn't see him
driving in his condition.

'Taxi. '

'We'll go in my car then.'

Before we left, I rang Maria from the club call-box.

'It's going to be a long night,' I told her and explained I was
taking Lucky to the Masquerade. 'I'll probably stay at the flat
tonight. No sense in waking you. I'll be home before lunch.'

The Masquerade was packed. Tommy McKale had decided
to cash in on the start of the football season and was holding
a Footballers Wives Fancy Dress Night. Nearly all the men
were wearing soccer strip and most of the women looked like
extras from a Channel Five late night movie. It was a dangerous policy. Punters from rival teams, fuelled by strong drink
and aroused by the sight of a number of Page 3 wannabees,
hired by Tommy to add colour to the proceedings, were
always likely to start a riot. The atmosphere as we walked in
was tense.

Tommy's grandmother, Dolly, greeted me at the door.
'Poor start for your team, Johnny,' I peered at her through the
pay box window. She was wearing a Liverpool shirt and a pair
of red shorts exposing her thighs, not recommended for a

woman of ninety. I averted my eyes.

'Everyone loses to Arsenal, Dolly.'

'Do you like my boots,' she said and lifted her leg in the air like Margot Fontaine. They were sparkling silver with high heels, more Gary Glitter than Roy Keane. Lucky turned away in horror.

'I couldn't see Vinnie Jones wearing those,' I said.

'Wait till you see Vince,' she replied.

Vince, the barman, was concocting a cocktail for a Kylie look-alike masquerading as a Manchester City supporter. He spotted me and cried out.

'Johnny. Can I do one for you?

'What is it?'

'A Multiple Orgasm. Would you like one?'

There were a few guffaws from fellows around the bar. I said I thought I'd stick to Scrumpy Jack.

Vince was wearing a red bandana tied round his shaven head, a Liverpool FC scarf swinging round his nipple rings as he pirouetted round the bar, and a pair of tiny red shorts that fitted too tightly for public decency.

Lucky said he'd settle for a bottle of Becks.

Tommy McKale came over as we were moving away from the bar. I introduced him to Lucky.

'He does a PJ Proby act,' I said.

'Really? Proby's got a big gay following hasn't he? We're putting on a Poofters Paradise Night next Sunday and I've been looking for a suitable act to complement the male lap dancers.' Tommy could never be accused of being politically correct.

Lucky said he'd be happy to do it.

'I take it you do split your trousers?' said Tommy.

'Oh yes.'

'You're on then. That'll get the shirtlifters going.'

I thought it time to get down to business. 'We came to see

you, Tommy, because Lucky here has been having a bit of trouble and he's looking for protection.'

Tommy's expression brightened. 'What sort of trouble?'

The DJ, dressed as a referee, was playing football anthems at top volume and I was finding it difficult to hear.

'Why don't we go and sit down somewhere quiet and I'll give you the full monty.'

Tommy led us to a quiet corner in the back bar where a Barry White CD played in the background and a few couples clung to one another on the small illuminated dance floor.

I continued the story. 'It started with death threats in the post. I suppose I didn't take it too seriously but on Thursday he was gunned down in Toxteth.'

'Bullet went into my shoulder,' explained Lucky, indicating his sling.

'Anyone you know?' asked Tommy.

I answered for him. 'Probably the Jenkinsons.'

Lucky coloured. 'That's crap. Why should the Jenkinsons bother with me?'

'You don't know? Then I'll tell you why, Lucky.' I was angry now. 'I don't like people pissing around with me. Something to do with your ex-wife maybe? She ran off with Jason Jenkinson and you weren't too happy about it. And don't deny it, Lucky. I've talked to your agent, Hymie Stein. He told me the whole story.'

Lucky was silent. Probably working out how much to tell us. 'OK. I'll admit it,' he said at last. 'Yes, all right, I did have trouble with one of the Jenkinsons. The bastard ran off with my wife. Wouldn't anyone be upset in my place?'

'So what happened?'

'What do you think happened? You know yourself what the Jenkinsons are like. They're scum and dangerous scum at that. They're lunatics. Wayne Jenkinson called round one day and took me to the cemetery to have a quiet word with me.

Asked me if I should let bygones be bygones.'

'Or?'

'Or I could choose my headstone.'

'I hope you didn't go for marble, Lucky, it's very expensive.'

He didn't appreciate the humour. 'I figured it was her choice, the wife I mean. If she'd rather have that ratbag than me, he was welcome to her.'

'A wise decision. So why are they shooting at you now?'

'They're not. I told you, it wouldn't be them.'

'You've really had no contact since then?'

'On my mother's life, Johnny. All that business happened over a year ago. As far as I'm concerned it's history now.'

'Is it history for them though? After all, you were near their patch when they opened fire on you. Are you sure you didn't catch a glimpse of them?'

'How many more times do I have to tell you? I never clocked the bastards.'

'Pity,' said Tommy. 'I was quite fancying a run in with the Jenkinsons. They need putting in their place.' He looked disappointed.

I kept on persevering. 'So who is trying to kill you, Lucky?'

'I really don't know. That's why I hired you.'

Tommy McKale spoke up. 'You want some muscle, son? I can provide it but I want to know the score, right? If I find out later you've been holding out on me...' He didn't need to finish the sentence. His expression was enough.

'Don't worry, I'm not.'

'Right. Well, I can let you have one of my men but it will cost you.'

'How much?'

'We charge £150 a day. He can start on Monday.'

'That's fine,' said Lucky. He turned to me. 'Worth it to stay alive eh?'

I did a quick calculation. That was over £1000 a week. Lucky would have to work six nights to cover that notwithstanding his own living expenses. On the other hand, I was forgetting about the size of his house.

'Do you have another income apart from the act?' I asked him.

'No. Why do you ask?'

'We've been to your house in Hoylake, Lucky. There's a million pounds of real estate there. You didn't buy that by singing 'Hold Me' on the rubber chicken circuit.'

'Then you've got the wrong place. No wonder you never found me last night.'

'Hymie Stein gave me your address. That's where he sends your contracts to.'

'He's made a mistake, I tell you. I'm in a little two up two down off the main drag.'

'Do you live there alone?'

'Since the wife left, yes.'

I didn't believe him but it would be easy enough to check. A bigger mystery was how he could afford to pay Tommy McKale, unless he had a lump sum salted away that we didn't know about. But that wasn't my problem. Tommy and Lucky shook hands on the deal and we all trooped back into the main bar.

Lucky Leonard was no longer my concern.

The sounds of Queen's *We are The Champions* reverberated through the club at a deafening volume. Groups of lads in various replica kits swayed and sang discordantly along. I didn't think the fighting would be long in starting and I was making my way towards the exit when I caught sight of a small blonde girl standing at the bar with a group of friends.

It was Hilary.

I knew, of course, that one day our paths would cross and we would meet up somewhere quite by chance and I knew too that I should keep walking, as Hilary still hadn't spotted me. But that thought lasted for only half a second. I went over.

'Johnny!' She seemed delighted to see me. The feeling was mutual. Hilary always had that uplifting effect on me. 'Fancy seeing you.' She kissed me on the lips and it felt good. And exciting.

'Who are you with?'

'Some girls from work. We've been on late duty so we thought we'd come out and relax and have a bop.'

I looked at her outfit. She was wearing a pair of tight indigo jeans that revealed the Calvin Klein waistband of her thong above the low-rise waistband, a sheer black top over a black bra that emphasised her ample cleavage and a short leather jacket. She'd have given the TV footballers' wives a run for their money any day.

She put her hand in mine. 'What are you doing here?'

'A bit of business with Tommy.'

'Back on the job then?'

'Something like that.' I didn't elaborate. Hilary had never been keen on my detective work. She preferred it when I was just a DJ on the radio.

We stood by the crowded bar, oblivious of everyone around us. Hilary squeezed my hand. 'Come on, let's have a dance.'

'For old time's sake?'

She grinned invitingly. 'Whatever.'

We walked back to the other bar, hand in hand in the way we had done for over twenty years. It felt quite natural for us to be together. On the dance floor, she put her tongue inside my ear and whispered, 'They're playing our song, sweetheart.'

I recognised the track. It was Dolly Parton's *I will always love you*.

She threw her arms around me and thrust her body into mine. I leaned down and kissed her urgently. Our tongues intertwined.

For a strange moment I felt myself standing outside my body, watching me holding Hilary and remembering the afternoon with Maria and Victoria. And then I was back in Hilary's arms.

I told myself it was only a dance, nothing more. Sometimes you can make yourself believe anything you want to.

When we woke up naked beside one another in my flat the next morning, I couldn't fool myself anymore. It had been a wonderful night but I knew I hadn't to let it happen again. But Hilary had other ideas.

She reached down to the side of the bed for her leather jacket that was lying on the floor and put it on without fastening it, allowing her boobs to protrude through.

'You look like Marianne Faithfull in that motorcycle film.'

'If only we had a Mars bar.'

'That was an urban myth,' I said. 'But I do have a Cadbury's Flake.'

Hilary giggled. 'You know where it goes.'

Eventually, I got up to make some breakfast, which I brought back to bed and we chatted together as if we'd never been apart.

'Have you heard from Mary since you came back?' she asked. Hilary knew every detail about my life.

'I got a postcard from her the other day. She's seeing a man from one of the budget airlines.'

Mary was someone I'd met at a jazz club in Javea. She'd put me up in her villa near Denia until I found myself a place of my own, an apartment in El Poblets. We'd gone out together on a casual, no-strings basis and had a good time but, after a few months, I became bored with life amongst the ex-pats and decided I needed to get back to Liverpool. Life on the Costa Blanca was hardly action-packed.

I think Mary was hoping for something to develop from our relationship. She'd been widowed early and didn't want to

spend the rest of her days alone. For me it was just an inter-
lude in my life. I booked my flight back, a few tears were shed
and we parted. I was glad she'd found somebody else.

I'd hate to think Maria or Hilary would do the same.

'Where are you going today, love?' Hilary asked, spreading
marmalade on a piece of granary toast and handing it to me.

'Nowhere special. I said I'd be back for Sunday lunch
about twelve.'

'We've still got a couple of hours then.' She smiled mis-
chievously.

'Enough time for another cup of tea and a shower,' I said
firmly, 'and then I'll take you home.'

'When will I see you again?'

I looked at her sadly. 'I don't know but we always keep in
touch, Hil, don't we?'

If parting was such sweet sorrow, why did we do so much
of it?

'I'll run you home and then I'll have to get back.'

'I know. Mustn't be late for Maria.'

Hilary lived on the Wirral in a cottage just outside Heswall.
As she climbed out of the car, I wondered if we would ever go
out together again. Maybe she read my thoughts.

'You will keep in touch, won't you, Johnny?' she asked
anxiously.

'I always have,' I said.

'It was nice tonight wasn't it?'

It was and that was the problem.

As I drove away, I realised I was not too far the house
where Lucky Learoyd was supposed to be living. It seemed a
good idea to nip along and see the so-called mansion for
myself.

I drove along Telegraph Road, into West Kirby, barely half
a mile away from Jim Burroughs' place, and out again towards
Hoylake and the house Lucky Learoyd denied he lived in.

Cameron had been right in one respect. The place was a like a palace. Think Castle Howard in miniature. I peered through the wrought iron gates. There were no signs of life and no cars in the drive.

Cameron must have been mistaken. This was a house for a captain of industry, a senior politician or a reserve centre forward with a Premiership club, Not the home of a second rate club entertaincr.

I pressed the button on the Entryphone. A voice answered almost immediately.

'Who is it?'

The voice belonged to Lucky Learoyd.

* * *

Chapter Eleven

'Lucky? It's Johnny Ace. Open the gates will you.'

Silence.

I pressed the buzzer again.

No answer.

Cameron had been right when she said there was no way in other than through the front gates and they were locked and, presumably, electronically controlled.

I tried ringing once more but Lucky was obviously not receiving visitors, at least not if one of them was me.

I went back to the RAV4, started the engine and cruised a few hundred yards down the road before doing a U-turn and parking facing Lucky's house.

I decided I'd give it ten minutes to see if anyone came in or out. I had been waiting only five when the gates slowly opened outwards and a black saloon with tinted windows glided out. It looked vaguely familiar. The driver took a left turn and the car flashed past me towards Hoylake. I managed to catch a brief glimpse of the driver through the front window. It looked like a woman with long hair. I couldn't see if she was carrying any passengers as the side windows were almost totally blacked out.

I turned back to look at the house. The gates were already closing. Too late to sneak in. I started the engine, turned the car round and set off in pursuit of the black saloon.

I put my foot down, expecting to see it ahead of me after a couple of turns in the road but the first car I caught up with was a Nissan Micra crawling along with a Sunday-driving pensioner at the wheel.

I overtook that only to find myself behind an Arriva bus pulling out imperiously from a bus stop. No sign of the car ahead and now I was stuck behind the bus. Steve McQueen never had this problem in *Bullitt*.

The clock on the dashboard said 11.30. Maria was expecting me at twelve. That settled it. Chase abandoned. I headed for the Wallasey tunnel, wondering about Lucky Learoyd. Why had he lied about where he lived? Who was trying to kill him and why? I had no answer to that but someone obviously believed he had a good reason to put Lucky away.

At least, I thought, he should be safe under Tommy McKale's protection so that was one less thing to concern me. I could worry about the rest later.

It was five past twelve when I drove through the gates of our Sefton Park house. I went inside to find Maria in the kitchen cooking the lunch whilst Victoria was playing on her swing in the garden with Roly, gnawing at an old bone, keeping an eye on her. I walked over to Maria and put my arms round her.

'Sorry I'm late.'

'How'd it go last night?' she asked.

'Hectic.' I gave her a brief rundown on the fire at Oliver Clarke's garage and Lucky's unlikely appearance at the Old Swan. 'At least I've got Lucky off my back. He's Tommy McKale's worry now.' I explained that the McKales were booked for bodyguard duties. I told her I'd been to check out Lucky's house and confirmed what Cameron had said about it. I didn't mention Hilary.

We had a quiet family day at home. Maria spent some time in her workroom working on a necklace she was making for her sister's birthday. I played with Vikki in the garden. At night, we watched Caroline Graham's *Midsomer Murders* on TV but I couldn't believe it wasn't really *Bergerac* transferred to the Cotswolds and my attention wandered.

The calm before the storm.

I was in the office next morning for nine o'clock. Maria was at home all day so I left Roly with her. He'd get more exercise in the garden than he would in my office. Cameron was already there when I arrived.

'Any word on Jeanne McGhee?' she asked.

'Nothing. But someone burned down Oliver Clarke's garage on Saturday night and it seems you were right about Lucky Learoyd. He does live in the Hoylake mansion.'

'But he told you he lived in a two roomed terrace?'

'Yes, but why.' A thought struck me. 'I've just remembered something Hymic Stein said. Lucky Learoyd was supposed to be working for him in Accrington last night. I wonder if he turned up.'

I picked up the phone and dialled Hymie's number and managed to get through to him first time. The answer I got was as I had expected. Lucky had done the gig.

We spent the next half hour going over developments.

'We need to look into Lucky Learoyd's personal life,' I said. 'If he's telling the truth about the Jenkinsons, then there's got to be somebody else out there with a grudge against him. Maybe from way back. And I want to know how he can afford a house like that and why he keeps it a secret.'

'I'm more worried about Jeanne McGhee.' Cameron said. 'She's been missing two whole days now.'

'You're right. She should be at work this morning, If not, we'll know there's something wrong. Let's give her a ring.'

I picked up the phone but, even as I dialled her office number, I wasn't hopeful. The receptionist answered immediately and I asked to be put through to Miss McGhee. The answer was the one I dreaded.

'I'm afraid Miss McGhee is away on extended leave.'

'When will she be back?'

'We're not expecting her back until next month. Can anybody else help you?'

I thought for a moment then told her I'd like to make an appointment with one of the directors.

'What name shall I say?'

'Johnny Ace.'

'Just a moment.' She put me on hold and I was treated to a polyphonic version of *Eine Kleine Nachtmusik* that I couldn't see making the charts. 'Hello?'

'Still here,' I assured her.

'Can I ask you what it's concerning?'

'Land purchase.'

Back to Mozart.

'Hello?'

'Yes?'

'Mr Taggart can see you at three o'clock.'

'I'll be there.'

I put the phone down. Cameron said, 'I take it she's not turned up?'

'Extended leave. Away until next month.'

'I don't like the sound of it at all.'

'Neither do I but, unless she gets in touch with us, there's nothing we can do.'

'I wonder if the police have heard from her?'

'If they have, they're unlikely to tell us. Anyway, I've arranged to see one of Stewart Davis's partners this afternoon. I may be able to find out more about this land deal.'

In the meantime, I was expecting Oliver Clarke. He duly arrived a little before eleven. I'd seen falcons with eyes less hooded and his thick white hair bore the texture of straw, a sure sign of stress.

'Showroom gutted, four cars destroyed, what next?' He laughed hollowly. 'What's left? I should say.'

'You've still got the garage,' I pointed out.

'And no chief mechanic to run it.'

'I take it you've had no message?'

'What sort of message?'

'From whoever is doing this. Ever since the vandalism first started, you've been convinced somebody is conducting a personal vendetta against you.'

'What else does it look like, for Christ's sake?'

'I'm not saying you're wrong, Ollie. In fact, I agree with you. Somebody wants you out of there. The big question is, why? And why haven't they made their wishes known?'

'How do I know?'

'Exactly. That's what I'm saying. If it was a revenge thing, you'd have expected some sort of message but you've not had slogans or graffiti painted on your walls or letters telling you to get out of town have you.'

He admitted he hadn't.

'Yet, if it's just the premises they want, why don't they just make you an offer? Have you had no other motor firms approaching you to buy the place?'

'No.'

'Have any of the other dealers suggested a merger?'

'No. I've been in the motor trade for thirty years as my own boss. People respect me for that and that's the way it's staying.'

'I wonder if any of the other dealers have experienced any trouble like this?'

'Not that I know of.'

'So we're back to why they want you out. How long have you been in the current premises?'

'In Chinatown? Ten years.'

'And business is good?'

'Fine. I know what you said about the insurance but it wouldn't pay me to torch the place. Check the books if you don't believe me. I'm making a good living.'

'You own the freehold do you?'

'Yes. I gave up renting when I bought this place. You're always at the mercy of greedy landlords.'

I let the allusion pass. Most people think of landlords as potential Van Hoogstratens. If they had to rent out their houses to some of the tenants I'd seen, they'd soon realise that the vilified Peter Rachmann had the only right method to deal with them.

'If you own the freehold then the obvious thing is they want the land. Has nobody made you an offer for the land as opposed to the business?'

'No.'

'Well don't be surprised if you get one and, if you do, let me know. Meanwhile, what's the latest with the police?'

'That Detective Inspector was round first thing. They're still waiting for the Health and Safety report on the ramp but he reckons the coroner will go for accidental death on Graham if there's no evidence the ramp was tampered with.'

'What about the fire?'

'Definitely arson, of course. The one good thing is it's made the police take the other things more seriously although I've not been able to tell Reubens any more than I've told you.'

'Has he expressed any opinion?'

'From the questions he asks, I'm sure he thinks it's a gang thing. You know, protection. I haven't paid up so they teach me a lesson. There's a lot of that heavy stuff going on in the city centre at the moment as you'll probably know yourself.'

'Always has been, Ollie. Nothing's changed since the Sixties in that respect.'

'And before that too, Johnny. The same families as well, like the Jenkinsons and the McKales.'

I didn't enlighten him as to my association with Tommy and Denis. But I thought it interesting that the Jenkinsons name cropped up again.

'Have they never approached you, Ollie, the Jenkinsons?'

'When I first came they did, but I knew some boys in Everton who'd give them a hard time if they came after me. I passed on the word and I've never been troubled since.'

I wondered, knowing what the city was like for gossip and how everybody seemed to know everyone else, if Ollie had heard any rumours about Lucky.

'Have you ever come across a singer called Lucky Learoyd, Ollie? He works the clubs with a PJ Proby tribute show.'

Ollie shook his head. 'Never heard of the guy? Why? Who is he?'

'His wife ran off with one of the Jenkinsons, that's all.'

'Let's hope he doesn't go after her then otherwise he'll find himself floating down the river on the next tide.'

There was little more to say. The police were far better equipped than I to deal with Ollie's problem, now that they had deigned to take up the case. They had the manpower and the forensics. But it wouldn't stop me from keeping my eyes open and asking round.

Cameron came in as Ollie left.

'No answer again at Jeanne McGhee's house. She could be dead inside there for all we know.'

I didn't think it likely. If she'd been abducted from work before Geoffrey reached her, they'd hardly have taken her home.

'Maybe I'll find out more this afternoon,' I said, 'when I go to her office and speak to her boss.'

We were interrupted by the promised visit from DI Reubens, together with Detective Sergeant Monk, in relation to the death of Ollie Clarke's mechanic. Monk's skin looked blotchier than ever whilst his superior bore all the signs of stress and overwork, furrowed brow and fidgeting hands. Perhaps Ollie and the two policemen would end up in the same clinic together.

'Did you know Graham Wharton personally, Mr Ace?'

'I didn't know him at all,' I replied truthfully.

'So you won't know anything about his relationships with the other staff at the garage or with Mr Clarke?'

'No, I won't. But do these questions mean you think Mr Wharton was deliberately killed by one of his own colleagues?'

'On the contrary. I've interviewed them all and there doesn't seem to be any motive for anyone to kill Mr Wharton. He was well liked at work, a happy family man, didn't owe money or mix in bad company. No, I believe the whole thing was a complete accident but we have to look at all possibilities.'

'What about Mr Clarke's theory, that the 'accident' was another in a long line of attacks aimed specifically at him.'

'In view of the fire on Saturday, we must consider that a possibility but I have to admit I don't think the two incidents are connected. Access being the main stumbling block to that idea. The other workmen would have noticed anyone strange entering the garage and messing about with the equipment.'

'Maybe one of his own workmen holds a grudge.' I suggested.

'In which case he'd have killed Clarke and not Graham Wharton.'

'True.' Unless, of course, he'd already set things in motion when Clark was underneath the car and it was too late to go back. But I didn't seriously believe that and certainly saw no point in saying it to Reubens.

'No, I'm just waiting for a report on the ramp from the Health and Safety people to confirm mechanical failure and then we can put this one to bed.'

There was a moment's silence. Maybe he was waiting for me to say venture some information but I said nothing and he changed tack.' I was surprised to see you at Mr Clarke's premises on Saturday evening after the arson attack.'

'Were you, Inspector?'

'You get everywhere, don't you Mr Ace?'

'I like to be where the action is.'

'You always seem to be in the right place at the right time

or could that be the wrong time?'

I ignored the bait. 'I do don't I? Perhaps I should buy a camera and become one of the paparazzi.'

He smiled dutifully and made a show of removing a shred of breakfast from between his teeth before asking, 'What's your take on the fire?'

I remembered what Ollie had told me about the police's view and thought it best to go along with their thinking. 'I can only think he's upset the wrong people.'

'Which wrong people would those be?'

'You know, one of the local gangs. The Holdens maybe, or the Jenkinsons.'

Did I imagine it or did his jaw stiffen when I mentioned the Jenkinsons?

'A drugs involvement perhaps?'

I was forgetting the Holdens' reputation as dealers. 'Good Lord, no. I was thinking more of protection. If anyone came demanding money, I couldn't see Oliver Clarke paying up without a fight.'

'Mmm.' He said nothing but he seemed quietly satisfied. Happy, perhaps, to have his own views endorsed.

I changed the subject before he could ask any more questions.

'What's the latest on the murdered vagrant?'

'Nothing at the moment. We're still waiting for DNA results. I take it you've still no idea how your card came to be in his pocket?'

'Not a clue,' I lied, 'and I don't suppose we'll ever know now.'

'I wouldn't be too sure of that, Mr Ace.' Sam Reubens looked determined. 'This case, as you show business people say, has legs. It will run and run. I take it you now know who the victim was?'

'I read it in the *Daily Post*. A fellow called Stewart Davis.'

'That's right. Did the name ring any bells with you when you read it?'

'No. I've never heard of the man.'

'He worked for a land and company called Oates International. You're into this property lark yourself aren't you?'

'I rent out flats. It's hardly in the same league.'

'Ah, you know Oates International then?' Reubens was not slow to pick up on things.

'Only by reputation. They're a London company looking for rich pickings on Merseyside since Liverpool won the City of Culture accolade.'

'There's more than a few of those around, I can tell you. Never mind City of Culture, if you ask me it's more like a city of vultures.'

'Could his death have been connected with his work?' I asked. I was anxious to find out how much danger Jeanne McGhee might be in.

'We've no motive established as yet,' he said guardedly.

'Oh dear, you aren't having much luck with your cases, are you Inspector?' I sounded like Paul Temple commiserating with the Chief of Scotland Yard in 1940.

'Fuck know's what'll happen next,' declared Reubens, his choice of words bringing me sharply back to the present. 'But something will turn up.'

I wondered how many more cases he was handling along with these two and he was happy to tell me.

'Two armed robberies in Croxteth last night for a start and a man shot in a pub in Huyton.'

'Jim Burroughs used to say, was there ever a night when there wasn't a man shot in a pub in Huyton?'

Reubens permitted himself a smile. 'A quiet night really, thank God. We've hardly enough officers to cover everything. Of course, at one time, policemen used to patrol the streets and catch criminals. Now, thanks to government interference in the name of political expediency, we're forced to spend hundreds of wasted hours filling in forms and completing fatuous public surveys just to reach some spurious target figure.'

I could imagine him repeating that speech at every police federation meeting whenever he got the chance. I said, 'It gives cushy well-paid jobs to a few thousand bureaucrats, I suppose, and keeps the unemployed figures down.'

Reubens warmed to his subject. 'When we do catch them, half of them never get locked up. It's no wonder the crime rate is rising inexorably. Did you know, to keep convicted felons at 1950 levels of incarceration, the prison population would need to be quadrupled. Prison might not rehabilitate them but at least they can't commit any more crimes while they are safely locked away.'

'Quite.'

'Now, when the prisons are full, instead of building more, they let the convicts out.'

'You couldn't make it up,' I agreed and decided I must have him on the show one night. He would make a good controversial interview and I could fit him in nicely between The Robins' *Riot on Cell Block Nine* and Webb Pierce *In the Jailhouse Now,* or maybe a bit of Gilbert and Sullivan, *A policeman's lot is not a happy one* to give it relevance. .

'I could murder a cup of tea,' he said. 'We're off to interview a rape victim next in Kensington. That was another one.'

'No problem,' I said and went into the kitchen to put the kettle on. I'd quickly learned that Cameron did not consider tea-making to be part of her remit.

We moved on to football over the tea and I told them I was an Everton fan. Sergeant Monk confessed that he supported Liverpool so we debated the wisdom of keeping Houllier on for another season.

Sam Reubens was of the opinion that professional football

was now the province of overpaid nancy boys and he had no time for it anymore. Instead, he admitted to being a enthusiastic follower of non-league football himself and, as a resident of Crosby, a regular follower of Marine in the Unibond League.

'I buy the *Non League Paper* every week and I go to watch The Mariners if they're at home. That is, if I can ever manage to get a Saturday off.'

'With all these rapists and gunmen running loose, you mean?'

The two of them stayed another twenty minutes chatting. I didn't know whether that meant less time for them to fill in forms or less time for chasing rapists. Perhaps they'd been hoping I'd let slip something about the murdered tramp but, if that were so, they were unlucky for I knew little more than they did.

They had only been gone a couple of minutes when the phone rang and Cameron came racing through.

'It's Jeanne McGhee. She's calling from a paybox. She sounds desperate.'

*   *   *

Chapter Twelve

'We'd given you up for dead,' I said.

'I've only got a minute.' She was out of breath like she'd been running.

'Where are you?'

'I'm in Preston.'

'What are you doing there?'

'It's a long story. Look, I can't talk now. I'll be back home tonight. Come and see me there and I'll explain everything.'

'Wait...' But she'd rung off.

I quickly dialled the number that was showing on the call display screen but it rang out unanswered and, after twelve rings, I gave up.

'How is she?' asked Cameron anxiously.

'I don't know. She wants me to go round to hers tonight. She's in Preston of all places. It seemed like she had to put the phone down suddenly, as if somebody was approaching the phone box.'

'Do you think she'll turn up tonight?'

'I don't know but we'll soon find out. Do you want to come along?'

She did. I think she felt she wasn't getting too much action sitting behind a desk every day. Didn't feel like a real detective. Hadn't she heard Sam Reubens say he spent half his time form-filling?

We sent out for a couple of pizzas for lunch. Cameron had brought in a bottle of Westons Organic cider, which turned out to be her favourite tipple next to champagne, and the two went together well.

Maria called to say she'd had an order for twelve of her bracelets from a jewellers in Grange over Sands. I was really pleased for her. I half expected Hilary to ring but she didn't and maybe it was just as well. There was no word from Lucky

Learoyd. I tried his number a couple of times but it rang out unanswered.

Cameron had spent the morning investigating Lucky's background but she hadn't got very far. The people who knew him, mostly agents and club-owners, knew him only as an act. I wondered if the best person to speak to in the end might be Jason Jenkinson.

At three o'clock I presented myself at the offices of Oates International for my meeting with Jeffrey Taggart. This was my chance maybe to find the underlying cause of the land deals that had led to the murder of Stewart Davis although, judging by my conversation with DI Reubens, the police had not come up with anything in that direction. I wasn't sure how I was going to approach the conversation but 'play it by ear' seemed to be favourite.

Taggart's office was on a different corridor to Jeanne McGhee's. He greeted me cheerily showing a set of gleaming white teeth that suggested regular visits to a cosmetic orthodontist

'Mr Ace. Very nice to meet you.' He spoke with a nasal voice. We shook hands over his oak desk and he directed me to the seat in front of it. 'You must excuse my cold,' he apologised and he took out a large handkerchief to blow his nose forcefully. He wore a navy suit with a wide white stripe, popular in Chicago during the Prohibition days, with those large lapels made to accommodate excessively floral buttonholes. 'I take it you're here in a professional capacity?'

'Depends on which profession,' I smiled back. 'I do own a property company if that's what you mean.'

His smile turned oily and stretched his full lips. Another millimetre and he would have cracked his cold sores. 'I was thinking of your business as a private detective.'

Taggart had obviously done his homework in the six hours since I'd phoned. Not a man to dismiss lightly.

'Probably our discussion could touch on both areas,' I said.

'Do I take it that the investigation part of your business might involve the unfortunate death of our colleague Mr Stewart Davis, because, if so, the police are already dealing with that quite adequately?'

I never take kindly to being warned off, especially by a smarmy honey-dripper like Taggart. 'Has Mr Davis's demise caused you some problems then?'

'Not really. Business, like life, goes on.'

'Do you think his death was in any way connected with any transactions connected to Oates International?'

'No I don't,' he snapped, 'and quite honestly, I can't see how it would concern you.' His smile was fading fast

'Mr Davis's personal assistant approached me...'

'Miss McGhee?'

'That's right. I'm here on her behalf. She's hired me to...'

'To find out who killed Mr Davis?' He finished my sentence like an eager contestant on University Challenge. 'What does she think the police are for?'

'No, nothing to do with Mr Davis. She hired me to protect her because she believed she herself was in grave personal danger.'

'Danger of what?'

'Danger of being murdered, Mr Taggart.'

'Why should anyone want to murder Miss McGhee?'

'Why should anyone want to murder Mr Davis?' That shut him up. I continued. 'I'm told Miss McGhee is on extended leave and...'

'She's suffering from stress. We told her to take a month off and ...'

I cut in myself. 'She never mentioned it when I spoke to her last night.'

'That's because I only discussed it with her this morning.' The answer was instant. If he was lying, he had it down to a fine art. 'She rang in sick and I explained that as Mr Davis was no longer with us, there was no immediate urgency for her, as his PA, to return.'

'I see.' I wondered if she'd been in Preston when she rang him.

'Does that answer all your questions, Mr Ace? If so, perhaps we could move on to your other reason for being here. Do I take it you are interested in one of our properties.'

'I'm curious about some land that you recently advertised.'

'Which particular area?'

'Between Toxteth and Dingle. I saw it in a recent brochure.'

'I'm afraid that land is already sold, Mr Ace.'

'May I ask to whom?'

'Certainly not. We operate a strict client confidentiality rule at Oates International.' The smile was long gone.

'What area exactly did the land cover?'

'I thought you said you had the brochure.'

'No. I said I saw it in your brochure. I don't have a copy of my own.'

'It's irrelevant now anyway as the land is sold. Tell me, is this something you were interested in purchasing for yourself or is it part of this investigation you are carrying out?'

'Why should it be part of any investigation?' I answered non-committally. 'I deal in property and that seemed like a promising deal. Have you anything else near to that area.'

'Regretfully no. We have prime land for sale in the Kensington, Walton and Garston areas but nothing nearer to town. You're a little late out of the starting gate, I'm afraid. Liverpool is today's London.'

'Perhaps you'd put me on your mailing list, Mr Taggart.'

'Of course. Leave your details with my secretary on your way out.'

I ignored the hint. 'Just one point; Miss McGhee told me

you were doing business with a Russian company, St Petersburg Properties. I wonder if you could give me a name for their contact man in the UK?'

'I'm sorry. I'm afraid that's not possible. And now, if you'll excuse me.' He stood up. 'I have a meeting to attend. Good day to you, Mr Ace.' He walked over to the door and opened it to let me out.

'One last thing, Mr Taggart. I'd like to know who you were dealing with in Leprechaun Developments.'

The answer was swift and came accompanied by the return of the oily smile. 'Never heard of them, Mr Ace, never heard of them. Goodbye.'

The sickly smell of his aftershave was still in my nostrils when I was back on the street. I didn't feel the meeting had achieved anything. In fact, it had alerted him to my involvement. I needed to do a lot more digging into Oates International.

'Another blank,' I said to Cameron when I got back to the office. 'He wasn't going to part with any information. We need to get hold of the people from Leprechaun Developments next. I don't know why Stewart Davis was killed or if Jeanne McGhee really is in danger but they are the people at the heart of this mystery.'

'I have some news,' she said. 'I've been trying to trace people who might know something about Lucky Learoyd and I've come across a man called Terry Farquharson who does a Jimmy Clitheroe tribute act.'

Was there no end to these acts? And who the hell remembered Jimmy Clitheroe these days? He belonged to a sadly forgotten army of Northern comics like Frank Randle, Al Read and Albert Modley.

'Well done, Ronni. Will he be performing it in the office or do you intend hiring the Empire Theatre to put him on?'

'What?'

'They'll be having Harry Champion lookalikes next,' I said.

Cameron looked at me blankly. Her musical knowledge didn't extend as far back as music hall.

'Wasn't Jimmy Clitheroe that little old man pretending to be a Lancashire schoolboy?' she said.

'I'm surprised you've heard of him.'

'They did a documentary on him on television a few months ago.'

'So who is this Farquharson person?'

'He's a comedian from Longton. He says he used to work with Lucky years ago. Long before he did his PJ Proby act he apparently worked under the name of Ben E. Prince.'

'Don't tell me, he did a Ben E. King tribute?'

'No. He was in a band called The Aliens. They came from Leyland. Lucky, or Benny as he was then, was the lead singer. They played mostly Tamla Motown and soul. '

'What did he have to say about Lucky?'

'He said he could tell me some stories so I said we'd go round and see him tomorrow. Is that all right?'

It was fine with me. Meanwhile, I had a radio show to do and then we were off to Birkdale for our meeting with Jeanne McGhee although I was doubtful whether she'd show.

Cameron met me out of the radio station at seven and we set off for Birkdale in the RAV4. She looked like she was dressed for the gym, in trainers and navy blue track suit, with her long red hair tied up in a bun.

It seemed strange going on such a mission with a young woman rather than a burly ex-copper like Jim Burroughs and I was slightly concerned about her safety if there was any trouble. As it turned out, I had no need to worry on that score.

'Nice area,' she commented as we passed the Round House opposite Royal Birkdale golf course. We turned up the road towards Jeanne McGhee's building. She seemed equally impressed by the landscaped gardens.

I steered the car down the driveway to the apartment entrance at the back. There were no other cars there. Perhaps the Honda Accord, which on my last visit I'd assumed belonged to Miss McGhee, was locked away in one of the three garages.

I rang the Entryphone and waited. Nothing.

Cameron looked at me. 'Are we too early?'

'She never gave a time, just said tonight.' I looked at my watch. 'Nearly eight o'clock. Seems like night to me.'

I tried the front door and, to my surprise, it opened.

'Let's go,' I said and we stepped into the hall. I pressed the lift button but no light came on and the doors didn't open.

'Doesn't look as if it's working,' Cameron said.

'Maybe the electric's off. We'll take the stairs.'

Miss McGhee's front door was on the second landing that we came to. I could hear a radio or TV playing inside. I knocked loudly. No answer.

'I thought I heard someone moving about,' whispered Cameron.

I listened. 'Not sure. It might be the TV.' I knocked again.

'Try the door,' suggested Cameron.

I turned the knob and pushed. The door opened. I stepped carefully inside and, without warning, a bulky figure rushed towards me holding some sort of weapon in his hand. Before I had time to react, he brought it down on the side of my head and I slumped to the floor.

Half-conscious, I tried to struggle to my feet but my legs collapsed beneath me. I shouted to warn Cameron but, through a haze, I watched in amazement as the man who had attacked me came flying backwards into the room, landing with a crash against a table behind me.

He was followed by Cameron who launched herself on top of him, grabbed him by the front of his sweater, yanked him forward then smashed the back of his head viciously down on the laminated wood floor. Twice.

'Are you OK Johnny?' She was hardly panting.

'I think so.' I rose to my knees then slowly stood upright. 'Be careful, there might be more of them.'

'I don't think so otherwise we'd know about it.' She looked pleased. 'I told you the judo would come in useful.'

'So it seems.'

She nodded. 'But I broke his nose as well, to be on the safe side. Ace Investigations has a reputation to protect. Can't have anyone attacking the staff.' She smiled and helped me to my feet.

'Are you OK?'

'Just dazed. Caught me by surprise,' I said.

'Sure.'

'We need to find if Jeanne McGhee's here.'

'You look down here,' she said, 'and I'll check out the bedrooms upstairs.'

I went over to inspect the man who'd attacked me. He was still out cold. Blood was still trickling from his nose and his right eye was colouring nicely. I put his age at around thirty five. He wore a pair of beige chinos and a nondescript polo shirt.

Luckily, the white leather furniture had escaped the bloodstains.

There was no sign of Jeanne McGhee in the kitchen or the bathroom. 'Any joy up there, Ronni,' I shouted up the stairs but she was already on her way down.

'Empty. But the place is immaculate, nothing disturbed, so whatever he was after in the flat must have been down here.'

'What about the study across the hall?'

We both went to look and it was obvious that this is where the intruder had been concentrating his attention. Drawers had been pulled out of a mahogany bureau, papers scattered everywhere, a filing cabinet overturned and books from a bookcase strewn across the floor.

Cameron surveyed the scene professionally. 'He can't have found what he was looking for or he'd been out of here. So what can it have been?'

'The deposit money's the obvious answer.'

'Mmm.' I went over to examine the bureau. 'Quite often these things have a secret drawer in them.' I opened the top of the desk and open and shut a number of small drawers, and pressed a few knobs until I heard a satisfying click and a the sidewall sprang open to reveal a narrow compartment. Inside was a sheaf of papers held together by an elastic band. I took it out and handed it to Cameron.

She leaned down to pick up a couple of papers and examined them carefully. 'This is interesting. These are copies of leases for properties in the Dingle-Toxteth-Chinatown triangle.'

'Let me see.'

She handed them across. 'These relate to properties that could well be on that land that Stewart Davis was selling.'

'I wonder why he never took them.'

'Obviously it was something else he was after but what?' I gave the papers back to her. 'Hang on to these, they might tell us something.'

I opened a small drawer at the back of the bureau and brought out a handful of twenty-pound notes. 'It can't have been money he came for. There's over three hundred pounds here, easy for him to find.'

'I suppose that's small beer if the deposit ran to several thousand.'

'We're assuming he's connected with Leprechaun Developments. He might just be a sneak thief.'

'A sneak thief would have taken the cash.'

'You're right. Let's see what's in his pockets, he might have some ID on him.'

We went back into the lounge.

'He's still out cold,' Cameron said. She delved in the pockets of his chinos. 'Nothing in here.'

'That's odd. No car keys or money?'

'She checked again. 'No, not even a mobile phone.'

'Odd.'

'I think he's coming round,' she said.

The man raised his arm slowly and rubbed his forehead.

'You've been in an accident,' I told him. 'And you're very likely to be in another so stay down there and when I ask you a question, answer it. Have you got that?'

He leaned forward and spit at me. I kicked him hard in the ribs and he cried out and rolled over.

'Question one, who are you and who sent you?'

'That's two questions,' Cameron pointed out to me.

'He gets a bonus point.' He said nothing. I kicked him again, this time on his broken nose. A mistake. I got blood on my new trainers. 'You're not going anywhere till you answer me so why don't you save yourself a lot of pain and tell me.'

'Should I break his fingers?' Cameron asked. Having seen her in action, I wasn't at all sure she wouldn't do it. Neither was our assailant because he held up his hand in a gesture of surrender.

'All right, all right. What do you want to know?'

'Your name.'

'Alby Durno and who the fuck are you?

'I'm Batman and this is Robin. What are you doing here?'

'I was sent to collect some papers.'

'What papers and who by?' It was getting tedious.

'Legal papers. Contracts. He said I'd find them in the apartment but they're not here.'

'Who is "he"?'

'I don't know his name. He rang me saying he'd been given

my number by a mutual friend. I had to come to this address, break in and take the papers to him and he'd give me £200 for it.'

'Where do you have to take them?'

'There's a pub down the dock road, the Bramley Moor. I'm supposed to meet him there at ten tonight.' It was eight thirty. Plenty of time for me to take his place.

'How will you recognise him?'

'He'll be wearing a blue suit and a red tie.'

The tie on its own would have been enough at the Bramley Moor. A suit and tie would stand out like a virgin in Ibiza.

Cameron asked a question. 'What was the name of the friend who recommended you for this job?'

'I don't know. He didn't tell me.'

'Do you think he's stupid?' Cameron asked me.

'If he was any more stupid, you'd have to water him twice a day.'

She gave him quick jab in the groin with her left foot.

'All right, all right.' Alby Durno put an arm to the floor and raised himself to a sitting position. 'It was a bloke called Jason Jenkinson.'

* * *

It was going dark as we approached the Bramley Moor along the uneven surface of the dock road.

We'd seen Alby Durno on his way. After a little painful prompting from Cameron, he produced his car key which, it turned out, he'd kept hidden in his sock. His money, mobile phone and house keys were locked in his car.

His Peugeot 306 had been parked discreetly round the corner, ready for a quick getaway if anything went wrong. Only things went more wrong than he'd anticipated.

I made a note of the registration number, put his key in my pocket and explained to him the benefits of missing his ten o'clock appointment.

'This guy isn't going to be happy if you turn up without the brief case. Your best bet is to tell your friend Mr Jenkinson, when he contacts you, that you couldn't do the job as there were people in the flat when you called round.'

As a parting thought, Cameron handed him a five pound note and advised him to take a taxi to the Infirmary to have his nose mended before it set in its current wrong position.

'How will I get home?' he spluttered.

'Not my problem. But I'll keep your ignition key at my office in case you ever want to collect it.'

I gave him the address but I didn't expect him to call and we left him standing in the road beside his locked vehicle as we set off for the Bramley Moor.

'Are we going in together?' Cameron asked, as we drew up outside the pub.

'Why not? If what Durno said is true and the man doesn't know him, we'll have the drop on him.

I locked the car and we entered the pub. Half a dozen men were standing round the bar and glancing between sups of beer at a boxing match on Sky. They looked at us curiously as we walked in. I ordered two ciders and we were given the ubiquitous Strongbow on draught.

And then I saw him. He was sitting at a table playing with a glass of whiskey. He was short, dark haired, about forty. He looked like he would be more at home behind a bank counter than a dockside drinking den.

We took a seat a couple of tables down from him. He ignored us. He was watching the door, waiting for a man he didn't know who would be carrying a black leather brief case. He was going to be unlucky.

'What's the plan?' Cameron asked.

'We can either wait till he leaves then follow him out and persuade him to tell us who he's working for...'

'Or?'

'Or we can follow him and see where he goes or who he meets.'

'I'd go for option two,' she said. ''That way we don't make ourselves known.'

'Option two it is then.'

'Where would you normally be on a Monday night?' Cameron's private life intrigued me. She spoke little of her family or friends. All I really knew about her was that she lived in a house near the Marina.

'Nowhere special at the moment but I've enrolled for a vocational music course at Hope University in September.'

We drank our ciders and watched the boxing match like everyone else. Two men in shirt and jeans came in and the man in the suit looked them up and down but they were regulars. The barman greeted them by name and pulled their drinks without asking. They both drank pints of bitter.

I wondered how long our man would give it before he realised his contact was not going to turn up. I reckoned on half an hour, Cameron thought an hour. She won. He hung on until last orders then, after glancing at his watch several times, he finally stood up, drained the last of his whiskey and headed for the door.

We allowed it to shut behind him before we followed him out. He was getting into a maroon Jaguar S-type. We sauntered to the RAV4 and let him move off before starting the engine.

We both headed towards the city centre. I kept a good distance behind.

'What's the word on Jeanne?' Cameron sounded anxious.

'I don't know but she has my mobile number if she wants to get in touch but I haven't heard from her.'

'What a bummer.'

I was worried too. She'd sounded vulnerable when she rang from the Preston callbox.'

We were passing the Liver Buildings. 'I wonder where he's heading?'

'Let's hope it's not London.'

'No, it'll be in Liverpool somewhere'.

I was right. He turned off at Upper Parliament Street and drove the full length until he came to Smithdown Road where he took a turn and headed towards Childwall.

We ended up in a tree-lined street off Woolton Road, big houses, nice area, befitting a car like an S-type. He drove into a gateway a few doors along. I drove slowly past and Cameron noted the house number.

'Electoral roll first thing tomorrow,' I said to her.

'I wonder how Jason Jenkinson is tied in with this. His name keeps coming up.'

'Yes, but only in relation to Lucky Learoyd until now.'

I took Cameron back to her car, which was parked outside the radio station. She drove a lilac Honda Jazz.

'Do you live on your own?' I asked her.

'Sometimes,' she smiled enigmatically. 'See you in the morning, Johnny.'

Maria was already in bed when I got back. 'There was a message for you,' she yawned. 'Jeanne McGhee rang. Said she'd ring you in the morning at the office.'

'How did she sound?'

'Strange. I couldn't hear what she said properly, she seemed to be whispering.'

'Did she say where she was?'

'No. Just that she'd ring back.'

'What time did she ring?'

'What is it now?' She sat up to look at the bedside alarm. 'Half past twelve. It must have been about eleven. I'd just gone to bed.'

'She was supposed to meet me tonight but she didn't turn up.'

'You'll find out in the morning I expect.' Maria lay back down and pulled the covers over her. 'Get into bed, Johnny.'

I didn't sleep well. I was wondering what had happened to Jeanne McGhee. What had prevented her from keeping the appointment?

I was in the office for nine the next morning. Cameron was already there.

'You're going to love this,' she said. 'You know who lives at that house in Woolton?'

'Surprise me.'

'Patrick Dixon'.

'So it was Stewart Davis's other partner who sent Durno to break into Jeanne McGhee's house. One of her own bosses, in fact.'

'And we know he got hold of Durno through Jason Jenkinson so that gives us a connection between Oates International and the Jenkinsons.'

'But what could Jeanne McGhee have in her possession that they want so badly?'

'It has to be those contracts we found at her flat, hasn't it?

Either she or Davis must have taken them from Oates' office.'

'Possible.'

'If there's anything incriminating about them, she could be trying to blackmail them.'

Nothing would have surprised me but I had other news to relay to Cameron.

'Jeanne McGhee rang last night. Maria took the call and Jeanne told her she'd be in touch today.'

'I can't work her out at all,' said Cameron. 'I've always been worried about Jeanne. After all, she did hire us to protect her yet now I'm not so sure she isn't playing a different game.'

Neither was I but I couldn't imagine what it might be and I didn't intend waiting around on the offchance she might ring.

'You'll have to deal with her if she calls because I want to go up to Longton this morning to see this Terry Farquharson bod. Where did you find him from, by the way?   I never asked you.'

'Spencer Leigh from Radio Merseyside. I thought if anyone would know about local singers, he would.'

'But Farquharson was with a group from Leyland, you said. That's not local.'

'No, but they played the odd gig in Liverpool. Spencer thought that Lucky might have played The Cavern with The Aliens in later years, just before the original club closed down, when Roy Adams was the owner.'

'And did he?'

'No but he did have a record of the names of the other group members and that's how I found Terry Farquharson.'

'I wonder if he looks like Jimmy Clitheroe.'

'You'll soon find out.' She gave me the address. 'I'll get you on the mobile if there's any word from Jeanne.'

It was another hot day and I had the air-con on full as I drove along the A59 through Ormskirk and Tarleton to

Longton. The journey took nearly an hour in the traffic. A canal boat might have been quicker.

Farquharson lived in a small detached bungalow just off the main road through the village. He opened the door to me himself. He may not have looked too much like Jimmy Clitheroe, his hair was curly with artificially blonde curls, but he was certainly the same height if not smaller. Four foot five at tops. His voice hadn't broken. He could have done an Aled Jones tribute as a sideline. Only the wrinkles and the liver spotted hands betrayed his age, the lines crossing his face resembling an aerial view of the approach to Clapham Junction station.

Behind him trailed a small brown and black mongrel shaped like a cocktail sausage with short legs and a tail like a Spanish fan.

'Johnny Ace,' I said, 'My partner rang you about Lucky Learoyd.'

'That's right, come in, come in. I've been expecting you.'

I followed him into the lounge and he waved me to a sofa. The dog sniffed my trousers enquiringly, detecting traces of Roly.

It was a tidy room. A three-piece suite matching the Axminster carpet; a china tea set in a glass fronted mahogany cabinet; a glass topped coffee table balanced on a carved wooden elephant; a widescreen TV and a magazine rack holding the *Daily Mail* and a copy of the latest issue of *The Stage*.

I sat down. 'Nice bungalow you've got,' I said, lifting my foot in an effort to dislodge his animal, which was trying to copulate with my left leg.

Farquharson gave a high-pitched scream. 'Down, Boswell. I'm afraid he's over sexed,' he explained. 'Shags anything that moves.' He chortled. 'He should have been a footballer. If he tries humping your leg, just kick him.' He didn't say where.

'You're a D.J. as well aren't you?' he said, settling himself down in one of the armchairs. His feet didn't reach the floor. 'I've heard your show a couple of times. What made you go in for this detection business?'

'The son of one of my friends was murdered and I sort of got involved and found I had a taste for it.'

'But you still do your radio show?'

'Oh yes. I guess the showbiz bug never leaves you.'

He grinned. 'I've just come back from the States you know. I played at this fella's 60th birthday party. I said to him, "Did you ever meet Elvis?" He said "no". I said, "Don't worry, you won't have long to wait".' He gave a squeaky laugh. 'The old ones are the best, eh?

I smiled dutifully. Terry continued. 'But you came here to ask me about Benny.'

'Or Lucky Learoyd as I know him. What is his real name?'

'Does Pavlov ring a bell?' he said and chortled. 'Sorry. Part of the act. Benny's real name? Benny Learoyd of course, though he used Ben E. Prince onstage because...'

'He sounded like Ben E. King. I know. '

'Better than that. Nobody could sing a ballad like Benny. You should have heard him do *Hurt* or *The Wonder of You*. He were magic. Better than Elvis.'

'So is PJ Proby,' I said. 'Was Lucky one of the founder members of the group?'

'No. Our lead singer had left and we advertised for a replacement and along came Benny.'

'Who was he with before The Aliens?'

'Only a local group. I forget their name. They used to play a lot of gigs at the Riverside in Banks. Do you know it?'

I did. I'd played there myself with The Cruzads, more years ago than I cared to remember.

'Of course. The caravan site on the bypass. Ron Naylor used to be the DJ.'

'He's still there is Ron. Still going strong.'

'What instrument did you used to play in the band?' I asked him.

'Drums.' I was about to tell him that I too had been a drummer until I realised it might start a five hour discussion on the merits of different drum kits.

Instead, I asked him if Benny had a daytime job.

'I don't know but if he had he didn't need it. His folks were loaded.'

'Really?'

'Yes. They owned this huge house and land in Hesketh Bank, out along the coastline. Long private drive to the door.'

'What was the father's name?'

'Victor.' It struck a chord immediately. Victor Learoyd. The name that Jim Burroughs had mentioned but he couldn't remember in what context. I would need to jog his memory.

Terry was still talking. 'Folks reckoned he were a gangster. He had a reputation as a very bad man. The kids used to call him The Devil and you know what they say about devils? If you don't pay your exorcist, you get repossessed.' He chuckled. 'Get it? Repossessed.'

'And you make a good living with this act of yours?' I asked incredulously.

'I sure do. Best thing I ever did, swapping a drum kit for this. Nobody else does Jimmy Clitheroe, you know. Not that I know of anyway. Nobody's small enough.' Again the laugh.

'But you don't look much like him, do you?'

'Don't I? Wait there.' He disappeared into the next room and came back minutes later, wearing a blazer and schoolboy cap, and struck a cheeky schoolboy pose, finger pressed to his lips. 'Eh up, don't some mothers have 'em.'

He hopped from foot to foot. 'My teacher says anyone who jumps in the river in Paris must be insane. In Seine. Get it?'

'I've got to hand it to you, Terry,' I said. 'That is good.'

And I meant it. The transformation was amazing. There was only a slight change in the timbre of his voice but he instantly became Jimmy Clitheroe.

He smiled gratefully. 'Not bad, eh?' He took off the uniform and I got back to the matter in hand.

'What did Benny's old man do for a living?'

'Officially he was a farmer. It's a big agricultural area all round there. But he had his finger in a lots of pies. Like I say, people round about thought he were connected with the Krays.'

'Did Benny have any enemies you know of?' It was a long shot. Somebody would have to have a pretty big grudge to hold it for over twenty years.

'Not that I know of. He was a likeable bloke. Why? Is he in trouble?'

'He's had death threats. My job is to find out who and why.'

Terry looked sombre. 'Can't help you there, I'm sorry. I've completely lost touch with him. When Benny left to go solo, the group packed in. Benny moved to Liverpool and worked the clubs but some said he were running a branch of his father's empire.'

'Was there any evidence of this?'

'Just rumours, you know how people talk?'

I thanked him for his help and stood up to go. Boswell resumed his attempted copulation so I kicked him as instructed. He yelped and ran behind the sofa.

Terry Farquharson put his stage gear back on and changed his voice. 'Here's one before you go. Do they call a hangover the wrath of grapes? Ha ha. All there with me cough drops, eh mister?'

'Great, "Jimmy".' I leant down to shake his hand and thanked him for his time.

It hadn't been a wasted trip in that I'd learnt something of

Lucky Learoyd's background. How it would all tie in with everything we knew I wasn't quite sure.

I rang the office only for Cameron to tell me that Jeanne McGhee hadn't been in touch.

'But somebody called Hilary phoned for you.'

'Oh yes?'

'She seemed to know you very well.'

I detected a certain curiosity in her voice. I hadn't told Cameron about the situation with Hilary but I realised I would need to one day.

'She does. Did she leave a message?'

'Only to ring her on her mobile.'

'Right. I thought I might pay a visit to Leprechaun Developments,' I said. 'We've always had them down as the number one suspects for Stewart Davis's murder. It's time I went to see what we're up against.'

* * *

On the way out of Longton, I stopped off at a Booths supermarket in the village and bought a sandwich and a couple of bottles of Cameron's favourite cider. I ate the sandwich and drank one of the bottles in the car park then set off back to town.

The drive took another hour. My worse case scenario of Hell would be to be permanently condemned to a life stuck behind a learner driver in a Toyota Yaris in city traffic on a hot sunny day.

Leprechaun's offices were in the old Cotton Exchange, a short distance from the entrance to Moorfields station. It was easier to park the RAV4 outside my flat in Waterloo Dock and walk over.

My first thought, as I walked into the reception on the second floor, was that they had not wasted much money on décor. The impression was that of a rented office with no attempt to create any individuality, the inference being that this not their home territory and they could move out without any trace at the drop of a hat.

A girl sat at the reception desk reading a June Francis saga novel. She looked up, almost surprised, when I walked in.

'Quiet afternoon?' I commented.

She looked flustered. 'Sorry.' She put the book down hurriedly. 'I suppose so. It goes in fits and starts.' The accent was Irish. Perhaps she'd come over with the firm from Dublin.

'Good book?'

Now she saw I wasn't going to complain, she relaxed a little. 'Yes. I like romantic tales. Can I help you.'

'Are either Mr O'Toole or Mr Flynn in?'

'Mr Flynn is. Do you have an appointment?'

'Do I need one?'

She looked sheepish. 'I suppose not. Who shall I say?'

'Johnny Ace.'

She buzzed through and seconds later a man in a shiny blue suit came out. He was big with shoulders like Superman and a neck like a bull, half covered by overlong hair, which reached over the collar of his striped navy suit. He belonged more in the wrestling ring than in a property developer's office.

'Mr Ace is it?' He shook my hand so hard that the pins and needles took a few minutes to subside. 'I'm Gene Flynn. What can I do for you?' His accent had a thread of American in it, more Boston Irish than Dublin Irish.

I gave him a card. He glanced at it and back at me.

'Private investigator? You're not investigating me, I hope.' He laughed as he said it. I imagined the hangman laughing like that before he dropped the rope. Think Vincent Price in the Edgar Allen Poe films. 'You better come into my office.' He turned to the girl. 'Maureen, two coffees.'

'Make mine tea,' I told her. 'Colour of an African woman.'

'Right, Mr Ace,' he said, when we were inside what was no more than a cubicle with a single window overlooking the street. For all their property interests, Leprechaun had not wasted money on surplus square footage for themselves. I sat on a plastic chair; he stood behind his desk with an impatient air. 'What's your problem?'

'I have a client called Jeanne McGhee. Her boss was a Mr Stewart Davis who worked for a company called Oates International. He was murdered a few days ago.'

'I read about it in the paper. What has it got to do with Leprechaun Developments?'

'Only that Mr Davis was in the middle of a deal with your company when he was killed.'

'He was indeed. But I don't see where your connection is here.'

'Miss McGhee hired me to protect her as she thought her own life might be in danger.'

'I'm sure you'll do an excellent job keeping her from harm, Mr Ace, but I still don't understand why you are here.'

'Before he died, Mr Davis had agreed to sell you a piece of land in Toxteth on behalf of his company. In fact, you had paid him a deposit to secure the deal.'

'I won't argue with you so far. But if you are about to suggest I had anything to do with his death, let me point out that we are the ones who lost out when he died. I found out that the contract needed three signatures from Oates International, one belonging to each partner. I had only Mr Davis's signature and neither of his partners were willing to sign.'

'Not even when you pointed out that you had paid a deposit?'

'They didn't accept that we had paid a deposit. On Mr Davis's instructions, I had paid the money into the private account of his assistant, Miss McGhee, instead of to Oates International. The company subsequently insisted they had no knowledge of this. I then found out that the money had been withdrawn in cash on the very day Mr Davis was killed.'

Flynn was becoming agitated, a film of sweat covering his brow.

'But have you not tried to recover it subsequently from Miss McGhee herself.'

'Certainly but with a total lack of success as Miss McGhee seems to be strangely unavailable.

'You have tried to get in touch with her then?'

'As she was the person named on the bank account, naturally we tried to contact her.'

'At Oates International's office?'

'Where else?'

'I thought perhaps you might have tried her home.'

'We don't have her address I'm afraid.'

'Have you ever done any business with Oates International before?'

'Never.'

'What did you know about them when you first contacted them?'

'We knew that they buy up pockets of land here and there until they can join them all up and market them as one potential redevelopment area, which is what this deal was.'

'So what reaction did you get from them when you enquired about your deposit?'

'Instant denial is how I'd describe it. Oates International said that as they had no record of us ever paying them the money in the first place, we could hardly expect them to refund something they'd never had. We paid Mr Davis in all good faith but I can hardly recover it from a man whose next appointment is at the Crematorium. Perhaps I too should hire you Mr Ace, to find out where our money has gone.'

I didn't take him up on his suggestion. 'Who did you see at Oates International?'

'A Mr Taggart and a Mr Dixon.'

'And they both affected not to know about any arrangement you had with Mr Davis?'

'Not totally. They knew we'd put in an offer for the land but, contrary to our belief, they denied they had accepted it. And they insisted that Mr Davis had neglected to tell them that we had paid a deposit to secure the deal.'

'And that was their excuse not to honour it?'

'Oh come on now, Mr Ace. If they genuinely didn't know about the deposit, surely that was understandable. They couldn't be expected to return money they had never received.'

'And you believed them?'

Gene Flynn looked at me sharply. 'I'd no choice but is there any reason why I shouldn't?'

I couldn't think of one. 'Tell me,' I asked him, 'were they prepared to reactivate the deal with you?'

'They said there were other offers in the pipeline and they would not be making a decision immediately.'

'Do you know who the other offers were from?'

'We weren't told.'

Maureen appeared with the tea and coffee. I took a sip of mine. It was light beige in colour and I'd tasted better cough medicine.

'So can I establish the fact that you feel it is Miss McGhee personally that you have the dispute with rather than Oates international?'

'That sounds to me, Mr Ace, like you are trying to create a motive for Leprechaun Developments to wish harm on Miss McGhee. Or is this visit really to warn us off in case we were already thinking of such a thing?'

'I'm sure you wouldn't dream of such measures, Mr Flynn. Especially now you are aware of my involvement. But I am interested in this piece of land you thought you had bought. What is so special about it?'

'Its size, its proximity to the city centre and the potential for both residential and commercial development.'

'It makes you wonder why Oates didn't want to keep it to develop themselves.'

'Oates are not builders, Mr Ace, they are just speculators. Buy cheap, sell dear, that is their policy. They look to make a fast buck and move quickly on to the next project. Our business is redevelopment.'

'You are still after this land then, despite the drawbacks?'

'Oh yes.'

'What do you know about a company called St Petersburg Properties?'

A glimmer of recognition flashed in his eyes but he quickly controlled it. 'Never heard of them.'

I didn't believe him. 'I've been led to believe they were after the same piece of land.'

'That's interesting. I wonder who they are.'

I wasn't about to enlighten him. 'Probably Russians with a name like that.'

In view of the fact that they boasted a Liverpool P.O. Box number, I considered it highly unlikely that they were Soviet citizens, but that was not something I was prepared to share with Gene Flynn.

'I don't suppose you have a plan of the land? Mr Flynn.'

'Not to hand, no. Still, that won't make any difference to your objective will it? Safeguarding the life of Miss McGhee I mean.'

It might well do, I thought, but I knew nothing that I said would make him produce the plan.

I wished him luck in securing his deal and managed to leave without shaking his hand again.

I walked back to the office and relayed the day's events to Cameron for her comments.

'From what you say, it seems like Oates International are the more likely candidates for Davis's murder,' she said. 'It was one of their directors that organised the break-in at Jeannie McGhee's and they would have a motive to kill Davis if they'd found out he was swindling them.'

'I'm curious as to why they should break into Jeanne's flat. It can only have been for those papers. I wonder what's in them that they want so badly?'

'We can soon find out. They're in my desk drawer. Should I get them.'

'In a minute. I just want to talk this through. I agree with you that Taggart and Dixon could well be the ones who arranged Davis's murder but I'm more worried about Jeanne at he moment. If they know she was in league with Davis, she could well be in grave danger from them.'

'There's always the possibility we mentioned earlier,' said Cameron. 'That those documents incriminate Oates in some dodgy dealings and Jeanne McGhee is blackmailing them.'

'If that were the case, then whether or not they fixed the Davis killing, that certainly gives them a reasonable motive for wanting to silence Jeanne for good.'

'Yes.'

'I've got to say, she's never been totally upfront with us.'

'I was thinking about that,' said Cameron, 'about her being upfront, I mean. You know, she could easily have been lying to you about handing over the deposit to Davis. We've only her word that she did so. It's quite possible she's kept the money for herself.'

'But it that's so, why come to me in the first place?'

'Protection, just like she said. Remember, Davis was already on the run so he knew somebody was after him, which is why he was carrying the Ace Investigations card. He just never got to you in time. The very same day that she draws the money out, he's murdered. She must have been afraid that whoever killed Davis would be after her next and that's when she comes to us.'

'But then there's this Irish mob that I've just been to see. That puts them in the frame because it's their money. They're determined to get their deposit back at any cost and if they think she still has it stashed away then I wouldn't fancy Jeanne's chances against them.

'So that's two sets of people after her that we know of.'

'I don't like it,' I said. 'Incidentally, did anyone come in for Alby Durno's car keys?'

'No.'

'Never mind. He probably broke into the vehicle himself. Breaking and entering was his profession after all.'

'That's true. I'm more concerned about Jeanne though. Don't you think it's very strange that we've heard nothing?'

'Apart from that message that she left last night with Maria, you mean? Yes, I find it very disturbing, Ronni. We have no idea whether she's dead or alive.'

We didn't have to wonder long. It came through in the four o'clock news bulletin on Radio Merseyside's Billy Butler Show.

'The body of a woman found on a railway line near Bootle New Strand Station this morning is believed to be that of 31 year old Jeanne McGhee, a company director from Southport. Police have not ruled out foul play.'

✳   ✳   ✳

Chapter Fifteen

'She was dead before the train ran over her, I can tell you that much.'

The speaker was Detective Inspector Sam Reubens. He had presented himself at the office less than half an hour after we heard of Jeanne McGhee's death on the radio and immediately explained the reason for his visit.

In Jeanne McGhee's pocket had been a Johnny Ace Investigations visiting card.

'Once may be a coincidence, twice and I'm looking for a plausible explanation.'

I pointed out to him that, unlike Stuart Davis, Jeanne had actually been a client. 'She came looking for protection,' I told him. 'After Stuart Davis's death, she was frightened that for some reason she might be next.'

'Her fears were justified weren't they,' said Reubens grimly, as he confirmed that it was murder and not suicide. 'Did she say what the reason was?'

'Not specifically, other than Davis seemed to be running some kind of scam on the property deals and she was involved with him.'

'Involved in what way?'

'They were having an affair.'

'Ah. Were they really? That gives us another suspect then.'

I raised my eyebrows.

'You should know that, Mr Ace in your line of work. The first rule of detection in a murder case, *cherchez la spouse*. Perhaps we should really be looking for Mrs Davis, the wronged wife. Hell hath no fury and all that. And, come to that, what if there's a Mr McGhee? He could be another candidate. Cuckolded husband seeking revenge.'

'I hadn't considered that angle,' I said 'I don't even know if she had a partner.' I realised I didn't know too much about

Jeanne McGhee at all. 'The impression I've had is that the murders were connected to the business deals.'

'They may very well be. We shall be looking very closely at the various operations of Oates International, I can assure you.'

No more closely than I was but that was something I was keeping to myself. I might not have been able to save Jeanne from her killers but I was sure as hell going to find them. I'd taken her money so, it was only right I should see the job through.

Reubens continued. 'You never mentioned any of this when we called yesterday.' Suddenly his tone became accusatory.

'I'd never really had a chance to talk to her properly,' I said. It sounded lame and Reubens knew it but he let it pass for the moment.

'But she hired you as a bodyguard. It didn't turn out a good result for either of you did it? Especially for Miss McGhee.'

I couldn't dispute it.

'So what went wrong?'

'Basically, she disappeared before I could set anything up. We agreed with her that my man would pick her up at her office after work on Friday but when he arrived there at the arranged time, she'd already left and we haven't seen her since.'

Reubens didn't look totally convinced.

'And you've had no other contact with her?'

'Yes. We had a phone call yesterday morning asking us to meet her that evening but she never kept the appointment. When I got home last night, she'd rung and left a message with my girlfriend apologising and saying she'd ring me at the office in the morning.'

'What time was that?'

'About eleven, Maria said.'

'It can't have been long before she was killed.'

'What time did she die?'

'Hard to say exactly but forensic put it around midnight.'

'If you're going to ask where I was...'

'Don't worry,' Reubens reassured me, 'I haven't got you down as a suspect though you do seem to turn up whenever there's a body.'

'When she called me yesterday morning, she was in a pay-box somewhere in Preston.'

'How do you know that? Did she tell you?'

'She said she was in Preston, and the word *payphone* followed by an 01772 number came up on the call display anyway, so she must have been speaking the truth. You should be able to identify where the paybox was from the phone records shouldn't you? But, if she was murdered in Preston, why bring her body to Bootle to throw on the railway line?'

'We don't know she died in Preston. We've no sightings of her at all yesterday. Quite possibly she was back in Liverpool when she rang you at night.'

'That could well be,' I agreed. 'When you say she was dead before the train hit her, I presume you still mean she was killed somewhere else, whether in Preston or Liverpool or wherever, and subsequently dumped on the line?'

'That's the most likely scenario, I think.'

'How did she die?'

'She was stabbed several times.'

'I see. And no trace of the murder weapon anywhere near the body?'

'No.'

'Which is why you assume the actual crime was committed elsewhere?'

'That and the time factor. The trains run every fifteen minutes. She was run over by the 6.59 from Southport so she was placed on the line roughly between 7.15 and 7.30 by which time she'd been dead for over seven hours.'

'Could she not have been lying there since last night and hit by several trains?' suggested Cameron.

'No. A driver would have seen her on the track even though he would have been unable to stop in time.'

'Her last known whereabouts seem to be when she left her office on Friday afternoon,' went on Reubens. After that, there's no trace of her movements all weekend until she phones you from a Preston public call box at eleven on Monday morning.'

'That's right.'

I thought about what Taggart had told me when I called on him at Oates International. He said Jeanne had rung in sick that morning and he'd told her to take a month's break. Where had she been when she phoned him? Let Reubens find that out for himself if he hadn't already.

'For which she fails to turn up and then she phones you later that evening, presumably to apologise, and an hour later she's dead. I take it you don't know where she was phoning from on that occasion?'

'I'm afraid not. Maria never thought to dial 1471.'

'Tell me, where exactly had you arranged to meet Miss McGhee?'

This was the dodgy part as far as Cameron and I were concerned. If the police were giving Jeanne's apartment a good going over, they'd be sure to find our fingerprints all over the place. Not to mention Alby Durno's blood on the carpet, the same blood that was on my trainers. And the state of her office would make it obvious intruders had been in.

I knew I'd have to tell Reubens sometime of our visit to Jeanne's but I'd been hoping it wouldn't have to be so soon.

Luckily, I was saved from making a decision by the ringing of his mobile phone.

'OK.' I heard him say. 'I'll be right down.' He turned to

me. 'Have to go. Something's come up. This rape case in Kensington; a man armed with a shotgun is holed up in a house in Jubilee Drive. An armed response unit is on its way. I'll be in touch.' He didn't add, "don't leave the country".

'Close,' said Cameron when he'd gone.

'Get those papers out from Jeanne's flat, Ronni. It's about time we had a good look at them. They seem to be the key to this whole business.'

She brought them over and we sat down to wade through them.

'They seem to be contracts for various land purchases, all in the same area.'

'Here's an interesting one,' I said. 'Oates International recently bought a builders yard just off Park Road. That's not too far from the Toxteth Triangle.'

'The what?'

'That's what I'm calling this piece of land that Stewart Davis was selling for Oates. The Toxteth Triangle. The three points of reference - the city centre, the Dingle and Toxteth. '

'OK, I get it. Let's have a look.'

I handed it across to her and she studied it carefully.

'The vendors haven't signed it,' she said. 'They must still be negotiating.' She picked up the next one. 'This one is signed. St James Street. A welder's workshop. Bought last month from a Mr Dave Collins. '

I looked at the price. It seemed a high price but not exceptionally over the top, certainly not high enough to suggest that Oates had paid over the odds to secure the deal. But there were other ways to persuade people to sell besides a generous offer.

'I wonder if they put any pressure on this Dave Collins to make him sell his business?' I said.

'Why should you think that?'

'Oliver Clarke. Don't you see? Ollie's place is roughly

inside that triangle.'

'But he said he hadn't had anybody after his business.'

'Maybe they're being clever. What's the betting they've been softening him up to put him in the frame of mind to sell. When he's totally fed up of the vandalism, not to mention the arson, they jump in with an offer too good to refuse.'

Cameron studied the next contract. 'There's a pub here, the Pig and Hamster, just off Northumberland Street.'

'Who owns that?'

'According to this, Oates International have bought it as a going concern from a Mrs Molly Laffin.'

'I can't see them going into the licensing trade. I wonder where Mrs Laffin ended up?'

'Another pub, perhaps?'

'Could be. Worth looking into,' I said.

'Do you think Leprechaun paid that deposit to Stewart Davis on the strength of these sales but some of the deals had not gone though?'

'So they forged the names? That could well be it. But, listen, Ronni, I've got to do my show at seven and I want to go home and get changed first We'll go through the rest tomorrow. In the meantime, see if you can find what's happened to the people who sold those businesses to Oates. If they've set up somewhere else, we might be able get hold of them and they could perhaps tell us something.'

'Before you swan off, did you remember to ring your squeeze?'

'Oh God, Hilary, I forgot. I'll do it now.'

I dialled her mobile number, watched closely by Cameron who had a quizzical look on her face.

'Hi Hil, it's me.'

'Johnny love. I'm so glad you phoned. I've seen an advert in the *Echo* for the Bamalama tomorrow night and it says Jim Burroughs' group's playing so I take it you'll be there?'

'Yes, it's a Merseycats Charity Night. I said I'd go down and support him. Why?'

'Nothing. Only I just thought you might want to take me with you. It'll be like old times. I presume the lovely Maria won't be going to anywhere like that.'

'No but...'

'I thought not. What do you say then, Johnny? Shall we go? I'll go in my own car so you don't have to take me home and it'll be nice for me to see Jim and everyone again. No harm in that is there?'

It was tempting and Hilary was speaking the truth, she did know a lot of the crowd who were likely to be there. They were people who'd seen us out together for years.

'OK, Hil. You win. I'll be going straight down after I've finished the show and written up the logs. So I'll see you there about eight.'

'See you tomorrow then, lover.' She blew me a kiss down the phone.

I put the phone down with a feeling of disquiet like I was about to go swimming in the sea knowing full well there were sharks in the water.

'Do I smell intrigue in the air?' asked Cameron.

I started to explain about Hilary but then I had a better idea. 'Why don't you come along tomorrow. You can meet my old partner, Jim Burroughs. I'm sure he'll have a lot to tell you about the job.'

'And Hilary?'

'I'm sure she'll have a lot to tell you as well.'

'Where's the Bamalama?'

'It's in one of those little side streets near the top of Upper Parliament Street. Most of the clientele are black. It used to be a blues club but nowadays it's hip-hop and rap. Got to cater to the younger generation.'

Cameron looked puzzled. 'Your chum isn't a rapper is he?'

'God, no. It's the old Merseybeat thing. All the old names from the Sixties will be there, Lee Curtis, Kingsize Taylor, Faron, Mike Byrne with Jukebox Eddie...'

'Stop, you're overloading me.'

'See you in the morning and try and find those people for me,' I instructed.

I stopped off at Aigburth Road on the way home to sort out a few things with Geoffrey about the properties and to tell him about Jeanne McGhee's death.

'That's my bodyguard duties finished then?' he said.

'For the moment.'

'I can't help thinking, if only I'd been earlier picking her up from her office.'

'I don't think it would have mattered, Geoff. Whoever it was would have got her in the end.'

'Maybe so.'

I was probably right but it didn't make me feel any better. After all, she had hired me to protect her. I just hoped Tommy McKale was doing a better job with Lucky Learoyd.

Whatever the motive was for killing Jeanne McGhee, I was sure it was all tied in with the land deal. And with the sort of money that was at stake, lives were dispensable. Including mine.

❖ ❖ ❖

Chapter Sixteen

Jeanne McGhee made the *Daily Post* front page headlines next morning. Police revealed that she had been killed before being flung onto the railway line and they appealed for witnesses who might have seen her over the weekend.

They also admitted that her death may be connected with the recent murder of the financier Stewart Davis.

When I arrived at the office, Cameron already had the names and addresses of the vendors on the contracts we'd found in Jeanne's flat.

'That was quick.'

'No sweat,' she replied. 'I rang the welding person, Dave Collins, and I was redirected to his new digits and got I straight through to the guy.'

'And?'

'He's renting a workshop near Kensington and he's on the premises all day so I said you'd probably call in sometime this morning.

'Fine. What about the other one?'

'The builders yard. A bit more tricky. They hadn't signed, remember, so I assumed they'd be in the same place but no, they've moved. I got wiped on the blower so I rang the Chamber of Commerce and they gave me a new label for them in Bootle. After that, easy-peasy, I was able to get their new digits from UK Phonebook on the web.'

'And did you get through?'

'Certainly did. I spoke to a Harry Howard. He's the site manager. He seems to know something about the move but he's working on a studio flats development off Upper Parliament Street all day.'

'So it looks like they did sell up, even though the contract we saw wasn't signed. That's odd. It will be interesting to hear what they have to say. Nice work, Ronni.'

She handed me a piece of paper. 'It's all written down for you.'

'Great. I'll go and see them both right now. Did you have any joy with that Mrs Laffin who had the pub, by the way?'

'Not yet. I'm still looking.'

'Right. I'll leave you to it then.'

I found Dave Collins' workshop without much trouble. It was in a converted garage up an entry at the back of some houses in Kensington. He was a stocky man, late fifties, dressed in an oily pair of overalls with goggles pushed onto the top of his forehead. Streaks of oil and grime on his forehead suggested he'd been brushing back strands of grey hair with his dirty hands.

He was working on the chassis of what looked to be two halves of an old Ford Escort, or possibly two Ford Escorts from different crashes.

'I'm interested in what happened to your old workshop' I told him after I'd introduced myself.

'Oh yes?' He carried on sorting spanners in a toolbox.

'Can I ask you who it was bought the place from you?'

'Why do you want to know?'

'A friend of mine owns some premises not far away and he's had somebody interested.'

'Good for him.' He moved over to his bench to pick up a crushed packet of cigarettes and coaxed one out.

'Only he doesn't really want to sell but they're putting a bit of pressure on him.'

Collins gave a throaty laugh followed by a cough after which he lit up his cigarette. 'That's what they do, ain't it?'

'Is that what happened to you?'

He stopped moving about and stared at me. 'They offered me forty grand for the freehold. I told them to eff off. I knew it was worth sixty. Then this other geezer came. Offered me fifty. I said the same to 'im.'

'Did they say who they were from?'

'The first fellow was from this firm called Oates International. I don't know about the second. He never said.

'But you sold to Oates International for fifty five in the end.'

'Only after I'd had the Jenkinsons round wanting to buy. You know the Jenkinsons?'

'By repute.'

'They offered me thirty five, thirty five, I ask you. They gave me forty eight hours to think it over. Told me I ought to worry about anything going wrong, like a fire.'

'What did you do?'

'Nothing. The fellow from Oates came back and…'

'Was his name Jeffrey Taggart?'

'No, Mr Dixon he was called. He was back less than an hour after Jason Jenkinson. Said his firm were prepared to go to fifty five but I had to sign within twenty four hours or the offer was withdrawn.'

'So you signed?'

'The next day. He already had the papers drawn up ready. I was glad to sign I can tell you. Because if the Jenkinsons got nasty when they found I'd sold to Oates, it wouldn't matter if they came back and burnt the place to the ground. It wouldn't be mine.'

'And did the Jenkinsons come back.'

He scratched his head, adding another black streak to the kaleidoscopic display on his head. 'That was the funny thing. They never did. Not a sign of them. But I'm not sorry I sold. I was able to pay off my mortgage and some debts and still have a bit put by. I'm just renting this place here, you see.'

'Did you never hear any more from the second people who called?'

'Not a word.'

'And you never found out who they were?'

'Never. Didn't matter though, did it?'

I said I supposed not. I thought it could have been Leprechaun Properties or, more likely, Jeffrey Taggart from Oates as a second string. It might even have been Stewart Davis.

'Is that all you want, mate? Only I've got a car to finish?'

I thanked him and went back to the RAV4. My next stop was Upper Parliament Street where Watson & Co were building a block of studio apartments for students, close to the ever expanding campus of the University of Liverpool.

The building work had reached the second storey and men in yellow hard hats were scurrying round the site. Most of them were stripped to the waist showing off their suntans and considerable amounts of builders' cleavage. I parked on the road and made my way through a gap in the fence surrounding the plot.

'I'm looking for Harry Howard,' I shouted up to a man halfway up the scaffold.

He jerked his hand towards a green Portakabin at the corner of the site. 'In there, pal.'

'Thanks.'

The door was shut so I knocked hard and a voice shouted me to come in. Inside was grubby with Just two plastic swivel chairs, an old plywood desk, a metal bookshelf filled with files and hooks all along one wall from which hung a miscellany of clipboards and keys.

'Harry Howard?' I asked.

'That's me.' He was standing by the window fixing a nozzle to a hosepipe. He wore a brown suit, thin striped tie and a light blue shirt, all of them covered with a layer of dust I put his age at late forties. His most noticeable feature was his height. The man was little more than five foot four. Chop his feet off and he could have helped Terry Farquharson out with his Jimmy Clitheroe act.

'Johnny Ace,' I said. 'I wanted to talk to you about the sale of the building yard.'

'That's right. Your partner said you'd be calling. Have a pew.' I wiped the seat of one of the chairs and sat down. 'What do you want to know?'

'Was there any pressure put on you to sell the old yard?'

'No messing with you, is there? Straight to the point. So I'll give you a straight answer. Yes, there was. Now bear in mind, I was not myself party to the negotiations. That was the Watson Brothers, John and George. They own the company. But I was made aware that I could well expect some, shall we say, disruption in the weeks before we sold up and moved to Bootle.'

'What sort of disruption?'

'Stuff going missing from the yard, scaffolding stacks upended, water in the sand and cement that sort of thing.'

'And was there any disruption?'

Yes. We ended up having to get a security firm in.'

'Who were the people negotiating to buy?'

'Now that, I cannot tell you. You would need to speak to one of the brothers.'

'Where will I find them?'

'Why, at Bootle of course. The new premises.' He gave a business card with a little map on the back.

I tramped back to the car. Bootle was where Jeanne McGhee's body had been found. Was there any connection?

The new yard and offices of the Watson Brothers were off Hawthorne Road. A length of barbed wire topped the eight foot high wall facing the street. An iron gate, open to admit lorries, had spikes at the top of each rail. The brothers had obviously taken their experiences in their last premises to heart. Stickers proclaiming that Hopkins Security was guarding the premises adorned every flat surface.

I walked into the yard and a sign on the wall directed me

to a brick built office where a middle-aged receptionist told me that John Watson would see me in a few moments.

I didn't have to wait long. Two minutes later, a muscular man in his late twenties dressed in jeans, a black cotton T-shirt and muddy Caterpillar boots marched into the office.

'John Watson,' he said, holding out a swarthy arm. 'I hear you've been looking for me.'

'I met your site manager, Mr Howard.' He put me on to you.'

'Harry? Yeah, a good bloke. One of the old school. How many men in his job do you see nowadays in a suit?'

'Not many,' I agreed.

'So what's your problem then, mate?'

'Harry told me about the trouble you had at the last place with vandals and suchlike just before you moved out and it seems you weren't the only one. Other businesses had the same problem.'

'Its this fuckin' City of Culture, ain't it?'

I recalled the comments made by DI Reubens. He'd called it 'a city of vultures.' Maybe there was something in that.

'I could get more for my Mam's garage now than her house was worth this time last year,' continued Watson and I didn't disbelieve him. 'Property sharks from London, Dublin, you name it, all out to make a fast buck out of the Scousers.'

'What I came to ask you is, have you any idea who it was that was putting the pressure on you?'

'Not a clue, mate. We had this spell where we had break-ins and stuff was damaged but after a while it stopped and we never found who was responsible.'

'And it was after this that the offers to buy came in?'

'Yes. The odd thing about it was we'd never put the place on the market or anything.'

'But you ended up selling to Oates International?'

He looked at me surprised. 'No. Who told you that? We

never sold to them.'

'Are you sure?' I said. This was an answer I was totally unprepared for.

'I think I know who I sold my own bloody business to, pal,' Watson said angrily.

I quickly apologised. 'Forgive me. I'm sorry. It's just that I could have sworn that it was Oates International who bought your old premises.'

'Oates were the first ones who got in touch with us, that's all.'

'So why didn't you sell to them?'

'Because the other lot came up with the best price in the end. The biggest bid of the lot.'

Again, his reply threw me. I'd not expected an auction. 'How did this bidding come about? Through estate agents?'

'We never used an agent. I told you, the place was never up for sale as such. One day this offer came in the post, completely out of the blue, from Oates saying would we be interested in selling the property? It was the first time we'd ever thought about it.'

'What did you do?'

'Nothing at first. Then a couple of days later, we gets another letter, this time from an Irish outfit called Leprechaun Developments who put in a bigger offer.'

'Didn't you think it strange, getting two offers like this out of the blue?'

'I suppose so. On the other hand, it made us think seriously about selling. George, my brother, knew of this bit of land going cheap in Bootle and we realised we could move the operation down here and make a few bob in the bargain.'

'Did either of them say why they wanted to buy your yard?'

'The way prices were going it was pretty obvious wasn't it? They were speculators. They weren't interested in the business, just the ground it stood on.

'So you sold to Leprechaun?'

'No we didn't. What we did, we got our solicitor on the job
and he sent out letters to the two parties who'd made the
offers, inviting them to submit sealed bids and, next thing, we
get three offers in, not two, and it was these new people who
came up with the best price.'

'Who were the new people?'

I waited for the answer, ready to be surprised, and I wasn't
disappointed.

'A Russian company called St Petersburg Properties?'

'Who did you say?' I couldn't quite believe it.

He repeated the name.

'And theirs was the biggest offer?'

'It was. Not by a large amount but enough to win it for
them.'

'And you didn't have any problems getting the money?'

'Just the opposite. It went through like bloody clockwork.
I've had more trouble in the past getting money for doing
someone's crazy paving.'

'Did you ever get to meet the people from St Petersburg?'

'No. Our solicitor handled everything.'

'Did you find out where they were based?' .

'No. I wasn't interested. Could have been Siberia for all I
cared so long as the money was kosher.'

I said, 'I don't suppose you know who was in charge of
their operation?'

'I know whose name was on the contract because I thought
to myself at the time, he didn't sound very Russian.'

I was suddenly very interested. 'Go on.'

John Watson said, 'His name was Learoyd, Victor Learoyd.'

* * *

Chapter Seventeen

'Are you sure?' I asked.

'Yeah. That was the name. Victor Learoyd on behalf of St Petersburg Properties. No mention of a Molotov or Sonovabich or anything like that.'

'Did you hear from Oates International again after the deal with Victor Learoyd had gone through?'

'Not a dicky bird. Why should I have?'

'No reason. What has Learoyd done with the yard?'

'Nothing as yet. I went past the other day, it's all boarded up.'

'And you don't know what his plans are?'

'No and I don't bloody care. We've moved on. The business is here now.' He glanced out of the window as a large lorry negotiated the entrance to the yard. 'If there's nothing more you want, I've got work to do. My supplies are arriving.'

'You've been a great help,' I told him. In reality, he'd only muddied the waters more than ever.

Before driving back to the office, I made a detour to the railway track near New Strand station to look at the spot where Jeanne McGhee had been thrown under a train. It was a bleak stretch of line running through an industrial wasteland of litter, derelict buildings and weeds. Not the best place to enjoy your last moments of your stay on this earth though quite probably she was already dead when she was brought there.

Who had killed her and why? Where was the missing money that Stewart Davis had supposedly taken from her account before he was murdered? Could Lucky Learoyd, Victor's son, who unaccountably was living in a mansion, somehow be connected to this affair and was his life really in danger and, if so, from whom? Where did the Jenkinsons fit in? Who wanted Ollie Clarke's property enough to torch his showrooms and kill his mechanic?

There were a million questions I couldn't answer and I drove back to the office more confused than when I started out.

One thing was clear, everything seemed to hinge on that one triangle of land that Stewart Davis had been trying to sell on behalf of his company, Oates International.

Cameron was waiting for news when I got back to the office but I was unable to enlighten her.

'It's like playing chess when all the pieces start to move in different directions than the ones they're supposed to,' I said. 'Did you find anything else in those papers from Jeanne's flat?'

'Only one that might mean anything. A Chinese restaurant in Park Road sold to Oates last month but the price looks dead cheap. Both parties have signed.'

'Let's have a look.'

She passed the forms across. It was called the Wong Foo and belonged to a Mr Kofi Borborkis who had supposedly sold it as a going concern to Oates, for just £20,000.

'Maybe it's still open under another handle,' said Cameron. 'It does say "going concern".'

'Perhaps we should take a little trip over there to find out. At the worst they can serve us lunch. And seal all these papers up in an envelope for me, Ronni. 'I'm taking them home with me tonight for safe keeping.'

When we arrived at the Wong Foo, we found the shop was empty and boarded up.

'It was only a takeaway,' I said, peering through the letter-box and seeing a frying range. 'There's a big menu board at the back with the numbered dishes.'

'There's a name over the door,' said Cameron, stepping forward to take a better look. 'Clarence Ho, prop.'

'He must have rented the place. Business can't have been

good.'

'Funny. I'd have thought it was just the place for a good chinese. What about upstairs?'

I stood back to the kerb and looked up. 'Flat above the shop. I think that's empty too. No curtains up.' I did the letterbox trick and saw papers and letters piled up behind the separate front door. 'Yes, definitely nobody living there.'

'So we've no idea were Mr Ho's gone.'

'Probably playing Father Christmas somewhere.'

'Ho Ho Ho,' echoed Cameron.

'Back to square one,' I said. 'If that's all the place was, the price is about right.'

'That just leaves that pub, the Pig and Hamster.'

'We can worry about that later. Let's go and have some lunch now.'

We went to the Italian Kitchen in Queen Square and ordered the Lunchtime Offer pasta with a carafe of red wine to go with it.

'Your big night tonight,' she said. 'You and your fly girl.'

'You keep your mouth shut,' I said. 'What about you? No men in your life?'

'Constantly.' She gave an enigmatic smile but was not any more forthcoming.

I changed the subject. 'Jim Burroughs will be at the Bamalama tonight. I need to find out what he remembers about Victor Learoyd.'

'I don't see how Learoyd fits in,' said Cameron. 'He doesn't appear to own any other properties in the triangle. Why buy that particular one?'

'According to Jeanne, St Petersburg were after the whole plot and Oates were lining up to sell it them. But who knows how much of that land Oates actually owned?'

We finished the meal and walked back through the square to the office. As we passed La Tasca, I glanced through the window and saw the familiar figure of Oliver Clarke in the company of a plump blonde-haired lady, enjoying a Spanish lunch. Judging by their body language, they seemed to be pretty close.

I quickly looked the other way before he caught my eye. I'd nothing new to tell him and I felt it better to back pedal until the police investigation into the arson attack had been concluded.

Back at the office, I rang the number I had for Lucky Learoyd but reached his Answerphone again. 'If I hear him telling me he is PJ Proby again, I'll shoot him,' I said.

Cameron laughed.

I was restless. So many avenues unexplored but every entrance blocked and the person most likely to shed light on the affair, Jeanne McGhee, was dead.

'I think I'll go and see Jason Jenkinson,' I said.

'Is that wise?'

'For want of anything better to do. '

'Do you know where he lives?'

'Tommy McKale will.'

I caught Tommy at his leisure centre, The Fitness Palace, "a luxury health and beauty spa in the heart of Liverpool's exciting Docklands". Or so the brochures said. I remembered it when it was a dilapidated old gym where Tommy, his brother Denis and half the city's gangsters used to work out. Now, it played host to Premiership footballers, footballer's wives and showbiz celebrities. As well as the gangsters.

'Come to try the weights, Johnny?' he said, as he greeted me in the foyer, 'or do you still rely on the old horizontal jogging for exercise?'

'I do a lot of thinking these days, Tommy. I'm told it reduces the calories.'

I asked him about Jason Jenkinson.

'Not a family you want to get involved with,' he warned. 'Is this connected with our mutual client, Lucky, the jilted husband?'

'Could be, I'm not sure. I think he'll fit in somewhere but it's really about this outfit called Oates International. They're a crowd from London who are buying up half the city by all accounts and they're using the Jenkinsons to persuade reluctant landowners to sell their property to them.'

'Sounds like a scene from the Old Wild West. Lee Marvin and Jack Palance driving the landowners off their land and Clint Eastwood riding to the rescue.

I remembered the words of The Coasters' song, *Along Came Jones*. '*If you don't give me the deeds to your ranch, I'm gonna throw you on the railroad tracks'*. That's where Jeanne McGhee had ended up.

'Yeah, that's about right,' I said.

'And you're Clint Eastwood?'

'Somebody's got to do it.'

We both laughed, he slapped me on the back and led me upstairs to the new Sports Bar. 'Get this man a cider,' he told the barmaid, 'and my usual.' His usual was a freshly squeezed orange juice.

We took our drinks to a table overlooking the new squash facility. Below us, two athletic women were slogging it out on court. They wore white shorts and those white sports bras guaranteed to control bounce. Both of them had muscles in places where other women just had tattoos.

We watched them for a minute or two and sipped our drinks then Tommy said, 'Strange character that friend of yours.'

'Lucky?'

'Did you know he lives in a bloody great mansion?'

'He denied it when I asked him. Swore he lived in a two up two down.'

'Bollocks.'

'I thought as much.' I explained how he'd answered the Entryphone when I'd called on Sunday morning.

'I went inside when I took Alec down yesterday,' said Tommy surprisingly. 'It's like Caesars Palace at Las Vegas in there.'

'Full of fruit machines you mean?'

'Fruit machines, arcade games, jukebox, cinema TV, you name it.'

'He's only on £200 a night doing his act.'

'Two hundred eh? He's not getting that at my place. I'm only paying him £150.'

'That's right, he's on the Masquerade on Sunday isn't he? If he lives that long,' I added.

'He'll live,' said Tommy, 'with Big Alec looking after him.'

'Where does he get his money, that's what I'd like to know.'

'His old man, of course. You never told me he was Victor Learoyd's boy.'

'You know Lucky's father then?' I should have realised that Tommy would know anyone with the slightest claim to a criminal record and, judging by what I'd heard from Terry Farquharson, Victor Learoyd was hardly Mr Clean.

'I know him by reputation. "Vic the Trick" they used to call him. Retired now of course. Must be over seventy. He worked the Lancashire coast Ran arcades and casinos in Blackpool and Fleetwood. He was a great card player himself, hence the nickname. Shame he was born too early.'

'Early for what?'

'Las Vegas hitting Blackpool. By the time it happens, Vic will be well rotted in his grave. He ran a girls operation too. It was a prime area for it, all those rampant day-trippers with stiff dicks desperate for somewhere to put them. You think Soho in the Fifties was naughty? It had nothing on Blackpool.'

It seemed a very different Blackpool to the seaside resort I'd been to with Maria and Vikki a few days before.

'I don't think he's fully retired,' I said, 'It looks like he's moved into property now.' and I told him about the Watson Brothers building firm. Victor bought it, under another name of course. St Petersburg Properties.'

Tommy laughed. 'That'll be because he married a Russian girl. Anna she was called.'

'She'll be Lucky's Mum, then?'

'I guess she will. So where does Lucky fit into all this?'

'I don't know. What do you think? What's he been doing all week?'

'Playing roulette in his games room most of the time, with Alec keeping an eye on him. Alec's a devil for the fruit machines. He's won more than I'm paying him.'

He paused to watch the squash game. The blonde girl was walking back towards us to take up her serve. She had full lips like Julia Roberts.

'I bet she gives good blowjobs,' commented Tommy in passing. 'Especially if she can take her teeth out. You wanted to know where to find the Jenkinsons?'

'Do you think it's them who are after Lucky?'

'Nah. If they wanted him out of the way, he'd be well gone by now. They don't mess about, the Jenkinsons. Write this down.' He pulled out a pocket diary and read me out an address. 'It's a big Victorian gaff off Lodge Lane. Half the bleeding family live in it.'

'Thanks Tommy.'

'I trust you'll be down Sunday then to see your mate perform for the gender benders.'

'Of course.'

'I noticed you with Hilary the other night. Just like old times. She's a nice girl that. I've not seen much of her while you've been away. Thought perhaps she'd gone in a nunnery.'

I assured him that was the last place Hilary would end up.

'And how's Maria and the kiddie? She must be growing up now.'

'Victoria's three now,' I said. 'They're both fine.'

He grinned broadly. 'Good. You'll have to bring Maria down the club one night.'

There was more chance of Everton winning the Champions League than me risking Maria and Hilary meeting but I just smiled back and told Tommy I'd see him at the weekend.

In the end, I didn't have time to see the Jenkinsons before I did the show. I wanted to go home, hide the contracts in a safe place and get changed before the Bamalama. The Jenkinsons could wait until tomorrow.

Maria had just arrived back with Vikki from nursery school.

'I'm going to watch Jim's band tonight, love,' I told her, 'so I'll probably stay at the flat as it's going to be after two when the gig finishes.'

Was I subconsciously leaving open the possibility that Hilary might stay at the flat again with me?

'Fine. Thank God I don't have to go.' Maria had seen The Chocolate Lavatory in the past and it hadn't been an experience she wanted to repeat in a hurry.

I showered and changed into a clean pair of combats and a Bootles T-shirt then spent half an hour playing football with Vikki in the garden. Never mind about it being just a game. The way women's football was taking off, especially in the States, it could well be a lucrative career option for her by the time she grew up.

Maria had bought some burgers and sausages so we had a family barbecue in the garden. Roly managed to eat five of the sausages that fell off the tray. I left for the station at five thirty.

I managed to give a plug for the Bamalama gig during the show and played a couple of appropriate records by Merseybeat stalwarts, R'n'B Inc.'s *Louie Louie* (the second most recorded song after *Yesterday* with over 1000 versions) and Pete James' self-penned *Doreen the Spaceman's Delight.*

I was on my way to the car park after the show when the incident happened. A dark saloon came speeding down the road towards me, braked heavily with a screech of tyres and a rear seat passenger poked a gun through the open window and fired three rapid shots. At my head.

* * *

Chapter Eighteen

The first bullet missed my ear by inches, the second was closer, the third caught me in the left arm.

By the time I'd reacted, the car was round the corner. A woman a hundred yards down the road screamed and a couple of people on the other side came running over. I assured them I was all right.

The bullet had nicked the upper part of my arm, below the sleeve of my T-shirt. It was only superficial and had already almost stopped bleeding. I wouldn't need stitches.

Was this a warning or was my assailant a lousy shot?

I rang Cameron on the mobile and warned her to be careful. Whoever they were, if they were after me they might well be targeting her too. And she'd asked if this job was dangerous!

The worrying thing was, knowing they'd missed me, would they try again?

Cameron thought the same. 'You want to be careful going home tonight,' she said.

I told her I was staying at the flat.

'Is it wise being on your own?' Her voice took on a mischievous tone. 'If, of course, you will be on your own.'

'No sense in waking everyone up at three in the morning at home,' I replied brusquely.

The Bamalama was already quite full when I arrived. The first band was due on at eight and the show was scheduled to carry on through until two with no less than eight groups performing during the night.

The owner, Jonas, greeted me at the door with a show of high fives. 'Johnny. Such a long time. Where yo' been. They said you was over in Spain or somefin'.'

'Yeah, and now I'm back. Nice to see you, Jonas. How's things?'

'You know my boy, Winston, and Shirley got married do

you, Johnny?'

I did, because Geoffrey had told me that Shirley, the Bamalama barmaid, had moved out of one of my flats in Princes Drive as she and her new husband had bought a house in the Docklands.   Shirley and I had once a thing going between us. She had been my confidante and a refuge when I needed it. I was glad she'd found someone who would take good care of her.

Another era passed, another page closed.

'I've signed the club over to them,' Jonas continued. 'I'm just the doorman now.' He chortled, obviously delighted with the new set-up.

'You'll be stopping brewing your own beer next,' I said.

'Hey, what's the matter with yo' arm, Johnny?'

'Caught it in a door, Jonas. Don't worry. It's cool.' I found I was talking more like Cameron every day.

Jonas said nothing but he wasn't fooled. Liverpool club owners and doormen knew a bullet wound when they saw one. They were hardly a rare sight in the city.

I went into the gents and washed the dried blood off my arm before seeking out Jim Burroughs. I found him at the side of the small stage, busy tuning his guitar. He was pleased to see me.

'Thanks for coming, Johnny. How's things?'

'Fine, Jim. And you?'

He put the guitar down. 'To tell the truth, I'm finding retirement hard work. There's bugger all to do all day except get harassed to death by the wife. You don't fancy taking me back on, do you, on a part-time basis maybe?'

'You wouldn't want it, Jim.' I held out my arm. 'See that. The first two bullets missed my head by inches.'

'Christ Almighty. Who've you upset?'

That was the million-dollar question. Who had I upset? There could only be Oates International and Leprechaun

Developments. I couldn't see Victor Learoyd wanting me out of the way. After all, his son had hired to me protect him although God knows who from. Favourites for the hitman role had to be the Jenkinsons, probably working for Oates. How long before they went for Ollie Clarke as well?

'I don't know but I wouldn't like to meet them when they're really angry.'

At that moment, I saw Cameron walk in and I brought her across to meet Jim.

'Your successor,' I said and watched the expression on his face as he took in her six foot tall slinky figure dressed in tight embroidered jeans and a black see-through muslin top with no bra. He looked gobsmacked.

'Hi,' said Cameron and kissed him on both cheeks. Jim looked quite rejuvenated by the gesture and kissed her back but, before they had time to talk, he was summoned back to the stage by the rest of the group.

'I hope you like Sixties stuff,' I warned Cameron, 'because you're going to hear a lot of it tonight.'

'I'm a floater,' she said. 'I like anything. Listen, the car the shooter was in, did you get the digits?'

'No, it happened too quickly.'

'Never mind. Probably a hot box anyway.'

'I couldn't even tell you the colour. Great witness I'd make.'

At this point, Hilary arrived. She was wearing black trousers, slightly flared, and a pink T-shirt with a lace up neckline. I introduced her to Cameron who looked her up and down then kissed her too.

'What would you like to drink?' I asked Cameron. She went for a Cosmopolitan cocktail, which she informed me they drank on *Sex and the City*. Hilary ordered her usual gin and tonic.

I left them to get to know each other and went across to

the bar where Shirley was serving. She was looking as gorgeous as ever. I congratulated her on her wedding to Winston.

'He's certainly better than that Rodney you once had,' I said, reminding her of one of her less salubrious exes. 'I'm sure you'll both be very happy.'

'We will. But how are things with you, Johnny?'

'You know, same as ever really.'

'Total mayhem, you mean?' She smiled. 'We had some good times you and me, and I really miss the flat. You must come over and see our new house sometime.

'That'd be nice, Shirl.'

But I knew I probably never would because our lives had moved in different directions. What direction mine would take, I could only guess but, whatever else, I knew Maria and Vikki always had to be part of it.

At a nearby table, I saw Kenny Leatherbarrow hammering an ashtray with his fingers. He looked very old since his stroke although he must only have been in his early sixties. The drink had taken its toll. Hard to believe he'd once been a fresh-faced drummer in a beat group with hopes of following The Beatles to stardom. He nodded at me vacantly. I don't think he knew where he was.

Shirley saw me watching him. 'Someone from his rest home brings him over once a week. He just sits there drumming away and they come and collect him at eleven. Shame isn't it?'

'Better than having to watch *Eastenders* I suppose.'

I rejoined Cameron and Hilary just as The Chocolate Lavatory started their set with Richie Barrett's *Some Other Guy*, a Leiber & Stoller number that practically every group on Merseyside played back in 1962. The two of them seemed to be getting on well.

'Hilary's been telling me about your double life,' said Cameron.

I groaned.

'And Ronni's told me someone shot at you tonight,' said Hilary accusingly.

'Probably mistook me for someone else.' I knew that wasn't true but I didn't want her to get alarmed.

'Didn't you say you were staying in town tonight, Johnny?' said Cameron, with an innocent look on her face. 'Better make sure you're not followed.'

Hilary was not slow to grasp the significance. 'Are you staying at the flat?' she asked.

'I told him I didn't think he should be there on his own,' Cameron's tone was mischievous.   I guessed there had been some secret girl talk going on between them and, somewhere along the way, I was being set up.

Hilary grabbed my arm and pulled me to my feet. 'Neither do I,' she said. 'Excuse us; we're going to have a dance.'

She pulled me to my feet and on to the dance floor. The Chocolate Lavatory were playing one of their rare slow numbers, The Crying Shames' version of The Drifters' *Please Stay.* Very appropriate.

'Twice in a week, Johnny my love. What can I say? Things are looking up.'

She wrapped herself round me as we danced, watched by the approving eyes of Cameron. As the group finished the number to a ripple of applause from the crowd, she threw her arms round my neck and kissed me lingeringly on the lips before we returned to our seats. I kissed her back. Hilary always made me feel happy.

The night went well. When The Chocolate Lavatory had finished their spot, Jim came over and joined us. He regaled Cameron with highly exaggerated and lurid accounts of some of our old cases and drank more Newcastle Browns than Rosemary allowed him in a week at home.

Onstage, groups came and went, each playing much the

same material as the ones before them.   Where would Merseybeat have been without Chuck Berry?

At midnight, Jim announced he was off home. Cameron had disappeared with Josh, one of Jonas's other sons, leaving Hilary and I alone at the table.

'Do we have to stay till two?' She looked at me pointedly.

I couldn't think of one reason why we should. We went over to say goodbye to Shirley before going out into the night air.

'We might as well go in my car,' I said, 'and pick yours up in the morning.'

The RAV4 was parked round the corner in a side road. As we came closer I thought I saw the shape of a person in the back seat.

I stopped on the spot. 'Hilary, go back into the club and wait for me.'

'What's the matter?'

'I think there's somebody in the car. Quickly, run.'

'Don't be stupid, Johnny. Don't tackle him on your own. Come back with me.'

'I'll be all right. I want to see who it is. Now go.'

She looked frightened, hesitated for a second then turned and scampered back to the Bamalama. I waited a few moments, pretending to search in my pockets, then carried on to the car and unlocked it with the remote from ten feet away.

I walked casually towards the driver's door but, at the last second, reached across and pulled open the rear door, holding it between me and my assailant who leapt out and lunged at me with a knife.

I spun round and kicked his arm below the elbow. It didn't catch the angle quite right. He held on to his weapon and jumped back ready for another attack.

He was white, early twenties and he looked fit. He bounced from toe to toe in his trainers, waiting for me to make a move. I stayed still, ready to counter attack when a second man jumped out of the car.

The odds weren't good. The second guy hurled himself at me, butting me in the head, knocking me backwards. I clung to him as I fell, pulling him down on top of me and held on to him as I waited for the shooting pain in my head to subside.

The first man hovered over us, waving his knife in the air, trying to find a way through our tangled bodies to slash my windpipe. I hung on as my opponent tried to roll beneath me and so expose my back as an easy target.

Suddenly, a car came down the road straight towards us, headlights blazing. The man with the knife immediately started down the road, towards the Bamalama. I brought my knee sharply into the groin of the man on top of me and followed it up with a finger jab into his left eye. He let go his grip and I forced him off me and brought the side of my hand up sharply under his nose before finishing off with a right hook that put him on the pavement. I lifted his head and banged it down one more time on the ground for luck. He slumped, comatose, into a foetal position.

The car pulled up beside me and the driver peered out. 'Now I know why I retired,' said Jim Burroughs. 'Want a hand?'

'Bit late aren't you? Where'd the other one go?'

'I think your new partner's got him.'

I looked down the road and there was Cameron dragging the knifeman by his collar. He seemed to be unconscious.

'Poor goof missed his footing as he ran past me,' she explained, 'and hit his head rather hard on that iron gatepost'.

We propped the two men against the wall. I picked up the knife, which had fallen in the struggle, and searched the other man. In his pocket was a gun. I transferred it to my jeans. It looked like he was the one who had shot at me earlier. Neither man stirred.

'Do you want me to phone our mob?' asked Jim, who still liked to think himself as a copper.

'No. Don't worry, Jim. We'll sort them.'

'If you're sure, I'll leave you to it, then,' and he drove off towards the tunnel and his safe haven in West Kirby.

'What are we doing with these wiggers?' asked Cameron. I looked at her vacantly. 'Wiggers,' she translated patiently, 'wannabe thugs.'

'I'll take their photos,' I said. I always carried a digital camera in the car. 'Show them to Tommy McKale. There's a fair chance he'll recognise them.'

'And then what?'

'He'll find out where they hang out and go round and have a quiet word with them on our behalf.' It was as much as I wanted to know about what happened to them next.

I took the camera out, snapped the still sleeping men, then opened the door for Cameron. 'Jump in, Ronni. I'll drive you back to your car. Where's Hilary?'

'I made her wait inside the club. I like her. She's a real hottie, Johnny.'

I agreed, without being quite sure what a hottie was.

'Nice fun bags. Sexy.' I looked at her queryingly. 'They called them boobs in your day.'

Once I'd seen Cameron safely drive away, I went back into the Bamalama for Hilary. She was relieved to see me and repeated how she wished I'd give up my dangerous occupation.

'I think it might be wiser if you went home, Hil,' I said. 'There's a possibility they might know about my flat and come looking for me. I don't want to put you in any danger. You've had enough of that in the past'

In actual fact, what I was more worried about was the fact that they might come to the house where Maria and Victoria were alone.

Hilary didn't argue. She didn't really fancy the idea of

more aggro. I dropped her off at her car and promised to give
her a ring then I raced off home to Sefton Park.

Maria half woke as I entered the bedroom.

'Is that you, Johnny. I thought you weren't coming back
tonight.'

I kissed her and told her I'd left the club early so thought
I might as well come home.'

'Hurry up and get into bed,' she murmured. 'Did you have
a good time? How was Jim?

I undressed and snuggled in beside her. 'Fine. Group was as
awful as ever but he enjoyed it.'

I didn't mention the shooting or the fight. No sense in
worrying her. But I knew it wouldn't stop there. I would have
to be on my guard whilst I tracked down who my enemies
were.

I put my arms round Maria and hugged her. It was good to
be home.

Cameron was already at the office when I arrived next
morning. Sometimes, I don't think she sleeps. The first thing
I did was load the pictures on the computer and print them
out.

'They are really peaked,' she commented, looking over my
shoulder.

'Peaked?'

'Ugly'.

I didn't disagree. Both looked athletic and muscular but
bore traces of previous battles in the form of facial scars. One
had a large curved nose that wouldn't have looked out of place
on a parrot, whilst his accomplice had four letters tattooed on
his forehead, H A R D, that I hadn't noticed at the time.

I'll take these over to Tommy,' I said, but before I had the
chance, we had an unexpected visitor.'

It was an excited Oliver Clarke. 'I've had an offer for the
business,' he gasped.

'It was on the cards.'

'You don't understand. It's a ridiculous offer but it was followed by a telephone call. This voice said: *"if you don't sell, you die"*.'

* * *

The official offer had been made, predictably, by Jeffrey Taggart of Oates International, who had called round in person at Oliver Clarke's garage. It was £30,000 short of the valuation that Ollie put on his business, even allowing for the burnt out showroom.

'What did you tell him?' I asked Ollie.

'I told him I wasn't remotely interested at that price, that I wasn't particularly looking to sell and he'd have to pay a damn sight more to persuade me to change my mind.'

'And what did he say?'

'He'd leave the offer with me and if I wished to reconsider I could reach him at his offices in Victoria Street. He was a greasy character, all false smiles and fake bonhomie.'

'Yes, that's a fair description of Jeffrey Taggart.'

'You know him?'

'I've met him, yes.'

'His manner soon changed when I said I wasn't interested though.'

'It would. How long after his visit did you get the phone call?'

'The phone call came first thing this morning. Taggart was round yesterday afternoon. I came straight over here to tell you.'

'I hope you don't want protection,' I said, 'because we have a poor record in that field.' One dead and one shot was not something to put in the brochures.

He sank into a chair and looked defeated. 'What do I do, Johnny? I've put everything into this business. It's my whole life.'

'If everything goes the way I think it will, Ollie, you'll have another offer later today for near enough the price you would sell for. And, if I were you, I'd take it. You don't need all this aggro.'

'After all the trouble these last few weeks, I'm very tempt-
ed. It's Graham Wharton's funeral tomorrow.'

'How's his family taken it?'

'His wife's devastated as you can imagine. A chap goes to
work as normal in the morning, perfectly fit, and never comes
home again.'

'How are they fixed financially?'

'He was in a pension scheme and she has a job.'

'What about insurance?'

'No idea. Unless he had an accident policy or a life policy
but I wouldn't know about that.'

'As his employer though, you might be liable.'

'I know. That's another headache.'

'Depends on the Health & Safety enquiry of course.'

He stayed another half hour going over the ramifications
of the latest development. When he'd gone, Cameron and I
tried to get a handle on the wider picture.

'As far as I can see it,' I said, 'Oates still own this parcel of
land that Stewart Davis ostensibly sold to Leprechaun.'

'Except for Ollie's little plot which it looks like they will
get pretty soon, and for real this time.'

'And except the Watson's' place, don't forget, which Victor
Learoyd bought.'

'Why did Oates allow that to happen I wonder?'

'God knows. Then there's the Chinese takeaway as well.
Mr Ho's. We don't know if Oates really owns that.'

'That's right. And what about the Pig and Hamster? That
could be another fake. Try and find where Mrs Laffin has
gone to while I take these photos to Tommy. I'll be back
later.'

Tommy McKale recognised the two men instantly. 'Bernie
Gibbon and Larry Tweedale. Muscle for hire.'

'Who sent them, that's what I need to know.'

'Leave it with me, Johnny. Have you been to see the Jenkinsons yet?'

'No, I got sidetracked.'

We were interrupted by the sound of the William Tell Overture.

'Is that your mobile ringing?' Tommy asked.

It was.

'Rossini,' he declared. Tommy was a master of general knowledge and trivia.

The call was from Cameron. 'I've located that Mrs Laffin,' she said. 'She's now the licensee of a pub in Wavertree called The Goose and Gander. Should be opening time by the time you get there.' I took down the address.

'Wonderful, Ronni. How ever did you find her?'

'I'm a detective, remember.'

'Wicked,' I said. This language business was catching. Soon we'll all be talking in txt.

The Goose and Gander was hardly the pick of the city's hostelries. It was small and squeezed in between a charity shop for starving Ethiopians and a shop selling discount beds. Sometime in the distant past, the outside had been painted a dark brown.

A torn, fluorescent orange poster in one of the grimy front windows informed prospective patrons that an exotic dancer would be appearing on Sunday lunchtimes. I didn't think she would affect the size of the congregation at nearby Holy Trinity too much.

I pushed open the door and went inside. My feet stuck to the carpet and the smell of stale smoke and beer was overpowering. I was confronted by a fat, blowsy woman in her early Fifties standing behind the bar wearing a nightdress and a housecoat. Her dyed blonde hair was in rollers and the previous night's lipstick was smudged over her cheeks.

I assumed she was the cleaner until she spoke in a gravely

voice.'

'What can I get you, luv?'

'I was looking for Mrs Laffin.'

'Her eyes narrowed. 'That's me. You're not from the VAT are you?'

'No. I'm from the radio. Johnny Ace.'

'Oh yes?' The reply was blank. She was not a listener.

'I'll have half of cider,' I said. I peered over the bar and saw her bare varicosed legs were encased in pom-pom slippers.

She moved towards the pump, pulled on it but no liquid came out.

'Friggin' 'ell, the fuckin' pump's gone.'

An elderly man holding an empty pint glass in one hand and a pipe in the other rose from a nearby table and staggered to the bar.

'Another in there, Molly.'

'You'll have to friggin' wait. I've got to get this chap his cider. Go and sit down,' she barked at him. He obeyed meekly. I wondered if all her customers were as docile but I doubted it. Judging by the state of the furniture, I reckoned there would be punch-ups in the snug most nights.

'Forget the cider,' I said. 'I just wanted to ask you if you were the lady who used to run the Pig and Hamster in Toxteth.'

'What if I was? What's it to do with you?'

'A friend of mine has a shop near there and he's been having trouble with people trying to force him out.'

'Well he will, won't he? They want the soddin' land to make a friggin' fortune, they're all the same.'

'Who was it bought your old place?'

'Why do you want to know?'

I produced a ten pound note from my pocket. 'To see if it's the same people who are pestering my friend. I'd be grateful for any help. I pressed the note into her hand and she trans-

ferred it into the depths of her sweaty cleavage before pulling
her housecoat defiantly shut.

'You tell me who's pestering your friend,' she demanded,
'and I'll tell you if it's the same people what bought mine.'

This was becoming hard work. 'A firm called Oates
International.'

'No, it wasn't them.'

'What! Say that again. You didn't sell to Oates
International?'

'I said not, didn't I? They was after it, but I gave them the
bum's rush. They was humming and hawing over the price so
I fucked them off and sold it to this fellow what said he did an
act in the clubs who had the readies. A fellow called Benjamin
Prince.'

I couldn't believe what I'd heard. Benjamin Prince. Ben E.
Prince. The early stage name of Lucky Learoyd. Lucky
Learoyd had bought The Pig and Hamster?

'Who did you say?'

'You 'eard. Are you deaf or something?'

'No. Just surprised.' Gobsmacked more likely. 'Was Mr
Prince a bloke of about fifty?"

'I'd say so.'

'Dressed a bit loud?'

'That's the one. But his money was good.' She took a long
swig from a nearby glass of gin. 'Look, I've told you all I
know, so if that's all you've come for, you can sod off.'

I was glad to get out into the street and fresh air. So the
contract we had back at the office, that had come from Jeanne
McGhee's flat, was a fake.

She wouldn't be aware of it but Molly Laffin was the one
person that could put Taggart and Dixon in the dock. She
would be able to swear that the signature on the contract was
a forgery.

But also, another twist in the tale, Lucky Learoyd was buying property in Liverpool. Could it be on his father's behalf? And why use the name Prince?'

I decided it was time I had a long talk with Lucky. I went back to the RAV4, which I'd parked in Church Road and rang his number on my mobile. To my surprise, he answered.

'I need to see you, Lucky. Can I come up to your place?' When he hesitated, I added, 'You needn't worry, Tommy McKale's told me all about the house.'

'OK,' he relented.

'I'll be there in half an hour.'

It was a little more than that as traffic was slow in the city centre around the Tunnel.

I drove up to the electric gates, which opened as I approached. Someone obviously was monitoring the CCTV cameras. Lucky came out of the front door to greet me. He was wearing a Hawaiian shirt featuring tropical birds of exotic plumage, a pair of white tennis shorts and a floppy white sun hat. His arm was still in a sling.

'Hi Johnny,' he said sheepishly.

'Two up two down, eh Lucky? Little terrace just off the main street? What the fuck was all that about?'

He looked embarrassed. 'I do have a little terrace, Johnny. The one I used to live in. I use it as a shagging pad since the wife left. Doesn't do to bring strangers to a place like this. Gives them fancy ideas, never mind the opportunity for a bit of light fingering.'

'What sort of women are you copping off with for Heaven's sake?'

'The sort you meet in clubs, what do you think? Where else would I meet them in my job?'

'You could try libraries. Possibly you'd find more refined types there.'

Even as I said it, I wasn't entirely convinced. I'd met some pretty rampant librarians in my time and some of the stories

Maria had told me about her colleagues suggested I wasn't the only one.

'I never read books,' he said.

'Are we standing on the step forever or are you going to show me round your mansion?'

'Sorry, Johnny. Yes, come in. Where do you want to start?'

'I think upstairs and we'll work our way down.'

Tommy McKale's description had been pretty accurate. All it needed was a Venetian canal running across the first floor and a couple of white tigers in the garden and we could have been in Las Vegas. I resisted the temptation to put money into any of the fruit machines.

'Is your old man's place like this too?' I asked him, as we reached the swimming pool flanked by plastic Roman statues. Very tacky.

At the mention of his father, Lucky became subdued.

'We didn't talk for years,' he said. 'When I left school, he wanted me to go into the business with him but I wanted to be a singer. Always have. Ever since I was a tiny kid in the school choir, all I've ever wanted to do was sing.'

'So what happened?'

'I walked out. At eighteen. I found myself a bedsit in Southport and joined a group.'

'This was before The Aliens, I take it? When you were Ben E. Prince?'

'Ben E. Prince and The Courtiers we were called. We got a lot of work. There were loads of venues around at the time and loads of bands, too. The Mersey Four, The Zeniths, The Smokestacks...'

'You played The Riverside I believe?'

'All the time. Great place for birds in those days.'

'I played there myself with The Cruzads.'

'Do you remember Jack Pass and Ralph?'

It was becoming a stroll down Memory Lane. Time to

move the interview on.

'Where did you meet your wife?'

Lucky's face darkened. 'Years later, after I joined The Aliens. We were playing at the She Club in Liverpool one night when Jenny came down with her mate and that was it. We started going out and two years later we got married. I left the group to go solo, the bookings were coming in and everything was hunky dory.'

'So what went wrong?'

'Nothing till she met Jason Bloody Jenkinson. He had a flash motor, villa in Spain, a pocket full of readies...'

'And a ten inch dick, I suppose, as well. Yes, I know the sort.'

'So she pissed off with him.' He sighed deeply. 'But we've already talked about that haven't we?'

'Were you living in this house when you were together?'

'No. We were in the one down the road.'

'The shagging pad?'

'It might only be small but she had it real nice. I was quite happy there until...'

I didn't give him the chance to get maudlin. 'So how did you manage to get this place?'

'The old man got in touch, after all that time. I'd had no contact with him since I left home but he'd obviously been keeping tabs on me because he'd heard about the divorce and what a state I was in. I almost topped myself, you know.'

'What did he want?'

'A reconciliation. I'm the only son and he's getting on. Immortality through the genes and all that. He accepts he was in the wrong trying to force me to do something I didn't want to.' Lucky looked down into the pool like Narcissus and was silent for a moment like he was reflecting on his life. 'He bought me this place,' he eventually said. 'So he'd know I'd be set up when he's gone.'

'And what do you have to do in return?'

He looked uncertain. 'I don't know what you mean.'

'The family business. Are you working for him in the end? And what is the family business anyway? Someone told me your father was a farmer.'

The reply came without hesitation. 'He was a farmer but he rents out most of his agricultural land now. He used to hire out gaming machines, too, in the old days when I was a kid, but now he's more into property. Says it's less hassle.'

It was hard to judge whether Lucky was aware of his father's reputation or whether he thought he had me fooled.

'Why do you tell people that you live in your old house?'

'Jealousy. Most folk don't like you to be doing better than they are, especially in this business.'

'You might have at least let me know when I was supposed to be protecting you.'

'Sorry. It's just that it's easier to tell everybody the same'

'Right, Lucky, the $64,000 question. Who do you think is trying to kill you?'

'I've honestly no idea, Johnny, but as I told you before, I'm sure it's not the Jenkinsons. That feud is long over.'

'Could it have anything to do with your father's activities in the property market Liverpool?'

Lucky frowned. 'Strange question. I don't have anything to do with the old man's business. Singing is my career, always has been. And I'm good at it. I'm not going to change now. Since I started the Proby act, I've never done better.'

'Then how come you've just bought a pub in Toxteth called The Pig and Hamster?'

His face became a contortion of confusion. 'How do you know about that?'

'I'm a detective and I'm good at it.'

'An investment. Everybody's saying how prices in the city are going to shoot up with this City of Culture thing and I was doing a gig in this pub on the Wirral when the owner told me his sister had a pub over the water and she was thinking of selling up.'

'That would be Mrs Laffin?'

'That's her. A right slapper she was. She'd been having a lot of problems with vandals and wanted rid quickly so I ended up getting it at a good price.'

This sounded like familiar Oates International strategy. But how had they managed to let someone else nip in and buy it from under their noses.

'Was nobody else after it?'

'Some big firm from London made an offer after she'd agreed to sell to me but they were too late. I'd gone down the day after I heard about it, took her straight to my brief and got her signed up the same day.'

Singer he may have been but Lucky had certainly inherited his father's nose for business.

'Why use the name Prince?'

'I didn't want anyone to connect me with the old man. I wanted to do this on my own.'

'You knew he was buying property in Liverpool then?'

'He'd told me he was but I didn't know where.'

'How often do you see him? Come to that, how did he first make contact you?'

'I'd been in a clinic for a month with depression. He came to see me there. When I came out, I went back home and stayed with him and Mum for a fortnight.'

'Had your mother never tried to get in touch with you all that time since you were eighteen?'

'No. I'd been disowned and she wouldn't have dared go against the old man's wishes.'

I guessed the Feminist Revolution would never breach the Learoyd household as long as Victor was alive.

'Then what happened?'

'He said he was buying me this house. I got myself a month's booking on a cruise ship and when I came back, it was all ready, fully furnished, the lot. We had a family party here to celebrate, him and my Mum came over for the night, and I haven't seen them since.'

'When was that?'

'The party? About three months ago, back in May.'

'And when did your purchase of the Pig and Hamster go through?'

'About three weeks ago.'

'Shortly before the death threats?'

'Yes. Good Lord, do you think they could have anything to do with that?'

'Could be. Have you had anyone on to you wanting to buy the place?'

'No. But nobody knows I've got it.'

Keep out of Liverpool or we will kill you, the note had said.

'Oh, I think you'll find, Lucky, that they do.'

* * *

After I left Lucky's, I stopped off at West Kirby to let Jim know everything was OK after the night before. Rosemary was out so we ended up going to the White Lion for a pint and a toasted sandwich.

We discussed the effect the City of Culture award had had on the city, in particular in relation to the property market and the speculators gathering from all over the globe.

'Or should we call them vultures now?' I said.

'It's certainly a rum business,' Jim declared, his mouth full of steak, mushroom and bacon. 'Some of these big property companies could teach the Mafia a thing or two.'

'The Mafia probably own the big companies these days, Jim. The career criminals have infiltrated the business world. They make their money in drugs and prostitution then buy their way into the City.'

Jim sighed. 'It was simpler when your average hoodlum wore a striped jersey instead of a striped suit.'

I laughed. 'Couldn't have put it better myself. Anyway, to change the subject, apart from the aggro at the end, did you enjoy the gig last night?'

'Brilliant, Johnny. What did you think of the band?'

'Excellent,' I lied. 'I think perhaps you could drop a couple of the Chuck Berry numbers though. They're a bit played out now. Maybe do something less well-known. 'Benny Spellman's *Lipstick Traces* for example or even something new.'

'It's getting the lads to learn them, Johnny. We don't rehearse you see so we have to stick to the old stuff that we know.'

'I suppose you're right.'

We chatted about old times and old cases. He asked what had happened to Linda Roberts whose sister Michelle had found hanging from the chandeliers in one of my flats at Livingstone Drive.

'She married Peter, her schoolteacher chum,' I said. 'They sent me an invite to the wedding but I couldn't go.'

'And how's Tommy McKale's security business doing?'

'Thriving.'

'I might have known it. And what about his mate, Big Alec?'

'Doing a job for me at the moment. I believe he's Worshipful Master at his lodge this year.'

Jim growled angrily. 'He was a right villain, he was. Killed at least two people that I know of, and God knows how many others that I don't, but we could never pin anything on him.'

I said nothing. Of such tales are legends made. Before I went to Spain, Hilary and I had been inside her house when a group of Animal Rights hoodlums had thrown a petrol bomb through the window. Big Alec had come to our aid and I must say I hadn't been too fussy about how he had treated them afterwards. With Big Alec guarding him, I knew Lucky Learoyd would be well protected and that gave me peace of mind.

Jim and I reminisced for another half hour before I dropped him off at home and drove back to the office to fill Cameron in with what had been happening.

'I wonder what Victor Learoyd will do when he finds out his son owns one of the plots on the land he hopes to buy?' she said.

'I don't know but, more importantly, what will Oates International and the Jenkinsons do?'

I didn't care to speculate.

'It's Graham Wharton's funeral tomorrow. I think I ought to go. It'll give me a chance to talk to Ollie Clark and see whether or not he's decided to sell to Oates International.'

'Where's it at?'

'Springwood Crematorium in Allerton at eleven o'clock.'

The place hadn't the happiest memories for me. It was there, five years ago, that Michelle Roberts had ended up.

'Do you want me to come too?'

'No, Ronni. It would be better if you stayed and looked after the office. I have a feeling things could be hotting up.'

'Have you heard from Hilary today?' She raised her eyebrows coquettishly.

'No. I said I'd ring her.'

'You're in a sketchy position with those two, aren't you?'

I would be, I thought, if I knew what it meant, but it didn't really need any translation. Other words like impossible, dangerous, and crazy came to mind. I wasn't so sure about 'enviable', though that was what Lucky Learoyd, in his position without a woman of his own, might have plumped for. In reality, it was the worst of both worlds.

'I guess so,' was all I said.

Before Cameron had a chance to reply, there was a knock on the door and DI Reubens and DS Monk strode in.

'Glad we caught you,' he said. 'We never finished our little chat the other day.' He closed the door behind him as if he was settling in for a long session. 'Tell you what though, I'm dying for a cuppa if there's one going.'

'I'll put the kettle on,' I said. I'd never dared asked Cameron to make tea although she had, on one occasion, offered.

'No dog today?' said Reubens, looking round the office for Roly.

'It's his day off.'

'Ah. We're still looking into Jeanne McGhee's murder,' he said, 'and I can't believe how many people there are who, for varying reasons, wanted her dead.'

'And who might they be?' I asked non-committally. 'And what are these reasons?'

'It all goes back to the murdered tramp, or Mr Stewart Davis as we now call him, seeing as how he wasn't a tramp at all but a city whizkid.'

I wasn't fooled by Reuben's insouciant manner and painstaking delivery. He was like a spin bowler churning out slow deliveries until, suddenly, he'd bowl a googly and hope to catch you out.

He continued. 'It seems Miss McGhee had been holding in her bank account the not inconsiderable sum of £50,000...'

The amount staggered me. 'How much?' I said. I couldn't believe I'd heard correctly.

'Fifty thousand pounds, paid into her account in the form of a cheque which had been given to Mr Davis by an Irish company called Leprechaun Developments as a deposit on a piece of land owned by Oates International. Mr Davis's company.'

Complicated but I followed it so far and nodded agreement.

'On the morning Mr Davis was killed, she withdrew this money in cash by prior arrangement with her bank. That money has disappeared. We also believe that Miss McGhee had in her possession certain contracts belonging to Oates International. They too have disappeared.'

He paused then, before I could reply, he bowled the rogue ball. It was short, sharp, swift and dramatic.

'What else did you take from Miss McGhee's flat, Mr Ace?'

I found it hard to take seriously a policeman who was younger and smaller than me. Apart from which, Sam Reubens was a likeable enough fellow who had the amiable air of a favourite young uncle at his nephew's bar mitzvah. As for DS Monk, he looked like he just wanted to be left alone with a full bottle of single malt.

'I didn't take anything at all,' I replied truthfully, glad he hadn't asked Cameron the same question.

'You do admit you were there then?'

'I can hardly deny it as you will have found my prints all over the room.'

I'd had my prints taken in the Michelle Roberts case when I was framed and arrested for a crime I didn't commit. They tell you that they destroy your records if you are found not guilty of a chargeable offence but I have always had my doubts about that.

'Why were you there?'

'Simple. I was about to tell you the other day when you got called away. How did the Kensington siege go, by the way?'

'Oh that. The police marksman shot him. Carry on with your story. You went to the flat.'

I explained to them that Jeanne McGhee had asked me to meet her at her home at eight o'clock but, when I arrived there, I found the front door to her apartment open and an intruder inside. I left out the bit about Cameron being with me.

'What happened to this intruder?'

'He ran away,' I said shortly.

'You didn't try to stop him?'

'I was taken by surprise. He ran straight past me.'

'You didn't recognise him?'

'No.'

'And Miss McGhee never turned up?'

'No.'

'So what did you do next?'

'I waited a few minutes and, when she didn't come, I shut the door of the flat after me and went home.'

'Did it not occur to you to ring the police?'

'I thought afterwards that the man might have been in her flat with her permission. I mean, he wasn't wearing a balaclava or anything.'

'Nice try but not credible. If he had good reason to be

there he would have spoken to you. Luckily, as he wasn't wearing a balaclava, you'll be able to give us a good description of him won't you?' He nodded to Jeff Monk. 'Sergeant.'

DS Monk took out his notebook and I furnished him with a rough description of Alby Durno, which would not have identified him in a line up of two.

'Sounds like The Invisible Man,' commented DI Reubens sarcastically.

He waited for my reply but, when none was forthcoming, came back with a different approach.

'When we inspected Miss McGhee's bank account, we also found she had written a cheque payable to Ace Investigations for £1000.'

'That's right. I told you, she hired me to protect her.'

'From whom?'

'That she didn't say. My job was to find out. All she told me was that she had received threats.'

'All she could expect one would think, given that she had purloined fifty grand of someone else's money. Is the tea ready yet?'

I made four cups and took one to Cameron in the outer office. The fifty grand had shaken me. I hadn't realised that Davis's cut would be so much. With stakes like this just for a mere backhander, no wonder people were prepared to kill.

'Is there anything else you'd like to tell me?' asked Reubens, sipping his tea with relish.

There was nothing in the world I wanted to tell him but I was sure there was plenty he wanted to hear.

'We've spoken to Davis's partners at Oates International,' he said.

'Oh yes?'

'They say they knew nothing about any deposit. They were negotiating with various parties over that particular plot and no decision had been made. Meanwhile, the partners at

Leprechaun Developments are very unhappy and want their money back. But you know this already, don't you, because you've been to see them both.'

I said, 'I've always maintained both murders are connected to this land deal but, as to who killed Davis or his mistress, I've no idea. I agree with you. It seems there's a veritable queue of people with a motive to kill both of them.'

Reubens agreed. 'And the opportunity too, given that Miss McGhee was missing the whole weekend and Mr Davis had spent his last five days alive living rough on the streets. They were walking targets.'

'I can't help you with any of your blank days, I'm afraid. I didn't know Mr Davis at all and Miss McGhee didn't contact me until after he was dead.'

Reubens sighed and drained his cup. 'I take it that now your client is deceased, your part in this investigation is over?'

'Put it this way,' I said carefully, 'I don't see anyone else paying me to continue it.'

'If you hear of anything at all that you think might be important, ring me.'

'I will, of course,' I promised. 'Are you going to the funeral tomorrow?'

'Mr Clarke's mechanic, you mean? Yes, are you?'

'I said I'd go. I've known Ollie since way back.'

'By the way, I never asked how it was you happened to be present at the fire at his showrooms.'

'Ollie was a client. He rang me, told me what had happened, someone had torched his showroom, and he asked me to go over.'

'Another one? All the people in my cases turn out to be your clients.'

'Not the Kensington siege,' I pointed out.

'Remind me. Why did Oliver Clarke hire you in the first place?'

'Because of the vandals. He didn't think the police were taking his complaints seriously so he asked me to look into it.'

'And what did you find?'

'The first time I went up to see him was when the ramp crashed down and killed Graham Wharton so that brought things to a halt before I'd had chance to do anything. After that came the fire and by then it was obvious that someone was after him for whatever reason.'

'The fire could have been a cleverly planned insurance job.'

'If it was, why hire me?'

'Try this for a theory, Mr Ace. Let's say all this was carefully planned in advance, set up for an eventual insurance scam. The talk of vandals was a smokescreen, building up to the fire. Hiring a private investigator to look into the so-called attacks, which he could have carried out himself, would serve to add credence to his story.'

That annoyed me. 'Would killing Graham Wharton add credence as well?'

'No need to get worked up. I was just putting forward a hypothesis. I've said before, we believe Graham Wharton's death was an accident. A faulty ramp.'

'Has that been confirmed?'

He looked uncomfortable. 'Well, not yet, but I'm sure that it will be in the next few days.'

'We'll have to see.'

'All right, let's look at it from your angle. If Mr Clarke is right about someone with a grudge against him, what do you think are the reasons behind it?'

'According to Ollie, he doesn't know himself and if has no idea, then I certainly can't say. My first thoughts are like yours however, he's upset the wrong people.'

I didn't mention the word *land*.

We left it at that. The two policemen left and Cameron emerged from office. She was astonished when I told her about the fifty grand.

'So much!' she exclaimed.

'Who's got it though, that's the question. It must be some-where.'

'If Jeanne did give it to Davis, he could have stashed it away somewhere.'

'Or whoever murdered him could have taken it.'

'Which suggests it wasn't Leprechaun Developments.'

'Why not?'

'Because they're making such a fuss about it,' said Cameron.

'Could be a blind, to cover the fact they killed him.'

'I don't go for that. One thing we do know, it isn't at Jeanne McGhee's flat and our burglar friend didn't take it. I think we'd have noticed if he had a thousand fifty pound notes on him.'

'How about Oates? They could have killed him and qui-etly kept the deposit.'

'Can't see it. I think they're more worried about the forged contracts. That's why Dixon arranged for the Jenkinsons to send Durno to burgle her flat.'

'But that suggests,' said Cameron thoughtfully, 'that Dixon and Taggart knew that Jeanne McGhee had the contracts. Now, how would they know that unless she was blackmailing them?'

'That's been your theory all along, hasn't it?'

'One of them. The other is that she'd stolen them and was now asking money for their return.'

'Either way, that's a good reason for booking the lady a pine box to nowhere. Like I just told Reubens, there's no end of people with motives to kill Jeanne.'

'Probably Leprechaun are favourites though. Fifty grand is a lot of dosh to lose.'

'Right. And if you'd met that Gene Flynn at Leprechaun,

Ronni, you'd not want to cross him.' I remembered the hand-shake. A slightly firmer grip and I could have lost an arm.

'Let's go over this carefully,' I said. 'As I see it, there are three alternatives. Jeanne hid the cash somewhere that we don't know about and it's still there, waiting to be discovered. Or Davis had it on him when he was murdered, which means the killer probably got it and it could be anywhere. Or, third-ly, whoever killed Jeanne got the money as well as a bonus.'

'And it could be anywhere again.'

'Yes.'

'There's another possibility,' said Cameron thoughtfully. 'Jeanne McGhee had another accomplice besides Stewart Davis and that person has got the £50,000.'

* * *

There wasn't a big attendance at Graham Wharton's funeral. The chapel was only a quarter filled.

A middle-aged woman, who turned out to be the Wharton's next door neighbour, explained to me why she thought this was. 'They were a quiet couple you see, kept themselves to themselves.'

I wondered. That usually meant *too stuck-up to bother with the likes of us* although, looking at her worn, soiled trainers, jogging slacks and black polo shirt, her only fashion concession to the occasion, I wouldn't have blamed them if that had been the case.

The front rows were taken up by family and friends. I tried to work out which of the young people there were the Wharton's three children and which were their spouses, or partners as the PC people insist we call them nowadays.

A lady at the front whom I presumed to be the widow, Mrs Wharton, was bent forward as if in prayer. She wore a black veil over her blond hair and I guessed the man with a consoling arm round her was one of their sons, which in turn suggested that the girl beside him, with a dummy-sucking infant draped over her shoulder, was his wife. She looked as if she might be pretty but, from where I was sitting, I only had a rear view of them all.

Oliver Clark and his staff took up two rows near the back. DI Reubens and DS Monk positioned themselves on the opposite side.

Graham Wharton had been a staunch member of his local Catholic church and his local parish priest had come along to perform the ceremony and treat the congregation to a brief résumé of the deceased's life.

We learnt that Graham had been a popular member of his church choir, was a stalwart of the bowling club and liked his home and garden. He was not a man for travel and adventure but enjoyed his fortnight's holiday in Llandudno once a year. He had always worked locally as a respected mechanic in the motor trade and was a keen viewer of *The Weakest Link* and *Coronation Street.*

It made Ken's life at the radio station sound quite dynamic.

'His unfortunate death at the early age of fifty-one', continued the priest, 'was a terrible tragedy,' at which point his widow emitted a low sob and the priest hurried into something in Latin that I didn't understand.

After the service, everyone trooped outside to examine and estimate the cost of the floral tributes.

'They say the murderer always comes to the funeral,' I remarked to Sam Reubens who was reading the names on the bouquets. 'So I wonder who'll turn up when they bury Stewart Davis.'

'When, being the operative word,' commented the policeman. 'His body hasn't been released yet from the mortuary.'

'What's keeping them? He's nearly been dead a fortnight.'

'Blame the boffins. If you ask me, it's all these books and TV shows glorifying forensic scientists. Place is full of trainees who can't wait for the next corpse to come through so they can get a slice for themselves so to speak. Universities are falling over themselves to set up courses on cadavers and crime scene investigations to satisfy the demand. At one time, most of the students would have been happy to be plumbers.'

'I suppose there isn't too much difference really.'

Reubens laughed and Jeff Monk chortled. They were probably finding the cremation light relief after the recent sieges, murders and rapes.

The lady neighbour came over to inform us that everyone was invited back to the Wharton's house for drinks and a buffet but we all declined. I figured the event would be confined to family and close friends. No place for strangers.

Instead, I sought out Ollie Clarke to see if there had been any more approaches from Oates International for his land. His staff had already gone back to work and he was walking slowly over to his car like a man in a dream.

'It's starting to get to me,' he said.

'Any more death threats?'

'No. But I'm not going to let the buggers beat me.'

'You're not selling then?'

'I didn't say that. I've not decided what to do. I'm still waiting to hear from the insurance about the fire. If they won't pay out I'll have no choice. I couldn't afford to rebuild on my own.'

'Any reason they wouldn't pay out?'

'Not that I can think of, but with all that's gone on, nothing would surprise me now.'

I left him to drive away and walked back to my own car. Reubens and Monk had already left and the Crematorium car park was filling up with new mourners for the next thirty-minute slot.

'What was it like?' Cameron asked when I got back to the office.

'A conveyor belt to Heaven,' I said. 'A departure every half hour.'

'I suppose as the population grows and the crematoriums get busier,' she mused, 'they will probably be able to cut the services down to ten minutes.'

To me, this conjured up a picture of crematoriums resembling the baggage sections at airports with lines of coffins bobbing along one after the other, all heading towards a gaping hole to be plunged headlong into a fiery pit.

I offered the thought to Cameron.

'Isn't that what they predicted in the Bible?' she said. 'I seem to remember the fiery pits bit at any rate.'

There had been no news during the morning.

'We need to speak to someone at Oates International,' Cameron said. 'If Jeanne had got another accomplice, maybe one of her colleagues can tell us who she was friendly with.'

'The trouble is, we know nothing about Jeanne other than she lived on her own and worked for Oates. Nothing about her family, friends, where she went socially.'

'We don't even know she lived on her own,' pointed out Cameron. 'That was a double bed in her flat.'

Stewart Davis stayed with her, remember. When his wife went away.'

'Yeah, that's true. So she lived alone. Unless, of course, she did have a fella and sent him packing for a week.'

'Clutching at straws, Ronni.'

'I suppose so.'

I looked at my watch. 'It's nearly one o'clock. Why don't we walk over to Oates and see if we can see any of the staff coming out for lunch.'

Oates International office was only a five minute walk away and, as luck would have it, I recognised a girl coming out of the doorway.

'That's the girl from Reception,' I said. 'I couldn't mistake that hair.' It was bright red and cut in a spiky style. She was dressed in black trousers and a skimpy top. I put her age around twenty. 'Let's go.'

The girl turned to walk in our direction. As she came closer I stood in her way.

'Excuse me. You work at Oates International don't you?'

I was glad I had Cameron with me. Such forward behaviour would probably be construed as sexual harassment in a modern British court. Or, even worse, stalking.

Funny how sexual harassment never works the other way. Man talks dirty to a woman, she has him arrested. Woman talks dirty to a man, she charges £5 him a minute.

In the event, the girl turned out to be quite pleasant. I'd

been expecting 'what if I do?' but instead she said, 'You're the man who came to see Mr Taggart the other day.'

'That's right.'

'How can I help you?'

I introduced her to Cameron. 'This is Ronni, I don't know your name.'

'Erica.' She and Cameron exchanged "hi's".

'Are you going for lunch?' I asked her.

'Only for a sandwich and a quick drink. I usually go to Starbucks.'

'I just wanted a word with you about Jeanne McGhee. You may remember I came to see her a few days before I saw Mr Taggart.'

'I remember now.'

'Let us come with you and we can all have something to eat while I explain.'

She was happy with this so we walked along and I let Cameron chat to her about girlie things. They seemed to get on well.

Once we had sat down with our food, I explained to Erica about Ace Investigations and what I needed to know.

'Jeanne had hired us to protect her but she disappeared immediately afterwards. We need to know if she had any close friends at work.'

'Or, indeed, any you know of outside work,' added Cameron.

Erica looked doubtful. 'I can't really say. She wasn't particularly close to anyone in the office, didn't mix that much.'

'Why do you think that was?'

'Well, for a start, she wasn't in the main office with the rest of the girls. She worked for Mr Davis as his personal assistant and had her own office. When she wasn't in there, she was in with him.'

No innuendo or sly giggle. Erica gave no indication that

she thought there was anything more in the relationship.

'Besides,' she continued, 'she was older than most of us.'

'She was only about thirty.'

'There's a huge gulf between twenty and thirty,' Cameron assured me and Erica nodded agreement.

'She was quite sophisticated. Preferred meals in nice restaurants to clubbing it. She lived in a posh flat in Southport.'

'Did she live on her own?'

'As far as I know. Might have had a rich boyfriend, I don't know.'

'What about friends outside work?'

'A woman did call for her occasionally. Looked a bit like her, might have been her sister.'

'But you don't know her name or where she lived?'

She pondered for a moment then shook her head. 'I think it was Farnham or something like that. I really can't remember. We see so many people. Sorry.'

'Would anyone else in the office know?'

'I don't think so. I don't know. Can you tell me why Miss McGhee was killed?' Erica looked very young as she asked the question, and not a little nervous.

'Don't worry, I don't think you're in any danger. Miss McGhee had some problems in her personal life.' Some problems indeed. Fifty grand's worth of them not to mention a married lover with his head sliced off.

We paid for Erica's lunch and walked her back to her office. As we said goodbye and thanked her, a man emerged from the doorway on his way out. He stopped dead when he saw Cameron and me. It was Patrick Dixon, Jeffrey Taggart's partner and the man in the Bramley Moor. I quickly smiled at him and, before he could speak, turned to Erica. 'If you think of anything, give me a ring.' I pressed a business card into her hand and walked away followed by Cameron who said, 'He recognised us.'

'I know. That'll give him something to think about.'

'I wonder what he'll do? Try to contact us do you think?'

'Or try to kill us maybe?'

'Perhaps he'll send the Jenkinsons round,' she laughed.

I said, 'This is where the police have the beating of us, Ronni. They have access to lists of all Jeanne's mobile and telephone calls, know everyone she's been in touch with. They can go through all the things at her flat, address books and the like, not to mention all the records at Oates International office as well. And there's the forensic tests for DNA and fingerprints plus the manpower to go round asking questions. Sometimes I think we should stick to debt collecting and searching for missing cats.'

'Missing cats sucks but I'm game for chasing the welchers.'

At least I'd know what to do in future if I got any non-paying tenants. Set Cameron onto them. She'd probably frighten them more than Geoffrey.

'I'm going to go down to the Planning Office this afternoon,' I told Cameron. 'See if I can find out anything there.'

Life these days is all about networking and luckily I had a contact in the Planning Office. Bob Dix had worked in local government all his life but for about ten years in his early twenties, he'd played keyboards in a band called Not Mozart and we'd done a few gigs with them. We met up again when I started buying property and Bob finished his surveyor's exams and moved into the planning department. Who better to know what was going on in the turbulent world of property development?

'What brings you in, Johnny?'

He'd put on a lot of weight since his performing days. The buttons on the single-breasted jacket of his suit strained to accommodate his swelling beer belly and his neck had become so thick that, if he ever packed in the planning office, there'd be an opening for him as a Sumo wrestler. But he was a jovial man. In his case, fat was happy.

'Curiosity, Bob.'

'You're not thinking of building a shopping mall in London Road by any chance?'

'Worse places to build one, Bob. London Road needs something. No, I want to build a giant Macdonalds on top of Anfield and put those Red supporters out of their misery.' Bob was an Everton supporter too so he appreciated the joke.

Bob put on his serious face. 'So, what can I do for you?'

'There's a big area of land just off Chinatown towards Toxteth and the Dingle. A company called Oates International owns most of it.'

'I know Oates. London firm, specialise in buying up odd bits of land and tying them into a package deal.'

'Then they lend the purchaser the money to pay for it so they cash in twice.'

'Interesting. I didn't know that bit, but go on.'

'I need to know how many properties in that area, I call it the Toxteth Triangle, are owned by people other than Oates and who those people are.'

'Don't want much do you? Hang on, I'll get a map out and you can pinpoint the area for me.'

He went over to a large filing cabinet and opened a drawer.

'It won't be a hundred per cent accurate,' I warned him, 'but I've got a fair idea of the boundaries.'

Bob pulled out a big sheet and spread it over the table. 'Have a look at this.'

I'd never be so crass as to offer Bob money. Government officials don't take bribes, we all know that. Having set the bait, I changed the subject.

'I went to a Merseycats do the other night. Jim Burroughs' band was playing.'

'Not The Chocolate Lavatory? Are they still going?' Bob grimaced. 'Sounds horrible.'

'Never thought of making a comeback yourself, Bob?'

'Not in a million years. I'm past all that.'

'Me too. Prefer to watch other people do all the work. Incidentally, I've got a couple of tickets spare for that Sixties Revival show at the Empire next month, if you and Alice can use them.'

'That's very civil of you, Johnny.'

'Fine. I'll drop them in next week.'

'I'll be here. Now then, have you found out where you are on that plan.'

I traced the area for him with my finger and he noted the outer limits.

'Leave it with me, Johnny. I'll see what I can dig up for you.'

'Much appreciated, Bob. Thanks a lot.'

I walked back the short distance to the office. As I climbed the stairs, I saw the door was slightly open. Odd. Something was wrong. I dashed up the last few steps and rushed inside. The desk had been overturned. The chair, fax, phone and photocopier were lying in a heap on the floor. Beside them was Cameron, unconscious, a pool of blood beside her head.

* * *

Chapter Twenty-Two

She tried to force a smile through her swollen lips. 'I told you that Dixon man might send the Jenkinsons round.'

Cameron was sitting up, dazed and still bleeding slightly from a cut on the head.

'How do you know it was them?'

'I heard the first sleazebag shout out 'Jason'.'

It had all happened very quickly, before Cameron had had time to defend herself. The first man had stormed into the office, made straight for Cameron sitting behind her desk and smacked her in the face, causing her nose to bleed and splitting her upper lip. The second man, the one called Jason, concentrated on throwing the furniture around.

'I'll have to make sure I bring Roly with me tomorrow.'

When I was living at Waterloo Dock, I always brought him to the office rather than leaving him on his own at the flat. Since I moved to Sefton Park, with Maria usually being at home at some time during the day, I've tended not to bring him as often.

Cameron dabbed at her head with a hanky. 'After he'd hit me, he threw me to the floor and I hit my head against the sharp edge of that metal filing cabinet.'

The said cabinet was lying on its side, drawers open and papers flung all over the floor.

'What were they after?'

'Nothing. They didn't take anything. They just said, "stay out of other people's business or we'll be back and next time you'll know we've been".' She shuddered. 'They said they'd leave a permanent reminder.'

I fought to keep my temper. The Jenkinsons would pay for this but not immediately. All the women's magazines tell you that revenge is best served cold. Never underestimate the wisdom of *Woman's Own*.

'Well, you said you liked a good scrap,' I reminded her.

'I did?'

'At your interview.'

'The things people will say to get a job.'

'You sit down and I'll make a cup of tea. Then I'll clear this mess.'

'I'll help you. I'm OK now.'

'No. You've had a shock, if nothing else. Take it easy for a few minutes.'

'You're the boss.'

'And the best tea-maker.'

I didn't believe the intruders had just come to warn us off. I was sure they were looking for the contracts and was glad I'd hidden them safely at home.

I gave it twenty minutes while Cameron got herself together then, between us, we started to rearrange the furniture back in its rightful place. Hardly had we put the phone back on its hook before it rang. I picked it up.

'Is that Johnny Ace?' Female. Breathless.

'Yes.'

'Its Erica.' A slight hesitation in case her name didn't register. 'We had lunch.'

'Erica, of course I know it's you.' For no other reason than I didn't know anyone else called Erica.

'Its about Miss McGhee.'

'Yes?'

'You wanted to know about anyone she was friendly with.'

'Yes.'

'Well, that lady came into work this afternoon, the one I thought might be her sister.'

I stopped her. 'Are you at the office now?' I was worried one of the partners might be listening on the extension.

'No, I'm on my mobile. I'm going home. I'm just on my way to the station.' Hence the breathlessness. She was walking.

'Fine. Go on. Did you find out her name?'

'Yes. It's Mrs Farley.'

The name meant nothing to me. Erica described her as about the same age as Jeanne McGhee; smart with a posh accent. When she'd called at Oates International previously, Jeanne had usually taken her through into her own office.

'What struck me as odd,' continued Erica, 'was she wanted to go into Miss McGhee's office. I told her I couldn't let her do that and she got quite stroppy. Said she thought she'd left some papers in there and wanted to march in on herself and get them.'

'Did she say what these papers were?'

'No. I asked her but she said they were private.'

'What did you do?'

'I told her I'd bring Mr Dixon or Mr Taggart to see her. It was up to them if she went in, not me.'

I could see Erica would make a fine Jobsworth one day complete with peaked cap and clipboard.

'And did they let her go in?'

'I didn't fetch them. As soon as I said I'd fetch one of the partners she got all nervous and told me it didn't matter, and not to bother them.'

'Can you tell me anything else about this woman?' It was a vain hope but worth asking.

'As a matter of fact, I can. When she realised she couldn't get into Miss McGhee's office, like I say, she became quite agitated and fiddled in her handbag for a hanky. And she dropped her diary. I only noticed it when she'd gone. I looked inside for her phone number and I was going to call her to tell her, but then I remembered what you'd said so I rang you instead.'

I took back all the unkind thoughts I'd had of her. 'You're wonderful, Erica. Where is the diary now?'

'I've got it with me here.'

'Where are you?'

'In Moorfields, just coming up to the station.'

'Wait for me outside. I'll be there in five minutes.' Thank God for a city centre office.

'Erica from Oates,' I said to Cameron. 'She's waiting outside Moorfields station. Will you be all right here on your own for a few minutes?'

'Don't be silly, of course I will. I'm fine now. Anyway, they're hardly likely to come back again so soon.'

'OK. I won't be long,' As I spoke, I was already halfway out of the door. I took the stairs two at a time and legged it along Dale Street up to Moorfields.

Erica was waiting obediently at the foot of the station steps. She held out a small russet brown diary. 'Here it is.' She looked anxious. 'You will return it to her, won't you?'

'Personally,' I promised. 'Don't worry. And I'll tell her that it was you who handed it in. You never know, she might give you a reward.'

Erica smiled shyly. She really would have to change her hairstyle, I thought. The punk overtones quite belied her nature.

'I listen to your show sometimes,' she said.

'That's nice. Would you like me to play a record for you?'

'Play one for Danny. That's my boyfriend.'

'I'll play it tonight. Anything special.'

'You choose.'

I thanked her for getting in touch and she hurried for her train. I rang Cameron on the mobile. 'Lock the office and I'll pick you up outside.'

'Where are we going?'

'I'm going to the radio station but I'll give you a lift home on the way.'

'I've got my own car haven't I?'

'Are you sure you're OK to drive though?'

Cameron assured me she was so I said I'd see her on Monday. At least she would have the weekend to get over her ordeal.

My car was in the multi-storey off Moorfields. Once I got inside, I took out the diary. The owner's name was Adrienne Farley. Inside, the personal information section gave me details of her blood group; doctor; next of kin; car, motor insurance driving licence and various telephone numbers; and her address. She owned a livery stables out in the country close to Preston.

Could that have been where Jeanne McGhee had spent her last weekend alive?

I put the diary back in my pocket and set off for the station. I was running late and I knew Ken would be getting in a state.

It was a lively show. There had been some controversy the night before at a poetry reading in the city when a member of the audience took exception to one of the poems, which referred to teenagers dancing like 'epileptic Quasimodos'. Quite a fracas ensued, a novelty at a poetry reading, but it made interesting copy for the reporters present. It also gave my listeners the chance to either rail at 'those foul-mouthed arty-farty hooligans' or defend a person's right to free speech and liberty, depending on which soapbox they were standing on.

A man from Runcorn rang to say the poem was offensive to spastics whereupon the next caller complained that the Cheshire caller was even more offensive than the poet was, as you weren't allowed to say 'spastics' anymore. Then someone came on to blame legendary comedian Bernard Manning for lowering the country's moral tone in the first place.

A lady from Knotty Ash brought a modicum of balance to the proceedings by saying she was appalled at the way writers were drowning under the insidious tide of political correctness sweeping over the country. However, the whole thing went pear-shaped when some clown rang in to say he had a joke that would leave any epileptic sufferer in fits, at which Ken almost had an embolism.

All good clean fun and great for the listening figures. I couldn't see it happening on Shady Spencer's show.

I thought about playing a John Cooper Clark track next but that might have inflamed things even more so, instead, I played Elton John's *Song for Daniel* for Erica's Danny.

After I'd finished the programme, I met Maria at the Liverpool Academy of Arts in Seel Street where June Lornie was putting on one of her famous exhibitions.

This one featured figures sculpted from waste metals such old car exhausts and pipes. I expected it to be more of the modern 'emperor's clothes' crap but, in fact, it was very clever and some of the creations quite appealing. Maria liked it too and I ended up buying her a bow-legged steel chicken that had probably been part of a Ford Fiesta in an earlier life.

Alongside the sculptures was a collection of illustrated poems in frames and an exhibition of celebrity portraits painted in a colourful primitive style, both created by local artists.

'Nobody can say we are not a cultured city,' I remarked.

Maria agreed. 'Quite. I've seen worse than this in the Prado in Madrid. I just hope it's a success.'

We went for a late snack in the Crowne Plaza, relaxing on the huge settees in the lounge before driving home to relieve the babysitter, the teenage daughter of one of Maria's friends.

'How's the case going? Maria asked me later. We were in the conservatory having a glass of wine before bed.

I told her about the intruder and the attack on Cameron. She was horrified.

'What are you going to do?'

'I'm taking Roly to the office with me. He's being promoted to Chief Guard Dog.' Roly turned round and wagged his stump as I spoke. He was lying beside the open door. It was a warmer than usual August.

'Is Cameron all right?'

'Fine. Just a bit bruised. She's tough that girl.'

'How are the cases going?'

'I've found a new lead. Friend of Jeanne McGhee's who lives in Preston. I thought I'd go and see her in the morning.'

First of all I had my bedtime reading. Mrs Farley's diary.

I checked her list of contacts in the Addresses section and immediately a name on the pages sprang out and hit me.

Victor Learoyd.

* * *

Chapter Twenty-Three

I ran down the other names. Nobody else I knew apart from Jeanne McGhee but the Victor Learoyd entry intrigued me. What could be the connection between Mrs Farley and Lucky Learoyd's gangster father?

I moved on to the diary entries but found nothing remarkable. Sadie Farley seemed to spend most of her time attending horse shows, giving riding lessons and running her stables. She dined out locally with her husband and friends once or twice a week, they had attended three concerts at Preston Guild Hall and, scattered throughout the year, she had had regular meetings with Jeanne McGhee.

The last entry involving Jeanne was Friday August 8th, when they had met for lunch at Ask Pizza in Queens Square, Liverpool at 1.30 p.m. Ten days before Jeanne was murdered.

'Should be an interesting day tomorrow,' I said to Maria who was catching up with the entertainments section of the *Liverpool Echo*. 'This woman has seen a lot of Jeanne McGhee. She could know something about what was going on.'

'Don't forget, I'm taking Vikki over to Bakewell to see Robin so I shan't be back till late. Aren't you going to the football match in the afternoon?'

'Certainly am. First home game of the season. I shan't miss that.'

'I'll leave you to sort yourself out then.'

I set off early next morning. I had thought of ringing first but decided that would make it too easy for Mrs Farley to dismiss me if she didn't want to talk. Besides, I wanted to see her reactions when I mentioned Jeanne.

I wasn't sure exactly where the stables were situated so I switched on the RAV4 Sat-Nav, punched in Adrienne Farley's address and instructed it to guide me straight to her home. Not always a good idea. Sat-Nav is great for finding a street once you reach a town but often it can take you on a horrendously circuitous route to get you to that town in the first place.

This time, I was surprised to find I was being led down a string of country lanes until I ended up outside a riding stables somewhere near Midge Hall and the metallic voice announced, 'You have now reached your destination. The route guidance is now finished.'

I wasn't going to argue. I got out of the car and looked around. A sign on a five-barred gate informed the world that this was Farley's Livery Stables. New wooden fencing enclosed the surrounding fields where several horses were grazing. Amongst the buildings nearest the road, I could pick out an indoor school, a couple of barns storing hay and straw, two long rows of stables, an office and a large detached bungalow, presumably where the Farley family lived.

I made for the bungalow. Two rings of the Westminster chimes brought a lady to the door who did indeed bear a remarkable resemblance to Jeanne McGhee. She wore jeans, a T-shirt and a pair of trainers.

'Mrs Farley?' I asked.

'Yes.' She was polite and friendly but then, so far I was a potential customer. That might change when she learnt the reason for my visit. This could be the lady, after all, who was Jeanne McGhee's accomplice. The missing £50,000 could be lying in the corner of one of those stables. Or was I being fanciful?

'My name's Johnny Ace.' No sign of recognition. 'We have a mutual friend. Jeanne McGhee?'

She looked startled. 'Have you not heard? Jeanne's dead.'

'I know. That's why I'm here. I was with her on the Friday of the weekend that she died. Did she never mention me to you?'

'No. I don't think so. Who are you exactly?'

I handed her a card. 'Jeanne hired me to protect her after

Stewart Davis was murdered. She feared her life was in danger.'

Her expression was grim. 'You better come in.' She led the way into a dining kitchen at the back of the bungalow and we sat down at a large pine table. 'What can you want from me?' she asked.

'When did you last see Jeanne?'

'On the Thursday before she died, which means you saw her after I did.'

'What do you know about her relationship with Stewart Davis?'

'I know they were having an affair, if that's what you mean.'

'Had it been going on for long?'

'No, not really. They'd only met a few weeks ago when she went to work in Liverpool.'

'You knew Stewart Davis was murdered, of course.' She nodded. 'Did Jeanne give any indication to you as to why she thought he'd been killed?'

'We talked about it, obviously. It was all to do with this land deal wasn't it?' She looked at her watch. 'Goodness, it's nearly ten. I've got to change the children over in the indoor school. Do you want to follow me down the Yard? There's some spare boots in the porch. It can get muddy by the taps.'

The green Wellingtons were tight but I managed to force my feet into them. She pulled on a similar pair and led the way across the yard. Children from pre-school age to teenagers were busy grooming their ponies outside the stables whilst others were practising jumps in a nearby field.

Some older riders, setting off on a hack, passed us. I was surprised to see a couple of women in their sixties mounted on creatures at least 16 hands high. I gave them a wide berth. Horses are fine except they have no brakes and no steering wheel and they crush you to death if they roll on you.

A queue of youngsters with their ponies was waiting outside the indoor school. Two of them were talking on mobile phones. Adrienne supervised the changeover as the nine o'clock group rode out to make way for them.

'Let's go back to the house and I'll make some coffee,' she said when the last rider had disappeared into the school.

'Do I call you Adrienne?' I asked.

'My friends call me Sadie. It started out Adie, short for Adrienne you see, and somehow metamorphosed into Sadie.'

'I see.'

'At school they called me Ariadne because we did Greek and one girl couldn't say Adrienne so she called me Ariadne instead and I was stuck with it right through to the sixth form. I like Sadie better.'

'You and Jeanne look very alike, Sadie,' I said, as she put the kettle on. 'Are you related?'

'Everyone thinks that. No, we're not, although we've known each other since we were at University.'

'How often did you see her?'

Before she went to work in Liverpool, Jeanne worked for an estate agent's in Preston so we saw quite a bit of each other. Since she moved, we spoke two or three times a month on the phone and met up for lunch a couple of times. Her voice choked. 'This has been a terrible time.'

'When did you find out that she'd died?'

'Not until the day afterwards. Wednesday, I think it was. I rang her at work and they told me then.'

'Do you know who her next of kin were?'

'She had no close relatives. She was an only child and both her parents were dead. You say she hired you to protect her. Who from?'

'She didn't know who the people were. She received a threatening phone call at the office shortly after Davis was killed which is why she got in touch with me. I called to see her at Oates International last Friday morning and arranged

for someone to be with her when she finished work that night
but she had already left when my man got there. That was the
last known sighting of Jeanne until her body was found on the
railway line on Monday night.'

Sadie started to cry.

'I need to know where she spent last weekend, Sadie, and I
was hoping you could tell me.'

'I've no idea. I haven't seen her for over a fortnight.'

'You went to Oates International's office yesterday. Why
was that?'

She stopped and looked at me. 'How do you know that?
Have you been checking up on me?'

'I'm told you wanted to get something out of Jeanne's
office but they wouldn't let you go in. What was it you wanted from there, Sadie?'

She coloured. 'Nothing important. Jeanne had some photos of mine, holiday snaps I lent her. I thought they might get
lost when they cleared her office.'

I didn't buy that at all but I let it go for the moment.
Instead, I handed her the diary that Erica had picked up.

'You dropped this in Reception.' She took it from me in
some confusion. 'Don't worry, I haven't read it,' I lied, 'apart
from getting your address that is.'

I don't know whether she believed me. Had I been in her
place, I certainly wouldn't have done.

She gave a nervous laugh. 'There's nothing in it, nothing
personal that is. Just appointments.'

'Anyway, you've got it back now.'

'I hadn't noticed I'd lost it. Shows how much I use it.'
Another nervous giggle.

Time to hit her with another question before she recovered
he composure.

'Sadie, can you tell me what has happened to the £50,000
that Jeanne took from her bank account the day that Stewart

Davis was killed?'

She looked suitably shocked but was it an act? I could not honestly tell. Suffice to say, she swore it was the first she had heard of such a sum. She had no knowledge of any of her friend's financial transactions and could not imagine how she could acquire such a sum.'

'Did you not realise Davis was involved in a some sort of business scam and Jeanne may have been helping him?'

'No. She only told me they were having an affair.'

'Did she often go out with married men?'

'No. It was the first time I'd known her do it.'

'Did she have a regular boyfriend when she lived in Preston?'

'She was living with a solicitor in Fulwood. They'd been together for over three years.'

'So why did she leave?'

'Basically, he wanted children and Jeanne didn't. He was a homebody. She wasn't the maternal sort. Bruce started seeing someone else, Jeanne found out and that was it. End of love story. She moved out, bought the flat in Southport and left them to it.'

'Was this long ago?'

'No. Only about four months ago. She found this flat in Birkdale and started to look for jobs in Liverpool. She wanted to break all ties with this area. When the Oates job was advertised in June, she applied and got it.'

'When did you say you last see her?'

'A fortnight ago yesterday. We had lunch in Liverpool.' This tied in with her diary entry. Friday August 8th 1.30 p.m. Ask Pizza. Three days before Stewart Davis was killed.

A thought struck me. Jeffrey Taggart had sent Alby Durno to search Jeanne's flat. Whatever Jeanne had hidden there, and I presumed it was the fake contracts, could Sadie Farley have been looking for them too?

'When did you last go to Jeanne's flat in Southport?' I asked her.

'Not since she moved in. Why?'

'You haven't got a key?'

'Goodness, no. Why should I have?'

'Someone broke into Jeanne's apartment last Monday. I wondered if you knew what they might be looking for.'

Sadie looked concerned. 'I've no idea.'

I left it there. I knew I wouldn't get any more out of her but there was something in Jeanne McGhee's office that she badly wanted to get her hands on and I needed to find out what it was.

She walked with me to the car. A couple of 4x4's with horseboxes attached were negotiating the path to the gate.

'One last thing. How well do you know Victor Learoyd?'

This time she was shaken.

'How do you know I know him?'

'Don't you?'

'Yes, but he's just a family friend.'

'Of you and your husband?'

'Peter doesn't know him,' she said hurriedly.

'Oh.' I waited.

'I met him at a horse show about six months ago. He helped me with some problems I was having at the stables.' She didn't elaborate.

'Did Jeanne know him as well?'

'She met him once. We were at Aintree for the Grand National meeting. Jeanne was there with a party from work.'

'The estate agents?'

'That's right. Corporate guests.'

'The prawn sandwich crowd as Roy Keane would say.' But the reference to Manchester United was lost on Sadie.

'And you were there with Victor Learoyd.'

'His son was there as well,' she added quickly. Anxious,

perhaps, to dispel any suggestion that she and Victor were a cosy twosome.

'Lucky?'

'Pardon?'

'Sorry. His real name is Benny. Lucky's his stage name.'

'Benny, that's right. Late forties. A rather flamboyant dresser.'

'That's him.'

So Lucky wasn't as estranged from his father as he had pretended.

'And do you still see Victor?'

'He's a good friend,' she said guardedly.

I'd heard that before. But Victor Learoyd was seventy, over thirty years older than Sadie Farley. On the other hand, he was rich and rich counts. Maybe the stables weren't paying their way.

'If I think of anything else, I'll ring you,' I said.

'Do. And thanks for bringing my diary.' Sadie Farley shook my hand and walked off towards the stables.

Curiouser and curiouser…

As for what Sadie was searching for. The odds were that Jeanne had told her she had the fake contracts and Sadie was trying to get them back.

I drove back to Liverpool, stopping off a couple of miles past Ormskirk at the Royal Oak at Aughton for some lunch on the way to the match. A new season and it was like there'd never been a summer break. The crowds were milling outside Everton's grounds. Graham was selling copies of *When skies were grey* next to the police horses in Goodison Road and the Winslow was packed with the same old faces.

The Blues won the game, 2-1 against Fulham. Naysmith and Unsworth scored. Nobody got too excited. Fulham were widely tipped for the drop come April so beating them was no big deal.

I went straight home after the match and took Roly a long walk in Sefton Park. We were by the Palm House when my mobile rang. It was Lucky Learoyd.

'Johnny. I need help.'

* * *

Chapter Twenty-Four

'Where are you, Lucky?'

'I'm in the Highland Home pub near the docks. Do you know it?'

'Know it? I was there the night The Berry Pickers nearly got beaten up by a crowd of drunken sailors in 1966.'

'Wayne and Jason Jenkinson are waiting outside for me. I'm trapped, Johnny. You've got to get me out of here.'

'What's happened to Tommy McKale's man?'

'Alec? He's somewhere near the Pier Head.'

I managed to get the story out of him. Basically, it was a variation of the carjack routine. Lucky and Big Alec were driving over from the Wirral on the way to Lucky's gig. They'd halted at the traffic lights coming out of the Birkenhead tunnel when two men walked up to the car. The first man opened the driver's door and pulled Lucky out onto the road. Alec jumped out to help but whilst he was grappling with the second man, Lucky was bundled into the back of a waiting white van and driven off.

'How many men were there altogether?'

'Two in the van. One had a tattoo on his head, looked dead hard.' The two men who had attacked me outside the Bamalama, the ones Tommy McKale had identified as Tweedale and Gibbon. 'And the two Jenkinsons were waiting to drag me out of the car.'

'Are you sure it was them?'

'Of course I'm bloody sure. My wife ran off with one of them didn't she?'

'But you've sworn all along that it wasn't the Jenkinsons who were after you.'

'Well I was bloody wrong, wasn't I? Look, can you come and get me or not?'

He'd managed to escape when the back door of the van

blew open as they turned a sharp corner into Upper Parliament Street. They'd chased him as far as the pub but, as there was only one entrance, Lucky knew he couldn't escape.

'Where exactly are you?'

'I'm in the Gents,' he said, 'but the window's barred and there's no other way out.'

'You could ring the police.'

'I don't want them. Can't you come, Johnny?'

'It's going to be half an hour, Lucky. I'm in the middle of Sefton Park with the dog.'

'I'll wait. They won't be able to drag me out in front of the customers.'

I remembered what had happened in the pub in Huyton but refrained from alerting Lucky to the possibility that they could easily walk in and shoot him on the spot.

'Stay locked in the Gents. You'll be safer.'

As I was talking, I'd started walking back home. Ten minutes later, with Roly safely in the house, I was on my way to the Highland Home.

I slowed down as I came up to the pub and immediately noticed two men loitering by the door. I recognised them immediately. They were the two men who had taken a shot at me outside the Bamalama Club. The Jenkinsons.

I didn't hesitate. I threw the wheel to the left, mounted the pavement and drove straight at them. The nearside bumper caught the first one just hard enough to hurl him against the wall of the pub. His brother threw himself out of the way in time to avoid the front offside wheel but as he scrambled to his feet, I threw open my door which smashed him full in the face. He crumpled back to the ground.

I went over to survey the damage. He was out cold. I ran into the pub. No sign of Lucky. I raced through to the Gents and knocked on the door of the cubicle. 'It's Johnny,' I shouted.

I heard the bolt being pulled back and the door slowly opened. Lucky peered out. 'Don't fuckin' stand there, let's go,' I screamed, grabbing him by the collar and dragging him towards the toilet exit.

He followed me through the pub. A couple of startled drinkers turned round but we were out of there in seconds. Our two antagonists were still lying in the road. I didn't wait to check on their health but jumped into the driving seat and started the engine. Lucky leapt in beside me and we sped off down the road.

I wondered what had happened to Big Alec.

'Where are we going?' Lucky asked.

'To see Tommy McKale in case he's heard from Alec.'

It was only a short drive to The Fitness Palace. Tommy was in the bar chatting with his celebrity clients. He excused himself when he saw us enter and came straight over.

'It's tomorrow night you're on the club, Lucky, not tonight.'

'Tonight, I'm supposed to be in Cheshire at a British Legion function.'

'What time are you due onstage?'

'Not until ten.'

'You'll make it,' I said.

'All my gear's in my car.'

I explained to Tommy what had happened. He looked grave when we said Alec was missing. I didn't fancy the chances of anyone who did any damage to Tommy's friend.

'I'll try his mobile,' Tommy said. 'Go and get your friend a drink. He looks like he needs a stiff brandy. I can only apologise for letting him down like this.'

'Nobody could have anticipated this,' said Lucky.

Tommy disagreed. 'In our job, you have to anticipate everything.'

We went over to the bar and ordered a cider for me and a

whisky for Lucky.

'I'll come with you on this booking tonight,' I told him, 'just to be on the safe side, though I doubt those two will trouble you again tonight.'

'I can't go if I don't get my car back. All my stuff's in there, backing tapes, costume, the lot. I can't do the act without them.'

'And tomorrow you're on the Masquerade.'

Before Lucky could dwell on the fact, Tommy came over. 'Everything's sorted. I've spoken to Alec. He's sound. He's bringing your car over now,' he said to Lucky. 'He didn't know where you were.'

'What about the two men? It was Gibbon and Tweedale by the way.'

'Is that who they were? Alec very kindly rang for an ambulance for them and, as far as I know, their condition is not life threatening.'

I didn't press him for details. Lucky's face was a picture.

'Always had a soft side to him did Alec,' continued Tommy. 'A lot of people wouldn't have bothered. He'll be round with your vehicle in a few minutes. You must excuse me now; I've got my guests to attend to. I'll see you both tomorrow down at the club.'

'Fucking assholes,' I heard him mutter under his breath as he walked away.

'Not a man to cross,' ventured Lucky.

'Better to have him on your side,' I agreed. 'Come on, drink up. We've got to get to Cheshire.'

Big Alec was waiting for us outside with Lucky's car. He didn't show any sign of injury. He apologised to Lucky for the snatch. 'Took me unawares, squire. Won't happen again.'

The evening at the British Legion passed without incident. Lucky went down a storm. When he lay on the stage with a naked knee protruding from his split trousers, three old ladies at a table close to the stage leapt from their seats and ran over to clutch his legs. Their combined ages would have represented a respectable innings for the England cricket team.

'They love it when I rip open the Velcro,' he said as we were driving home.

'Yes, I noticed. Pity they were in their seventies. Do you never get any younger people at your gigs?'

'Rarely,' replied Lucky. 'Sometimes I get lucky and one of the barmaids I take home will be under forty.'

No wonder his guests never got taken to his real home.

It was one in the morning when he dropped me off at my car outside Tommy's gym.

'Go straight home and stay there till tomorrow night,' I said. 'I'll see you in the Masquerade at nine.'

Sunday was a quiet day. Maria had only arrived back a little while before me so we had a lie-in. Nothing about the previous night's 'accidents' was mentioned on any of the local radio stations. In the afternoon, we took Vikki for a run to Ladygreen Nurseries to buy some plants for the garden and stayed for something to eat in the coffee shop.

'Are you staying at the flat tonight?' Maria asked.

'I might as well. It's going to be two o'clock by the time I get away.' I remembered what had happened last time I went to the Masquerade.

Lucky was due onstage at eleven o'clock but he had already arrived at nine when we got to the club. Judging by the queue outside, Tommy's faith in the power of the pink pound seemed to be well justified.

'Give it another ten years and they'll outnumber us,' he grinned as he watched Dolly's fingers moving faster than Jerry Lee Lewis as she stacked the notes in the till. 'At this rate, I'll be a millionaire by Christmas.'

The first act on the bill featured a male stripper whose act made use of some rather offbeat props including a rubber snake, two golf balls, a tub of Flora Sunflower spread and a blow up poster of Tony Blair.

I stood at the end of the room furthest from the stage quietly drinking my cider. Lucky was in his dressing room preparing for his spot. Vince, behind the bar, was in his element, surrounded by an admiring group of acolytes.

And into the club walked Hilary.

She made a beeline for me. 'I knew you'd be here tonight. You never rang me,' she said accusingly, slipping her hand in mine, 'but I'll forgive you and let you buy me a gin and tonic.'

She looked enticing as ever with a sheer top, bare midriff and tight black trousers.

I waved Vince over and ordered her drink.

'Who's the new DJ?' she asked then she leaned closer and whispered. 'Are we at the flat afterwards?'

I quickly glanced across to the rostrum. A swarthy man of mixed race was playing a Kylie Minogue track. I recognised him immediately as Sonny Loumarr, a villain who'd once broken into my flat with his partner in crime, Teddy Twigg. Twigg had tried to knife me but caught Loumarr instead, ripping him open in a place which might have qualified him for the title role if they ever filmed the life story of Allesandro Moreschi.

'Christ, not enough that the place is owned by gangsters, now they provide the entertainment as well.' I avoided Hilary's second question and reminded her who Sonny Loumarr was.

'I remember. That was when you took me to that Stripes Club with those handcuffs and whips and things.'

'They probably sell them over the counter in Woolworths these days.'

Tommy McKale came over, pleased to see Hilary again. I commented on Loumarr's presence behind the turntables.

'The punters like a bit of criminal glamour in the club, Johnny. Now Ronnie's gone, Biggsy's on his last legs and Mad

Frankie Fraser's busy with his tours, we're reduced to using 'C' list gangsters but, don't worry, it's in Sonny's contract that he hasn't to do any of the customers over while he's working in my club.'

'Very reassuring,' I said.

'Is your boy nearly ready then?'

'I'll go and fetch him.'

I left Hilary by the bar and walked across to Lucky's dressing room. He looked very nervous.

'I'm worried Johnny. There might be somebody out there waiting to have a go at me.' He took a swig from a pint glass on the table. 'Dutch courage,' he said ruefully.

'I thought you once told me you didn't drink between shows.'

'I don't usually. A fan sent it over.'

'You have fans?' I wanted to lighten the mood, make him forget he might be in danger although I never really thought anyone would harm him here.

Wrong again.

A roar of applause went up as Lucky took to the stage. It had been a shrewd move on Tommy McKale's part to book him for this event as he had obviously had a big following amongst the gay fraternity.

Dressed in what looked like red velvet pyjamas and cowboy boots and sporting a long pony tail, Lucky minced towards the spotlight singing *Hold Me* in a high Gene Pitney voice, thrusting his crotch suggestively at the audience.

I rejoined Hilary at the bar and we watched him run through his repertoire of PJ Proby's greatest hits. Everything was going well until the penultimate song.

Those who had seen Lucky's act before knew immediately that something was wrong when he missed the high note that closed *Maria*.

Maria was never the easiest song to sing at the best of

times. I'd seen Proby himself make seven false starts at it in a desperate attempt to hit the right key, and his was the hit recording for Christ's sake. But Lucky Learoyd's devoted fans knew their idol had never missed that note in his life and they were alarmed.

Even casual onlookers at the Masquerade Club that night, who'd never seen Lucky before, didn't take long to realise in horror that they might never see him again as, seconds later, the hapless entertainer clutched his throat and slumped to the floor with a strangulated cry.

If there were any doctors in the packed crowd, none of them rushed forward. I didn't blame them. The way things are today, they'd probably be sued by the bereaved family if he didn't pull through.

A curtain was quickly pulled across the stage and Sonny Loumarr stuck on a Perry Como track. I didn't think *Magic Moments* quite fitted the occasion but nobody seemed to notice. A few couples even took to the floor for a late evening grope but most people were busy speculating about what had happened to Lucky.

Vince behind the bar, always an opportunist, opened a book. The smart money was on a heart attack but quite a few people were taking 3-1 on a stroke. Vince was offering 8-1 on a brain haemorrhage, which I thought generous, mainly because I always believed a brain haemorrhage was the same thing as a stroke anyway. One punter put fifty pounds to win a grand that Lucky had choked on a bone from one of The Masquerade's infamous chicken pies.

Somebody phoned for an ambulance. I hoped Lucky could hang on. With the current state of the NHS, if he croaked we'd have to pack his body in ice in case it decomposed before the vehicle finally arrived.

He certainly didn't look so good though as he lay on the bare boards of the stage behind the curtain.

Tommy had joined me in the rush backstage. 'Unfortunate choice of name in the circumstances,' he commented as he gazed down at the supine singer.

'Lucky, you mean? At least he isn't dead?'

'Yet,' said Tommy, forebodingly.

Being a qualified nurse, Hilary had rushed round to help. She loosened his collar, listened to his breathing and felt his pulse. 'I think he's been poisoned,' she announced.

'The beer,' I said. 'In his dressing room. He said somebody had bought it for him. They must have slipped something into it.'

'That's a relief then,' said Tommy. 'Someone just having a giggle. At least we know it wasn't personal. Couldn't have handled another cock-up after yesterday's fiasco.'

'Do many people get their drinks spiked in the club?' I asked, thinking back to all the ciders I'd drunk there.

'Happens all the time. Someone's probably slipped him a roofie. He'll come round.'

Which was the reason, of course, why most young people in pubs drank straight from the bottle these days.

I helped Hilary pull Lucky into a sitting position and we propped him up against the side wall.   Hilary wasn't too happy.

'This is the second time this week something like this has happened. Why does trouble always follow you, Johnny?'

'Must be my appealing nature. Listen, he's coming round.'

Gurgling noises were emanating from Lucky's throat as, slowly, he regained consciousness. He turned his head and focussed his eyes on me.

'What happened?'

'You passed out,' I reassured him 'Don't worry about it. You're going to be fine. I'm going to take you home.'

Lucky groaned.

'I'd better stay with him tonight,' I said to Hilary, explaining that I was supposed to be guarding him. 'It's the second time in two days he's been attacked.'

Hilary wasn't happy but could hardly argue. She didn't fancy another night of terror from possible attacks. She'd had enough aggro with my cases over the years to last her a lifetime.

The ambulance still hadn't arrived when we left. As it was far from unknown for paramedics to be beaten up whilst on duty, I was only surprised they ever turned out at all.

I drove Lucky home to his Hoylake mansion. He was half asleep and with little memory of the night's events but otherwise all right. In the end, Big Alec turned up to mind him so I was able to leave them to it.

It was still only one o'clock when I got back to Liverpool but I didn't call at the Masquerade for Hilary. Instead, I drove straight back to Waterloo Dock to get a decent night's sleep.

Come Monday morning, I needed to have a long hard look at the cases before someone else was killed.

※ ※ ※

Chapter Twenty-Five

Roly and I were in the office for eight thirty sharp, Roly in his new role on official guard duty. He stretched out on his usual blanket, seemingly unaware of his new responsibilities.

Cameron arrived dead on nine, recovered from the attack by the Jenkinsons.

It was a fortnight since she had started in the job yet we had the same three cases going, all still unsolved and I felt it was time to take stock and consider new angles.

'What happened with Mrs Farley?' she asked.

I gave her a brief rundown of my morning at the livery yard. 'She wants to get her hands on something that she thinks could be in Jeanne McGhee's office but God knows what that is. And there's a tie-in with Victor Learoyd too.'

'How does she know him?'

'She met him at a horse show.'

'Perhaps he's giving her one?' suggested Cameron with the indelicacy for which modern girls are famous. She shuddered. 'How gross. He must be nearly seventy.'

'So's Mick Jagger and it doesn't seem to have cramped his style. You could be right but I think with Adrienne Farley it may be more of a financial arrangement.'

'Talking of the Learoyds, how's things going on with Lucky?'

'Don't ask. A weekend of chaos. Doesn't do much for our reputation as bodyguards.'

'That's down to your friend Mr McKale, not you.'

'True. Incidentally, I must introduce you to Tommy.'

'I think so. He sounds cool.'

'Where was I?'

'A weekend of chaos.'

'That's right. Since Saturday, whilst in our care, he's been kidnapped, attacked and poisoned.'

'All at the same time?'

No. The attacks were down to the Jenkinsons, obviously on orders from Oates International.'

'What happened?'

'They hi-jacked Lucky's car coming out of the tunnel and the Jenkinsons dragged him out and drove off with him. He managed to escape and was holed up in the lavatory at a pub near the docks. I had to go and rescue him.'

'What about the Jenkinsons?'

'Got in the way of the car,' I said shortly.

'Boss.'

'You can take it they won't be in circulation for a good while,' I promised her.

'That's a relief. At least they won't be able to come after me again.'

'The other two were the same ones that shot at me when we came out of the Bamalama. Big Alec took care of them.'

'I won't even ask.'

'Best not to.'

'You've not told me about the poisoning,' she said.

'Oh no. Well that appears to have been a separate issue. Someone slipped him a roofie in his beer at the Masquerade.'

'No? Before or after he went onstage?'

'Before. Didn't do much for his singing. He got a quarter way through his act before he collapsed. But he's back home now with Big Alec minding him.'

'Right. And what's the latest on the Mohair Man?'

'Ollie, you mean? Definitely the Jenkinson mob behind the vandalism and the fire. Trouble is, making anything stick. We know who they work for, Oates International, but we need some cast iron evidence to pin it on them and I don't know where we're going to get it.'

'So far we have them down for intimidation and forged contracts. Is that it?'

'Yes, but meaningless until we get Molly Laffin's signature.'

'And the biggest puzzle of all, where is Jeanne McGhee's fifty grand.'

'Don't you mean Leprechaun Developments' fifty grand to be strictly accurate?'

'Whatever.'

'Disappeared without trace.'

'Dare we mention the question of who killed Jeanne and her ragbag lover?'

'I know what you're saying. Basically, we're hardly any further forward than we were at the beginning. I think we need divine intervention. Do you know any good psychics, Ronni?'

But we didn't need to call on the supernatural because, just at that moment, Bob Dix came up with a lifeline.

Cameron took the call and handed the phone to me. 'It's the guy from the planning office for you.'

'That was quick, Bob,' I said.

'It might be nothing, don't get your hopes up. Do you want to pop into the office sometime? I've found out a couple of things that might interest you.'

'I'll be there in twenty minutes,' I told him.

'Could this be the big breakthrough?' I said to Cameron, reminding her, as I left, that she had the dog to protect her. Roly wagged his stump in support but didn't move from his blanket.

Bob Dix was sitting at his desk in the Planning Office looking remarkably cheerful for a Monday morning.

'Nice weekend, Johnny?'

'So so. I've known better.'

'Well I can cheer you up. You wanted to know if anyone other than Oates International owned a piece of that land that you showed me?'

'And were there many?'

'A few. I've made a list for you. But before I give it you,

I'd like you to tell me why you need to know?'

'Simple, Bob. I believe that Oates International might not own all the properties that they say they do.'

'That wouldn't surprise me. Here you are then, see for yourself.'

I took the piece of paper he handed me and studied it. There were only four names, St Petersburg Properties (Watson & Co), Oliver Clarke (Oliver Clarke Motor Showrooms), Benny Prince (The Pig and Hamster) and, the last one we still had to check out, Kofi Borborkis (The Wong Foo).

'Tell me about the Wong Foo takeaway?' I said. 'We had a look at it last week and it's all shut up. According to the name above the door, a Mr Clarence Ho was running the business but he seems to have gone AWOL.'

'He's probably fled back to the rice fields,' said Bob. 'Funny you should pick on this one, Johnny. There's a very weird story behind it. The Wong Foo was originally called the Crete Café and the proprietor was another Greek gentleman called Nikos Zagorasis.

Zagorasis put a sign up in the window saying the business was for sale and along came Mr Ho who decided it would make an ideal takeaway and made him an offer of £20,000, being under the impression he was buying the freehold from Mr Zagorasis.

The deal went through, Mr Ho moved into the flat above the shop and took over the running of the business. He changed the menu from Greek to Chinese of course, but otherwise the shop kept open throughout the changeover.'

'I suppose chips are chips in anyone's language.'

'The customers continued rolling in and everything was hunky-dory for a while until, a few weeks later, a big bearded Greek fellow marched into the shop, said his name was Kofi Borborkis, he was the owner of the property and demanded

£1000 from Mr Ho for the month's rent.'

'I thought you said Ho bought the freehold.'

'No, I said he thought he was buying the freehold. There's a subtle difference. He'd actually only bought the business. Mr Borborkis still owned the actual building. Borborkis was supposedly Zagorasis's cousin.   They'd worked the scam between them.'

'Surely the solicitor would have sorted all that out.'

'Ah, now there's the rub. They didn't use a solicitor. Believe it or not, Ho handed over twenty grand in cash to Zagorasis.'

'You're joking.'

'Obviously a tax dodge of some sort.'

'Or money laundering,' I suggested. 'But Ho must have been crazy paying in pound notes. Did he get a receipt?'

'Yes he did, but all it said was "Received £20,000 for Crete Café" and that could mean either for the business as a going concern or for the property, depending on how you wanted to take it.'

'So what happened?'

'Ho was told to fork out for the rent by the end of the month or they'd shoot him as a matter of family honour.'

'Pardon me but are these the same Greeks that invented Civilisation?'

'Distant ancestors.'

'And did Ho pay up?'

'He tried to sell the place on at first but, without the proper documentation, he was stymied. Borborkis still held the deeds to the property and nobody would pay £20,000 ingoing just to rent a takeaway, especially at that exorbitant rent.'

'Not round there at any rate.'

'So, when they came calling for the rent, Ho paid the first instalment to stop them shooting him.'

'And Zagorasis and Borborkis came out of it with the twenty grand, an extra thousand for the rent and got to keep the deeds of the building as well? Not a bad result for them.

'Not only that, Johnny, they got their café back too.'

'How come?'

'Simple. Ho disappeared. The next day, the shop didn't open and nobody's seen Clarence Ho since.'

'Presumably he pissed off back to China before anything else happened to him.'

'Either that or he ended up in the Greek yoghurt and feta cheese,' smiled Bob. 'Well, does that help you in your quest, Johnny?'

'It certainly does. You see, I've got a contract that shows Oates paying £20,000 for that property from Mr Borborkis.'

'And we know Borborkis still owns it.'

'So this contract I've got is a fake.'

'It would appear so.'

'Which means if I could get Mr Borborkis in a witness box...'

'You'd have a case against Oates International.'

'So where do I find Mr Borborkis. I've been to the shop and it's all boarded up and the flat upstairs is empty.'

'That's because Mr Ho had friends in the neighbourhood who didn't like to see their countryman stitched up. Mr Borborkis and his cousin had to make a speedy getaway themselves.'

'It never pays to cross the Triads. Anyone could have told them. I would imagine Oates tried to buy the property when Ho first advertised it but Ho disappeared before they could set it up.'

'Surely though, once Oates found out that Borborkis was the rightful owner, they'd have been able to buy it from him without any trouble?'

'Maybe, but perhaps not at a price they wanted to pay. Then again, we don't know that Borborkis and Oates ever got to talk. It could be that by the time they found out who really owned it, Borborkis and his mate had done a runner too, just like Mr Ho.'

'You're right.'

I took a moment to consider the implications. Time had been against them at Oates International. Stewart Davis was well on with the deal to sell the whole area of land to Leprechaun and they had St Petersburg waiting in the wings, so had they faked the contract with Borborkis's name on it to get the deal done, the same as with Mrs Laffin?

'I don't suppose you know where Borborkis and Zagorasis went?' I asked Bob.

'As a matter of fact I do. The two of them moved up to Scotland and opened a similar business in Dunoon. I believe it's called The Minoan Bull.'

'Will there be much demand for Greek haggis in Dunoon?'

''Probably not but at least they should be safer than if they'd stayed in Liverpool.'

I thanked Bob for all his efforts. 'By the way,' I said, 'I managed to get you these,' and I handed him the tickets to the Sixties show.

He put them in his pocket gratefully. 'Let me know how you get on, Johnny.' I promised I would.

Back at the office, I discussed developments with Cameron.

'We've got two potential witnesses against Oates now,' I said. 'Molly Laffin and this Kofi Borborkis.'

'But we still don't know where Jeanne McGhee's £50,000 is and we still don't know who killed her or Stewart Davis.'

'One thing at a time, Ronni.'

'They're all connected. Find one and the rest will follow. Trust me. In the meantime, I think I'll go and have a word with Oliver Clark and see if he's had any more approaches from Oates. Will you be OK on your own?'

'I'm not on my own am I?' She pointed to the dog who

opened one eye and growled on cue.

Ollie was in his garage, overseeing the day's repair jobs. A Nissan Primera was parked up on the ramp and one of Ollie's workmen was standing underneath examining the exhaust

'It's working again then?' I said to him, 'the ramp.'

'Oh yes.' He didn't seem inclined to talk.

'Any word from Health and Safety about the accident yet?'

'Not yet. I daresay they'll get round to it.'

'What about Oates International? Have you heard any more from them?'

'I'm signing on Wednesday,' he admitted. 'They've made me an offer I can't refuse.'

'Horse in your bed, you mean? Or, in your case, a Ford Fiesta.'

'Nothing like that, Johnny. Hard cash.' I waited for the rest. 'They upped the offer by twenty five grand.'

'I thought you said their first offer was thirty grand short?'

'Yes, well, you've got to give and take in business haven't you? You should know that.'

'Does this mean you're going to retire now?'

'Not likely. No, I'm buying a place off Prescot Road. Showroom and garage with a petrol station at the side. One of the big oil companies is selling it off. Too good to miss.'

'I see. No news on the insurance?'

'I had a letter this morning as a matter of fact.'

'They've paid up?'

'Not yet but it looks promising. They seem to have accepted it wasn't a put-up job.'

'That's good. And no more vandals I take it?'

'No. I think torching the showroom frightened them. Caused more damage than they intended.'

I didn't agree with him. The way I figured it, the fire had been their masterstroke, the final straw to persuade him sell up, and it had worked. But I didn't say so.

'How about the death threats?'

He looked uncomfortable. 'Death threat, Johnny. There was only one. Irrelevant. Just some nutter. Everyone gets them.'

Strange how people can rationalise things. They make a decision they're not really happy with and then try to justify it to convince everyone, and most of all themselves, that they've done the right thing.

It never works. I wondered how long it would be before Oliver Clarke admitted it was a mistake, selling his showroom to Oates International.

※　※　※

Chapter Twenty-Six

I wished Ollie luck anyway and walked back to the RAV4. That was one of my three original cases all wrapped up, albeit with little input from me, but things had moved on from there. The task now was to gather evidence against Oates International, which might lead to the unravelling of the rest of the mysteries. The murders.

It seemed a good time to go back to Molly Laffin. I wanted to make sure she would be willing to give evidence confirming that the signature on the contract we held was not hers.

The Goose and Gander was as unwelcoming as ever. A bunch of workmen were discussing football at the bar, two pensioners sat glumly apart in the snug and, in the background, a sound system pounded out muffled music by Guns'n'Roses. Pat from Livingstone Drive would have loved it. She was a big heavy metal fan. Personally, I preferred *Since I don't have you* by The Skyliners.

Behind the bar, Molly Laffin was serving a dark-suited sales rep with a pint of non-alcoholic lager. Instead of the nightdress and housecoat of my previous visit, she wore a bulging white T-shirt emblazoned with the slogan 'Try these for size' and a red skirt that ended six inches too far above her knees to conceal the cellulite of her thighs.

'You again,' was her greeting. The genial British pub landlady.

'I need to talk to you,' I said and ordered a glass of cider.

'Strongbow all right?' she asked then added, 'we've no other.'

'Nobody ever has,' I said. 'Do you do food?' It was coming up to one o'clock and I hadn't had lunch.

'Sandwiches.'

'I'll have a tuna on brown.'

'Only white bread.'

'Tuna on white then.'

'No tuna. Egg, ham or cheese.'

I settled for the cheese, bought her a gin and tonic and retired to a nearby table with my drink. When she brought the sandwich over, I asked her to sit down for a moment and explained about the fake contract.

'What do you want me to do about it?' she asked.

'Just sign an affidavit to say that the signature on that contract with Oates International is not yours.'

'What's in it for me?'

'Nothing.' Giving her money would smack of bribery in a court of law. Besides, where was my income coming from? With Tommy McKale looking after Lucky Learoyd, the only paying client I had in this case was Jeanne McGhee and she was dead. 'But you can't have people going around signing your name.'

'I suppose not.'

I tackled the cheese sandwich. The bread was stale and the cheese was hard as if it had been retrieved from an overnight stay in an untouched mousetrap. I washed it down quickly with a mouthful of cider.

'So will you agree?'

'I suppose so.'

We left it that I would bring my solicitor round to the pub along with the fake contract and she would confirm in writing, witnessed by him, that it was not her signature beside her name.

And having done all that, what next? Hand the whole lot over to DI Reubens, I supposed. Let him take the kudos for uncovering a fraudulent racket and collect a few brownie points for myself along the way.

I went back to the office where Cameron was talking to someone on the phone. 'Just a minute, he's just come in,' and, covering the mouthpiece with her hand, whispered, 'It's Victor Learoyd. He wants to talk to you.'

'OK.' This was a surprise. I took the phone from her. 'Johnny Ace.'

'Victor Learoyd.' The voice was deep and resonant and authoritative. 'I think we ought to meet.'

'Where do you suggest?'

'Come up to my place. You know where I am.' It came across as a command rather than a suggestion. I looked at my watch. It was two o'clock. I had to be back in town for six to do the show.

'I can spare you an hour,' I said.

'That will be ample. I'll expect you at three.' The line went dead.

'I wonder what he wants,' I said to Cameron.

'There's only one way to find out.'

'I'm on my way.'

Roly looked disappointed not to be getting the trip. I threw him a biscuit on the way out.

I drove along the coast road through Southport to The Plough and turned left into the country village of Banks. The long road from Banks to Hesketh Bank followed the line of the coast of the Ribble Estuary, but up to mile inland. In the olden days and right up to recent times, scores of shrimpers plied their trade in these waters.

Victor Learoyd's palatial residence was not unlike his son's house only even grander. The approach alone was a half-mile journey along an avenue of tall conifers and electric gates guarded the entrance to a courtyard in from of the house itself.

The house was huge. Roly Howard, manager of Sam Reuben's favourite football team, runs his own window cleaning business, and I reckoned he could have made a good living there without ever leaving the building.

It was two fifty as I drove up to the house. Someone was obviously manning the CCTV video because the gates opened slowly when I was within a hundred yards of them.

I parked outside the front door alongside a Land Rover Discovery and a black Bentley saloon.

Before I could ring the bell, the front door opened and a middle-aged lady enquired if I was Mr Ace. I said I was and she led me into a large drawing room.

Gilt-edged Victorian paintings lined the walls, mostly featuring horses and country scenes. Two heavily jewelled chandeliers hung from the ceiling and an old-fashioned Symphonion in an ornate wooden, glass-fronted cabinet stood at the side of the marble fireplace.

'Have a seat. Mr Learoyd will be with you shortly,' said the lady and she crept quietly out.

I had hardly had time to sink into the gargantuan settee when Victor Learoyd, proprietor of the mysterious St Petersburg Properties, made his entrance.

'Mr Ace. We meet at last'

He held out his hand and I stood up to shake it. He was a big man, all muscle, well over six feet and broad as a club bouncer. Despite approaching seventy, he stood erect and boasted a thick head of suspiciously dark brown hair, which I suspected owed everything to Clairol.

'Do sit down,' he instructed and joined me on the settee. 'I believe you have been guarding my son.' He was not a man to waste his time on small talk.

'I arranged for a friend of mine to look after him.'

'I know of the McKale Brothers. He'll be safe with them. What's your interest in the property game?'

I took it as read that he wasn't referring to my own portfolio.

'My client was Jeanne McGhee from Oates International. She was murdered last week.'

'I know that. Who do you think killed her?'

'Someone connected with the property business, that's for sure.'

'What do you know about me?'

'You run an outfit called St Petersburg Properties that, for some reason best known to yourself, you lead people to believe is a Russian company.'

'Go on.'

'You made a bid for a piece of land between Toxteth and the Dingle which is supposedly owned by Oates International but an Irish company called Leprechaun Developments is in competition with you for it.'

'Why do you say *supposedly* owned?'

'Not all the properties on that land belong to Oates. You yourself own one of them for a start.'

'You know which one?'

'Watson and Co. the builders.'

'You've done your research pretty well. So who owns the other ones that Oates have been unable to buy?'

'There's a pub called the Pig and Hamster.'

'Oates own that.'

'No they don't.'

'Then who does?'

I wasn't going to betray Lucky by telling Victor that his own son had bought it. 'I don't know but I spoke to Mrs Laffin, the licensee, who's now running the Goose and Gander in Wavertree, and she said she'd be willing to swear that she didn't sell the Pig and Hamster to Oates International.

Victor Learoyd looked thoughtful. 'Anyone else?'

'Besides you? Only a Chinese takeaway off Park Road.'

'Who does that belong to?'

'The proprietor was a Mr Clarence Ho who ran the business but it's closed down now. The actual building is owned by a Greek man by the name of Borborkis.'

'And does he live on the premises?'

'No, he moved to Scotland and opened a Greek restaurant in Dunoon with his cousin.'

'I see.'

It was my turn for questions. 'So why do you want to see me, Mr Learoyd?'

'I thought that, with your connection to the late Miss McGhee, you might be able to acquaint me with what's going on in Liverpool at the moment and you have been very helpful so I won't take up any more of your time.'

'Are you still hoping to buy the land from Oates International?'

'Who knows?'

'You asked me before whom I thought killed Jeanne McGhee. Who do you think killed her, Mr Learoyd.'

'I have no idea. That is not my business.'

'And what about Stewart Davis? He was working for Oates International so you must have come into contact with him.'

'No. I dealt only with the other two partners. I never met Davis. These people are not my concern.'

'I met a friend of yours recently. Adrienne Farley?'

'Mrs Farley and I have a business arrangement together.' He stood up. 'Thank you so much for coming Mr Ace.' He reached for my hand before I could move it away and, as he took it, guided me into the hall. 'I'm afraid I have other appointments and must leave you. Goodbye now.'

He walked me to the front door without another word and shut it firmly after me.

It was easy to see why his son had left home. Victor Learoyd wasn't a man you'd want to disagree with. I could imagine the teenage Benny facing his father's wrath when he told him he wanted to be a singer. He'd done well to get away.

I just hoped that the gift of the Hoylake mansion wouldn't be used to draw him back into his fathers' clutches.

I drove back to town along the coast road. On my right, was the distant Irish Sea with Blackpool Tower looming from behind the Lytham skyline whilst on my left, hundreds of sea birds gathered in the marshes.

How many houses would be standing on that stretch of land in a hundred years time?

A new bridge was being built connecting the seafront to the Promenade. It was of an eye-catching futuristic design that sat uneasily amongst the Victorian and Edwardian architecture of the town. But then, the conglomeration of painted aircraft hangers that made up the Ocean Plaza retail park would have looked more at home on an estate in Speke than on the once golden sands of a seaside resort.

At least the Pier was still standing.

Back in Liverpool, I picked up Roly from the office and took him for a walk. We both needed the exercise. There had been no word from Lucky since The Masquerade. No word from Hilary either but I suspected I should have been the one to phone her, if only to make sure she got home all right from the Masquerade.

We walked up to Lime Street alongside the Library and Walker Art Gallery then past the Empire Theatre and station and up Renshaw Street till we came to Liverpool 8, the heart of the student quarter. There was an empty table on the pavement outside the Quartet in Falkner Street.

I fixed Roly's lead to the chair to reserve my place and also to prevent him from taking off down Hope Street on his own. Any chance to escape and he'd be away. I went inside the café to order a pot of tea and apple cake when I noticed a couple in the corner, heads together, chatting earnestly. The man was Oliver Clarke and the woman was the same blonde I'd seen him with at La Tasca the week before. I felt I recognised her from somewhere, but I couldn't recall where except that it was in the last few days. After the sighting at La Tasca.

They hadn't seen me. I picked up a *Daily Post* to read and I took it outside to my table where Roly was patiently waiting.

Who was the blonde and why did I feel she was significant?

'I think I'll take an early night,' I said to Cameron when we got back to the office.

All of a sudden, I felt the cases were sliding away from me, if indeed there was a case left at all. Ollie's vandal problem was solved. Lucky was in Tommy McKale's care.

There was the question of Jeanne McGhee's death, of course. As she had been my client, I felt an obligation to find her killer but I was becoming resigned to the fact that this was in the hands of the police and, unless I turned up something unexpectedly, it was best left to them. They had the greater resources. All I had to do was tie up the Oates forged contracts scam, pass it over to Sam Reubens, and I was out of it. Time to move on to a new case, whatever that might be.

I couldn't have been more wrong.

The news came on the Radio Merseyside breakfast show early next morning. The details were sketchy but I got the gist of it.

Basically, the report stated that police officers had been called to a public house in Wavertree in the early hours of the morning when a middle-aged woman, covered in stab wounds, stumbled out of the building and collapsed in the street.

Two teenage girls on their way home from a nightclub in the city called an ambulance but the woman died of her injuries an hour later in hospital.

Police gave the woman's name as Margaret (Molly) Laffin, the licensee of The Goose and Gander and asked for anyone who was in the pub that evening or who may have seen anyone hanging round the premises to get in touch with them.

* * *

Chapter Twenty-Seven

'It could have been a domestic quarrel,' said Cameron. 'It doesn't have to be connected to the case.'

Cameron had heard the news on the wireless as well and had come straight down to the office for 8.30am. I was already there.

'True'. It was a plausible argument. Molly Laffin was the just type of person to be stabbed by a jealous lover/partner/wife. Or, come to that, by any of the yobbos likely to frequent a dive like the Goose and Gander.

'I mean,' continued Cameron, 'I haven't seen her but from how you described her...'

'I know. A slut in slippers. Yet, I still think it's because of that contract. Too much of a coincidence. The very day she agrees to give evidence against Oates, for that's what it amounted to, she's killed.'

'And in the same way Jeanne McGhee was killed. Stabbed.'

'Several times. Seems like whoever did it enjoys it.'

'If it's the same person.'

'The Jenkinsons have to be favourite. Oates International is clearing up after them. Tying up the loose ends.'

'I thought you said they'd not be around for a while after Saturday night.'

'They're a big family, the Jenkinsons.'

'But who knew that you'd been to the Goose and Gander and arranged for her to give evidence against Oates? You only went there yesterday lunchtime.'

'God knows.' And then it hit me. Victor Learoyd. I'd told him about Molly Laffin. But why should he tell Oates International. And, if he didn't tell Oates, did that mean he himself was in some way instrumental in the landlady's death? 'I told Learoyd about Mrs Laffin,' I confessed to Cameron.

'So? What motive would he have for killing her?'

'I don't know but I also told him about Borborkis.'

'But he's in Dunoon. Three hundred miles away.'

'With Mrs Laffin dead, he's the only person left who represents a danger to Oates International. Ronni, I should go over
there immediately and get him to sign a statement in front of
a local notary. It's our only chance to get the evidence to give
to DI Reubens and it may be the last chance if I don't make it
in time.'

'What about the threats and the vandalism? Are the
Jenkinsons going to get away with that?'

'Possibly they will but not the murders.'

'You reckon they murdered Davis and Jeanne then?'

'Probably Molly Laffin too but I'll worry about all that
when I get back.'

Cameron looked at her watch. 'You're going to drive to
Scotland now?'

'No, I'll go by train. But I am going now. I'll take the car to
Preston station and pick up the London-Glasgow express.
It'll be quicker than fighting my way up the M6.'

'What about your radio programme?'

'Phone them up and tell them I'm sick. They'll easily get
someone to step in.' Maybe they'd resurrect Shady Spencer
who was last heard of playing records in a supermarket,
unseen by the general public.

I checked the train times on the Internet. There was a train
out of Preston at 11.15am that got into Glasgow just after
two. I could catch the 11.25 connection to Gouruk in time for
the 20-minute ferry ride across to Dunoon.

'I reckon I could be there for four o'clock,' I told
Cameron. 'That would give me an hour to find a notary and
take him to Mr Borborkis.'

'You don't know whereabouts in Dunoon the café is,' said
Cameron.

'There can't be too many Greek cafes in a town as small as

Dunoon. The Minoan Bull shouldn't be hard to find.'

The timetable was very tight, no room for any delays.

'I've got two hours to get to Preston, park the car, buy a ticket and board the train.'

'You'll do it.'

The first part of the operation went according to plan. When the 11.15 drew into Preston station on its journey from London Euston at 11.19am, less than five minutes behind schedule, I was waiting on the platform with my first class ticket.

It was the second and third legs of the journey that went belly-up. How many times had I heard the words "We apologise for the delay…"? The power had failed between Lockerbie and Carstairs. We glided to a crawl before shuddering to a halt.

If my hunch was correct, and the Jenkinsons, or other hit men, were also on their way up to Dunoon, how far were they behind me? Were they at this moment racing up the A74, making up mile after mile as I sat marooned and helpless in the train? I looked across the fields and felt like Richard Hannay in *The Thirty-nine Steps* although I elected not to jump out of the carriage onto the line and make my way on foot across the moors.

By the time the train limped into Glasgow, I'd missed not only the designated connection to Gourok but also the express service after it and when I finally arrived at the port I was in time to see the ferry halfway into its twenty-minute sail to Dunoon.

The weather had taken a turn for the worse and a cold wind was blowing as I stood on the jetty and waited for the boat to return. Dark clouds hovered over the mountains restricting visibility and, though Dunoon was only five miles across the Firth of Clyde, I could hardly make out its coastline as the first drops of rain began to fall.

While I was waiting, I phoned Maria who was a little surprised to hear I was somewhere in the Scottish isles when she was expecting home in a couple of hours.

'It's going to be tomorrow night when I get back,' I told her. 'If the station rings, Cameron's told them I'm off sick.'

It was well after five when I stepped ashore at Dunoon quayside. The rain was now lashing down as I walked up to the main street.

It didn't take long for me to find The Minoan Bull. It was not far along Argyll Street from the ferry terminal and it was shut. A notice on the door informed patrons they were open for business from 6 p.m. till 'Midnite'.

I wandered across the road and went into the Di Marcos bar to while away the half hour wait. I sat by the window drinking a glass of cider. A few bedraggled trippers occupied the tables around me. Come six, I went out again. The rain had stopped and a shaft of sunlight was shining through the clouds.

I reached the café just as a large bearded man was turning over the closed sign on the door.

'Mr Borborkis?' He opened the door and looked me up and down.

'Who are you?'

'My name is Johnny Ace and I've come over from Liverpool to see you.'

This information did not go down well. He closed the door slightly and made sure his foot was behind it.

'What do you want with me?'

I pushed a card through the opening. 'Nothing to worry about but I think you may be in danger. Can I come in?'

He took the card, glanced at it, hesitated, then opened the door again and jerked his head to direct me inside.

The walls of the café were decorated with murals of Crete and a collection of model bulls adorned the shelves behind the bar area. The seats were wooden to match the tables on which straw tablemats were in place ready for the evening diners. I counted room for thirty covers.

He pulled out a chair for me and sat on one opposite.

'What is this talk of danger?'

'A firm in Liverpool wants to buy your property.'

'Which property? I own lots of property.'

'The Chinese Takeaway you swindled from Mr Ho. No no, don't get excited.' He had started to rise angrily from his chair. 'I'm not here on behalf of Mr Ho.'

'Then who are you here for?'

'For you. Have you heard of a property company called Oates International? They came to Liverpool a few months ago.'

'I don't know these people. What are they to do with me?'

Briefly, I explained to him that they wanted to buy the freehold of the building in Liverpool.

'For whatever reason, perhaps simply that they couldn't get hold of you, they drew up a contract to buy the property from you for just £20,000.'

'They've never been in contact with me.'

'They didn't need to be did they? They signed it for you themselves as the purchasers.

Borborkis jumped up. 'What! That's forgery.'

'So would you be prepared to sign a statement confirming that?'

'Just a minute, I fetch my cousin.'

He disappeared to the rear of the café and I heard his footsteps on the stairs. A short while later, he returned with a small sallow-faced man with a sly expression whom I assumed was Nikos Zagorasis.

On Borborkis's instruction, I repeated my story to his cousin. The two men then retired to the back of the café to whisper urgently to one another before Borborkis came back to me.

'Yes, we will both sign your paper and I need to see this contract you speak of. Have you got it with you?'

I pointed out that all he needed to do was sign a letter confirming he owned the Liverpool property and that he had not signed any contract to sell it either to Oates International or anyone else.

'This, of course, won't stop you selling it to them or anyone else at a later date.' I assured him, although I didn't think Oates International would be in the bidding once this came to light.

'It will need to be done in front of a notary,' I said. 'They will be closed now so it will have to be tomorrow morning.'

We made a tentative appointment for eleven o'clock. I said I would call to accompany him to the notary's office and get everything signed up.

After that, knowing how the two men had conned Mr Ho, I was quite happy for the Triads to find the two men and dispense whatever rough justice they thought might be appropriate.

In the event, the Triads were beaten to it.

I'd not packed for an overnight stay in Dunoon but I'd noticed the Argyll Hotel at the top of main street so I made my way back and touched lucky. They had just one room left that night.

I went back into town, found a Boots down the road from the hotel and bought the necessary toiletries. I noticed a few early diners gathering in the Minoan Bull already as I passed. Perhaps Mr Ho should have bought a place in Dunoon in the first place instead of Liverpool.

The Argyll Hotel dining room, the Clyde Suite, served me with a fine dinner and a bottle of White Zinfandel at a table overlooking the bay with its panoramic views. It was almost like being on holiday except I kept looking out of the window to see if I could spot the anyone out there resembling the

Jenkinsons.

I presumed, though, they would come by car, which meant they would be approaching from the opposite direction.

Back in my room, I switched on the TV to watch the news when my mobile rang.

'You never rang to see if I got home all right on Sunday,' said Hilary.

'Hil, I'm sorry. Things have been hectic this end.'

'Where are you?' she asked. I rang your office but Ronni just said you were out of town.'

Good old Cameron. I thought. Never disclose things on the phone. 'Scotland.'

'Scotland! What are you doing there? And why didn't you take me with you?'

I explained it was work and, anyway, I'd had to leave at short notice.

'We could have had a night together, Johnny. I've never been to Scotland.'

At that moment, all alone in my hotel bedroom, there was nothing I would have liked better.

'I'll be back tomorrow,' I told her. 'I'll ring you then and we can go for lunch or something.'

I slept well in the double bed but I was awake for eight and on the streets for nine after a large Scottish breakfast.

I'd checked the telephone directory for a list of solicitors and found a notary not too far out of town. His name was Wintersgill. Instead of the elderly be-whiskered Scotsman I was for some reason expecting, I found a young switched-on bloke whose accent betrayed a Southern England origin.

I explained the situation to him and he agreed to draw up a document and bring it to the Minoan Café at eleven for Mr Borborkis to sign.

The work done, my next call was on Mr Borborkis to let him know everything had gone to plan and he could expect us on time.

My first feeling of foreboding came when there was no answer when I knocked on the shop door. I had presumed that the two men lived above the shop but, thinking about it, that was probably not the case.

I should have enquired where their home was. Or homes. For all I knew, both men were married with families. They need not even be living in Dunoon. Zagorasis had run the Crete Café by himself in Liverpool. Perhaps he ran the Minoan Bull on his own and Borborkis was just visiting which meant Borborkis could live in Glasgow or anywhere.

All these doubts crossed my mind as I stood outside the café but, realistically, I was sure the two Greeks were in this together and I expected them to be there at eleven o'clock.

And so they were or rather, one of them was.

I walked up to Castle Gardens behind the landing stage and inspected the famous statue of Highland Mary, paramour of Robert Burns, then did a circuit Alexandra Parade beside the sea before returning to the café. Still no sign of the owners. Simon Wintersgill arrived at eleven prompt.

'Nobody in?' he enquired. 'I thought they were meeting us at eleven.'

'That's what we arranged. Perhaps they're inside.'

I couldn't see a bell so I knocked loudly on the glass-fronted door. No reply. I knocked a couple more times to no effect.

'Something's wrong,' I said. 'Stand back. You didn't see this,' I added and planted my right heel squarely over the mortise lock. The old wooden door swung open as the lock splintered and I led the way into the café.

All was silent. Wintersgill looked stunned as he followed me into the kitchens beyond as if he didn't quite believe what was happening.

'Upstairs,' I said. 'There's probably a flat above the shop.'

'I believe there is,' gasped the solicitor. 'This used to be a sweet shop years ago and the old lady who had it lived above the shop. We dealt with her estate that's how I know.' He was babbling. Perhaps he thought he ought to be making a citizen's arrest on account of my breaking and entering. Or was he debating how long he would get for aiding and abetting?

I reached the top stair, Wintersgill behind me. In front of us was a door marked Private. I could hear talking inside the room. I knocked. No answer. I tried the door. It opened into a lounge. The talking had come from a TV set in the corner. The room was empty.

I strode across to another door at the other side of the room and turned round to Wintersgill who was right behind me.

'This could be unpleasant.'

The door led to a small bedroom. Most of the space was taken up by a cheap flat pack double wardrobe in white chipboard, a matching chest of drawers with one of the handles missing and a double bed with drawers beneath. The pink Dralon headboard was slightly askew. The carpet was of a worn twist pile in a contrasting pink. The curtains were of an attractive multicoloured floral pattern but made of flimsy material, which allowed sunlight to pour into the room. A cheap woodchip paper painted in magnolia covered the walls and a slightly faded Vettriano print of The Singing Butler ensconced in a cheap dark wood frame hung on the side wall.

Borborkis lay on the bed, his face staring at the ceiling, his mouth open. His throat had been viciously sliced open and the dried blood saturated the pink and white duvet. His beard was caked with it. Some had splattered onto the Dralon headboard; more had dripped to the floor. There was probably more poured out of him than was left in his body. By his expression, he had been screaming at the moment he died but whether in fury or for mercy I could not tell. His eyes had a look of terror.

The noise behind me was Simon Wintersgill vomiting in a corner. It wasn't the sort of thing he was used to.

I was glad he was with me. The police always have the person who finds the body marked down as a major suspect so having a respected local solicitor in tow was a bonus.

The next question was, where was Nikos Zagorasis?

I let Wintersgill dial the local police on his mobile and resigned myself to a morning of questioning. What could I tell them? The dead man was to be a witness in a case of fraud and intimidation back in Liverpool but the defendants had got to him first End of story. Did I know who killed him? I had an idea but it was their job to prove it, not mine.

I would give them DI Reubens' name which I didn't think would please him and I knew I could expect a long and unpleasant interview with him when I returned to town.

The Strathclyde police force is the second largest in Great Britain and 'L' Division which covers Bute, Argyll and West Dunbartonshire is its largest division of which Dunoon is just a small branch. However, they were on the scene with alacrity, albeit the police station was only a few yards down the road.

I identified the deceased, gave my statement to an Inspector Pickford, furnished him with all my contact numbers and referred him to DI Reubens in Liverpool.

By two o'clock I was all done. I thanked Simon Wintersgill for his help. It was a morning he'd never forget. I just managed to catch the boat back to Gouruk where the Glasgow train was waiting in the station.

The last train from Glasgow to Preston left at 17.51. Time to have a late lunch. I'd not eaten since the Argyll Hotel breakfast I found a place called Miss Cranston's Tearooms just by Central Station in Gordon Street, where a Chinese girl called Ming served me with a delicious meal in surroundings redolent of architect Rennie Mackintosh's finest period. Tearooms in Glasgow at the turn of the century were as famous as the coffee houses in Vienna.

I walked across to Ottakars and bought a book for the return journey but I couldn't concentrate on it. The case was on my mind and I thought long and hard about recent events as the train hurtled through the Lowlands towards England.

The murders of Stewart Davis and Jeanne McGhee were still unsolved but my mind was on something else. A third possible murder that nobody had even suspected.

For I remembered where I had previously seen the blonde woman who was sitting in the Quarter Café.

✳ ✳ ✳

Chapter Twenty-Eight

The RAV4 was waiting for me in the car park at Preston Station and I was back home for 9.30 p.m.

Maria had a message for me. 'A Detective Inspector Reubens was on the phone for you,' she said. 'He wants you to meet him at his office at ten tomorrow morning. He didn't make it sound like a request as much as an order.'

Crunch time.

'Does Ronni know?'

'I rang and told her.'

I kissed her. 'What would I do without you?' And I meant it.

'I don't think that Ronni likes me?'

'What makes you think that?'

'Women's intuition. And half the time, Johnny, I can't understand a word she says.'

'Neither can I,' I admitted. 'I'm getting better but I could still do with a translator.'

'She is English isn't she?'

'I think she was born in Bradford but I suppose that counts.'

Maria smiled. 'Listen, I've had my dinner but do you want something to eat?'

'I wouldn't mind a snack. The food on the train came in those little plastic food trays like you get on airlines and it was just as inedible.'

We had sesame prawn toasts and a glass of wine. I brought Maria up to speed on the case and she told me all her latest news. Another gift shop, this time in Arnside, had bought some of her jewellery; Vikki had sung in the nursery school choir for the first time; Maria's friend at work, Jenny, had got engaged to her boyfriend.

It was all very relaxing but constantly at the back of my mind was the feeling that the following morning's interview was not going to be too pleasant.

And so it proved.

I reported to the police station at ten o'clock as requested. DI Reubens interviewed me alone in his office. His desk was littered with papers, telephone messages and too many half-empty polystyrene coffee cups. His caffeine intake can't have helped his stress problems.

He wasted no time with polite introductions. 'Deaths follow you like flies follow shit.'

'I see the Strathclyde police have been in touch with you.'

'They have indeed. What do you think you're playing at, interfering in matters that don't concern you?'

'Wrong,' I said. 'They do concern me. Oliver Clarke hired me to sort out the trouble he was having with the vandals targeting his property. Something, I might point out, the police were not too keen to investigate.'

'There's vandals everywhere. We can't look into every case. We haven't the manpower. He should have employed security guards.'

'I thought that's what we paid our rates for.

Reubens said nothing. I continued.

'I found out that the people behind the attacks on Mr Clarke's property were hired by the property company Oates International as a means of persuading Mr Clarke to sell out to them.'

'What has all this got to do with the murder of a Greek café owner in Scotland?'

'I'm coming to that. The man who was killed in Dunoon is a Mr Kofi Borborkis who also happens to own a property here in Liverpool. A property that Oates International want to get their hands on.'

'Are you suggesting that the people who set fire to your friend Mr Clarke's car showrooms are the same ones who killed Mr Borborkis?'

'Maybe not the same ones who carried out the killing but certainly sent by the same people.'

'Can you prove any of this?'

'That's why I went to Scotland. To get Borborkis to sign an affidavit confirming the signature beside his name on the contract was not his.'

'What contract is that?'

'Oates had drawn up contracts for all the properties they wanted to buy on this particular pieces of land. On the ones where the people would not sell to them, they simply forged their signatures. Borborkis's café was one of those.'

'Where are these contracts now?'

I opened my brief case and, with a flourish, laid them on the desk in front of him.

'All the evidence you need, except your two principal witnesses are now dead.'

He gave me a fixed stare. 'I won't ask where you obtained these.'

'It was Jeanne McGhee who originally removed them from Oates office.'

'For what purpose?'

'I think you can safely say, for her personal gain.'

'You mean Miss McGhee was blackmailing her bosses?'

'I cannot say for sure but, put it this way, they'd be pretty anxious to get them back.'

'By *they*, I take it you mean Mr Taggart and Mr Dixon.'

'The two surviving partners, yes.'

'Hence the break-in at Miss McGhee's flat?'

'Precisely.'

'Except you got the contracts not the intruder.'

'Yes.'

'And you still don't know who that intruder was?'

'Put it this way, the heavy mob Oates International were using were the Jenkinsons and friends.'

I didn't bother to describe the other two men who had attacked me just in case Big Alec had actually disposed of them. Not too many people had H A R D tattooed on their heads so one of them at least would be easy to trace. No sense in getting Alec into trouble.

'So this is why Miss McGhee hired you to protect her? Because she was frightened that her employers, whom she was blackmailing, would try to silence her. '

'Either them or the partners at Leprechaun Developments who thought she had their £50,000. And don't tell me what a cock-up I made of protecting her.'

I was afraid he was going to arrest me for withholding evidence but instead he rose from his seat. 'Before you go on, I need a coffee. Do you want one?'

'I'll have a tea if that's all right?'

It was. His manner had softened. I'd ceased to be the enemy. I was going to help him out with a case he was struggling with.

The tea tasted like diluted vinegar but it was the thought that counted. I took one sip and pushed it to one side. Reubens gulped his coffee eagerly.

'Right, Mr Ace. Is there anything at all you can tell me that might help in solving Miss McGhee's murder?'

'Not really. But certainly Oates International are guilty of fraud and intimidation.'

'But, if what you say is true and Miss McGhee was blackmailing the partners at Oates International, they could have hired the Jenkinsons to carry out her murder?'

In fact, I didn't think the Jenkinsons did kill Jeanne for, even as I was talking to the inspector, I suddenly remembered where I had first seen the black saloon car that came out of Lucky Learoyd's house that Sunday morning and a theory started to form in my mind. But I needed to work it through before saying any more to Reubens.

'They may have done. On the other hand, I am pretty certain they killed Borborkis. And Molly Laffin too,' I added casually.

'Who?'

'The landlady murdered in her Wavertree pub during the early hours of Tuesday morning. She used to own the Pig and Hamster in Northumberland Street. Oates wanted it but she sold to someone else so they forged her signature as well. Like Borborkis, they killed her to keep her from testifying. '

'Hold on. The Wavertree landlady. That's not my case. I'll have to inform DCI Hovden. He's dealing with that one.'

'I think you'll find it will be yours in the end,' I assured him and Reubens looked resigned

'I don't suppose you can tell me who killed Stewart Davis by any chance while we're at it?'

'Sorry. Nothing whatever to do with me.'

'Oh really? I thought you were working your way through my case file.'

'I think you have enough to go on with, Inspector. Oh, one thing you might not know though. Mr Borborkis had his cousin with him up in Dunoon, a Mr Nikos Zagorasis. He was the one who actually ran the café.'

'So?'

'He's missing.'

'Ah, well that's where I have news for you. Mr Zagorasis's body was washed up in the Firth of Clyde near Greenock late last night.'

'Oh.'

'But I don't think his death had anything to do with Mr Borborkis.'

'But it was murder?'

'Oh yes, but the way the execution was carried out, the Strathclyde Police believe it was committed by one of the Triads. He'd obviously fallen foul of the Chinese at some time.'

The news pleased me. Retribution for their treatment of Clarence Ho.

'To get back to where we started, is Mr Clarke selling his premises to Oates International then?' the Inspector asked.

'Depends if they're still around,' I said. 'And that depends on whether you can get the evidence to arrest them.' I stood up. 'Let me know if there's anything else I can help you with.'

'It wasn't an easy interview,' I said to Cameron when I got back to the office. 'But I think we've got Oates International all sewn up as much as we can. The Jenkinsons won't have any qualms about landing them in it if it gets them a shorter sentence. Reubens still suspects I know more than I told him though.'

'And don't you?'

'Probably, although I'm not hundred per cent sure how much. I have a vague theory which ties everything together but there are one or two missing links to sort out before I can make it work.'

'What are we talking here? Jeanne McGhee's murder? The attacks on Lucky Learoyd? The missing money?'

'You're forgetting Stewart Davis's murder, Ronni. They're all connected and, if I'm right, in a way we never originally thought of.'

'Go on then, hang it on me.'

'Not yet. I need to work a few things out first and talk to a couple of people.

What I had was little more than a hunch. A collection of random facts that, when I put them together, had a common denominator. And that common denominator was Victor Learoyd.

* * *

Chapter Twenty-Nine

Jeanne McGhee had been in Preston when she phoned me that Monday morning. Sadie Farley lived near Preston. Could Jeanne have spent that 'missing weekend' with her friend? If so, why had Sadie kept this from me? Sadie admitted she knew Victor Learoyd and I realised now that It was Jeanne's black Honda I'd seen coming out of Lucky Learoyd's mansion on the Sunday morning. Victor Learoyd was the only person I'd told about Molly Laffin and Kofi Borborkis. Could it be just coincidence that, within forty eight hours, both of them were dead or was there a more sinister meaning behind it all?

To mix metaphors, it was time to stir the waters, throw all the balls in the air and see where they came down. It might not be the way DI Reubens or the CID would have done it but I thought it worth a try.

My first journey took me to Midge Hall but I steered clear of the Farley livery yard. Instead, I drove around looking for public telephone boxes and the second one I came to was the one I was looking for. When I checked the phone number, I knew it was the same box that Jeanne McGhee had called me from that Monday morning. Less than twenty four hours before she was murdered.

I drove to Hesketh Bank on the offchance I would find Victor Learoyd at home and I touched lucky. As on my earlier visit to his son, my arrival was anticipated and the electric gates opened as I came to the end of the long drive.

Learoyd himself stood at the front door to greet me.

'Back so soon, Mr Ace. '

'I have a theory, Mr Learoyd, that I should like to try out on you. Will you indulge me? It won't take long.'

'Come into the sitting room. I confess I am rather intrigued.'

I doubted whether he would be so intrigued in half an

hour's time.

He escorted me into the room, gesticulated for me to take the settee and poured himself a malt whisky from a drinks cabinet in the corner of the room.

'Whisky? Or would you prefer something else?'

'I'm fine thank you.'

'Fair enough.' He made his way across the floor and held his glass up. 'Cheers.' He swallowed a good half of the liquid before putting the glass down onto a nearby coffee table and lowering himself majestically onto the settee like a king occupying a throne.

'Right, you have my full attention. What have you got to tell me?'

'I think I know what really happened to Jeanne McGhee, Mr Learoyd.'

'To whom?'

He wasn't going to make it easy.

'Let me tell you a little story. It's all about land and property and large fortunes to be made. When Liverpool was named City of Culture, everyone knew that property values were going to soar and the speculators moved in like hungry vultures round a rotting carcass.

'For some reason, Victor, you were a little late getting into the Liverpool scene. Oates International had got there some time before you and they had managed to acquire a prime piece of land with great potential near the city centre, an area I call The Toxteth Triangle.

'I say they acquired it. In actual fact, there were four properties on the land they still had to buy.

'You came along and immediately saw the potential of the plot and managed to snap up one of the last remaining businesses on it yourself, namely the Watson's' builders yard.'

'Go on.' Learoyd lit a cigar and blew a smoke ring into the air.

'You found out that Oates were preparing to sell the land on, to a Dublin company called Leprechaun Developments, so you quickly stepped in with a bigger offer. Two of the partners, Taggart and Dixon, wanted to sell to you, but the third partner, Stewart Davis, was anxious for the Leprechaun deal to go through.

'This was because, unbeknown to Taggart and Dixon, Davis was making a cool £50,000 for himself in the form of a deposit that he'd taken from the partners at Leprechaun, Messer's Flynn and O'Toole.

'Naturally, having paid the cheque to Davis, Leprechaun Developments assumed the land would be theirs. Then they got to hear that another bid was in the offing, so they threatened Davis that nothing had better go wrong with their offer or he would be killed.

'Davis realised that his partners were leaning towards accepting your bid rather than Leprechaun's so, fearing for his safety, he went into hiding, living rough disguised as a tramp.

'Now all this time, Stewart Davis was secretly having an affair with his PA at Oates, Jeanne McGhee, and he had arranged that the fifty thousand from Leprechaun was paid into her private bank account so it could not be connected to him in any way.

'It's here that the story becomes interesting.

'Unable to get hold of the reclusive Davis, O'Toole and Flynn at Leprechaun contacted Oates regarding their purchase of the property. Imagine their displeasure when they found that Oates knew nothing about the deposit they had paid and, furthermore, refused to sign the contract for the deal.

'On the morning of Monday August 11, Miss McGhee went to her bank to draw out the deposit money in cash. That same night, Stewart Davis was murdered. At first, I thought that Flynn and O'Toole had arranged his murder, having realised he'd conned them out of their so-called deposit, but I no longer think that.'

'Why is that?'

'You'll see in a moment. I believe that, once they heard that Davis was dead, Flynn and O'Toole turned their attention to the person to whom they had paid the cheque. Jeanne McGhee.

'On the Wednesday, Miss McGhee received a phone call saying if she didn't return the money, she would end up like her former lover. Dead. The call undoubtedly came from someone at Leprechaun. She naturally became very frightened. She realised she had got on the wrong side of some highly ruthless people and her life could be in danger. That is when she came to me for protection.'

'In the circumstances, not the best choice she could have made,' commented Victor smugly.

I ignored the insult, mainly because I could hardly dispute it. I carried on.

'What interested me was where had the money gone? Jeanne McGhee said she'd handed it over to Davis, suggesting that whoever killed him hit the jackpot and ended up with the cash.' I looked hard at Learoyd. 'But I am sure Jeanne never gave that money to Davis.'

Learoyd stayed silent and continued smoking his cigar.

'You see, I think Jeanne McGhee was playing a dangerous double game but one that she had planned soon after she joined Oates International and realised they were on the fiddle.

'Oates were forging contracts, signing the names of people that had refused to sell them their properties and claiming they had rightfully bought them.

'It is my belief that she seduced Stewart Davis and started the affair with him with the sole intention of using him to make money.

'Her initial plan was to get Davis to smuggle out the fake contracts, with which she intended to blackmail the other two partners.'

'Why would he go along with it?'

'Because he was smitten with her. She had led him to believe the two of them were going to run away and start a new life together. He was ready to leave his wife for Jeanne. She probably told him the money would go towards buying a love-nest for the two of them, and the poor sap believed her, but that was never going to happen.'

'Why not?'

'Because Jeanne already had a man of her own, someone she had recently met and fallen for. Or maybe fallen for is the wrong word. A calculating women like Jeanne doesn't fall for men. Let us say she found someone she regarded as a better meal ticket than Stewart Davis.'

'Even with the fifty thousand?'

'Her latest catch would have made her a lot more in the long run and, don't forget, she was getting the fifty thousand anyway because, once she'd safely collected the cash from the bank, Davis was a dead man.'

'So if you say the Irish didn't kill Davis, who did? Miss McGhee herself?'

I took a deep breath. 'You did, Mr Learoyd. I think you were Jeanne McGhee's secret lover. You met her when you were with Adrienne Farley at Aintree Races. She'd recently parted with her boyfriend. She'd probably heard about you already from her friend Mrs Farley, knew you were a wealthy man and set out to win your attention. You, in turn, must have been flattered to have a young woman like her in your bed.'

Learoyd said nothing but stubbed out his cigar heavily into a gold ash tray.

'After she got the job with Oates, she told you about Davis and the blackmail plot and you realised you'd found your perfect partner in crime. When she told you Davis was on the verge of signing up the Leprechaun deal, you dreamt up the idea of getting Davis to ask for a deposit, being careful to insist that the money went into her personal bank account, after which you killed him. And then you had the gall to out-bid Leprechaun for the land, knowing you had also got their £50,000.'

Victor Learoyd started to laugh. Not a good sign.

'You're talking complete madness, Ace. For a start, what possible motive could I have? I'm a rich man. Why risk a life sentence for fifty grand? It's peanuts to me, son. And, secondly, I deal in money not lives. And, thirdly, I'm seventy years old. That woman was barely thirty. There's no way she would look at me.'

'Money is a powerful aphrodisiac,' I said.

'It's obvious to anyone with a grain of sense that the Irish are the ones that did for Davis and then they got rid of Miss McGhee because she stole their money.'

'No, that doesn't add up because they never got their money back.'

'What about Oates International then?' said Learoyd. 'You've said that McGhee was blackmailing them. An obvious reason to kill her.'

'Indeed. And we already know that Dixon and Taggart at Oates had no compunction about hiring hoodlums like the Jenkinsons to wreck property and beat up, even possibly kill, innocent people. However, I think it was only later, after Jeanne had left, that they realised she had stolen their contracts. That's when they sent a man called Alby Durno to break into her flat to try to recover them.

'Of course, by this time, Jeanne was well gone. She left Oates office on that Friday night before the man I sent to guard her could reach her, probably leaving by a back entrance. She fled to her friend, Adrienne Farley, whom I suspect put her up for the night then brought her to you next morning.'

'Stop. Stop there.' Learoyd had jumped to his feet and waved his arms imperiously in the air. 'No point in going on with this charade. I can put a stop to your ridiculous theories quite simply. Wait there.'

He strode out of the room and a minute later returned with a programme and thrust it into my hand.

'Read that.'

It was a programme for an Agricultural Show up near Penrith for the weekend that Jeanne McGhee went missing. The speaker at the eight o'clock dinner on the Friday night was Victor Learoyd. He judged several classes on the Saturday and Sunday and was Guest of Honour at the closing dinner on the Monday.

'And if you check with the George Hotel at Penrith, you will find I stayed there from the Friday night through to the Tuesday morning and my movements over those four days will have been witnessed by several hundred people.'

'What about the previous Wednesday when Davis was killed?' As I asked the question, I knew I was clutching at straws.

'A Sportsman's Dinner in Lancaster. A group of us stayed overnight at the Royal Kings Arms. Two hundred people will confirm I was at the dinner all evening and drinking in the hotel bar until 3 a.m. I think you'd better leave now, Mr Ace.'

I knew he could easily have arranged for someone else to have carried out the murders but there was no way he was going to admit that to me. I gave it one last shot.

'Just one more question if I may. When I came to see you the other day, I told you about Molly Laffin and Kofi Borborkis being two people who could give evidence against Oates International.'

'So?'

'Did you pass that information on to anyone at all?'

'Why do you ask?'

'Because they have both been murdered in the last forty eight hours.'

'Yes, I told Jeffrey Taggart at Oates International,' said Victor Learoyd disarmingly.

'Whatever for? You must have known about their record of intimidation and violence?'

'Of course. But, Jeffrey Taggart and his partner had agreed to sell me the land. I didn't want to end up disputing owner-ship of different pieces of it.'

'So you let them do your dirty work and get rid of the two witnesses?'

'How Oates International conduct their affairs is no con-cern of mine. I just wanted to make sure that when they sold it on to me, I inherited the whole plot. How they acquired it was their business. Now, if you don't mind, you have taken up enough of my time. I don't want to see you here again, Mr Ace.'

I drove away from the Learoyd mansion feeling totally defeated. I was sure I had been on the right track.

As I drove back to Liverpool, I went over the case in my mind. Once Oliver Clarke put his name on the contract to sell his showroom to Oates, if he hadn't done it already, the final piece of the jigsaw was in place and St Petersburg Properties would purchase the lot. Oates was making their pile. Leprechaun had been squeezed out and lost fifty grand in the bargain. I couldn't see O'Toole and Flynn taking that lying down. After the Glasgow "Ice Cream Wars" of the last decade could come the Liverpool "Land Wars".

The big mystery was, where had the £50,000 gone if Victor Learoyd was speaking the truth?

I posed the question to Cameron when I returned after I had repeated my hypotheses to her.

She was quite impressed with my reasoning but found a flaw in the final argument.

'There's one thing you're forgetting,' she said.

'What's that?'

'There is one more property on that land that neither Oates or Learoyd own.'

I looked at her enquiringly. 'Go on.'

'The Pig and Hamster.'

'We've covered that. They forged Molly Laffin's name on the contract. That's why she was killed, to prevent her talking.'

'Yes, but don't you see, burger brain? She was the vendor. What about the purchaser? Oates has not threatened the new owner. Nor have they made an offer to buy him out, yet he could well testify against them that Molly Laffin sold to him not to Oates.'

'You're right.'

'So why haven't they killed him as well?'

And, in a blinding flash, the truth hit me. My theory itself was right but I'd got the wrong man.

'Of course,' I said. He was the man behind it all. He, not Victor Learoyd, was Jeanne McGhee's secret lover. He was the man who killed Stewart Davis and Jeanne McGhee. The man who now owned the Pig and Hamster. None other than Benny Learoyd, once known as Ben E. Prince, but lately as… Lucky Learoyd,' I said.

Cameron smiled triumphantly. 'Is the killer.'

✻ ✻ ✻

I went through to my own office and rang Tommy McKale at The Fitness Palace to see if he knew where Lucky was.

'As far as I know, Johnny, he's already left. They've gone to Anglesey on a gig.'

'Is Big Alec with him?'

'Yes. He's doing two nights up there, a social club in Holyhead tonight and a hotel dinner dance tomorrow. Do you want the addresses?'

I took them down in my notebook. 'Getting a fair bit of work at the moment isn't he?'

'Seems like it and its a little holiday for Alec.'

'Can you get hold of Alec, Tommy?'

'Yeah, on his mobile. Do you want his number?'

'No, you can ring him for me. I don't want to alert Lucky.' I outlined my theory to Tommy.'

'Phew, that's a bleeding turn up and no mistake.'

'If I'm right,' I said. 'And I think I am.'

'I'll brief Alec right away. When are you going?'

'Soon after lunch. I want to catch him before the show.'

'This time of year, all the traffic, I'd give it a good two hours to be on the safe side. They were leaving first thing this morning. Your mate wanted to do some fishing while he was over there.'

'I never knew Lucky was an angler.' But then, it seemed there was a whole lot I never knew about the man once known as Ben E. Prince.

I rang Cameron, told her I was going to Anglesey and asked her to man the office.

'Are you still off sick at the radio station?' she asked.

'Slipped disc. Can't walk.'

My next call was to the Liverpool Royal Infirmary where Hilary worked. I was in luck; she was on duty. I still felt guilty about leaving her at the Masquerade on Sunday. 'Just wondered if you fancied lunch?' I said.

'If you can wait till two. I'll be off duty then.'

'Fine. I'll pick you up outside the entrance.'

We went to the Albert in Lark Lane.

'I'm sorry about last Sunday,' I said as we waited for the Cajun chicken and chips. 'Only, with all the trouble the other night at the Bamalama, I didn't dare risk you getting involved in anything dangerous again.'

She put her hand over mine. 'That's all right, Johnny. I understand.' She raised her eyebrows reproachfully. 'I wouldn't have minded coming to Scotland with you though.'

'It was a last minute thing, Hil.'

'Is everything solved now with your case?'

'Not yet but I'm hoping it soon will be. After we've had lunch I'm off to Anglesey to tie up a few loose ends.'

'I could have come to Angelsey with you too but I'm on a split today.'

'Another time maybe.'

She squeezed my hand. 'I hope there will be other times, Johnny.'

And we left it at that. We talked about other things like hygiene in hospitals, Hilary's forthcoming holiday in Malta, The Zutons' latest CD, and mutual friends whom we didn't see much anymore. All non-explosive stuff. The meal was good and afterwards I took Hilary back to work and set off through the Wallasey Tunnel en route for Wales.

The traffic built up on the A55 coming up to Conwy but I shunted through without too much delay and carried on along the coast through Penmaenmawr and Llanfairfechan into Bangor and across to the Isle of Anglesey.

I passed RAF Valley as I came near to Holyhead. It was like old times. I'd played at the No. 10 Club there with The Cruzads in the Seventies when Mud were topping the charts with *Tiger Feet.*

The social club was down a side street close to the docks. It was not the most salubrious looking of venues from the outside, the usual graffiti on the concrete walls and litter in the potholed car park.

I checked my watch. Six o'clock. I was banking on Lucky and Big Alec arriving early to do a sound check before they booked into their hotel.

The front door was unlocked so I wandered inside. The interior of the club belied its external appearance with smart new furnishings, a large stage with purple curtains drawn across, a well-stocked bar, bright lights, a fair-sized dance floor and Chinese lanterns suspended over every table to create a late night romantic mood.

I walked up to the stage and peered behind the curtains and I'd timed it perfectly. There was Lucky setting up his equipment with Big Alec attending to some wiring. I walked through to them. Lucky was wearing a red T-shirt and the bottom half of a shell suit in bright orange.

'Johnny. What are you doing here?'

'I came to see you Lucky.' I smiled at him. 'How's it going? I believe you've been fishing?'

'Yes.' He looked uncertain.

'Catch anything?'

'Only a couple of pike.'

'Is there anywhere we can talk?' I motioned to Alec to join us.

'Give me a minute to fix this and we can go into the dressing room.'

The dressing room was well fitted out with a huge mirror covering one wall under which ran a shelf bearing an electric kettle and a packet of teabags with a jug of water and cups and saucers. A three-seater settee stood beside the adjacent wall and to the opposite side was a tiny annexe housing a sink and toilet.

I followed Alec and Lucky in.

'Christ it's like the London Palladium,' I said. 'Half the places we played at, we had to get changed in the Gents.' I motioned to the settee. 'Have a seat, Lucky.'

Big Alec took a place next to him. I sat on a stool by the mirror and opened my notebook.

'I've been working on your case, Lucky, and the good news is, I think I've solved it.'

A puzzled expression crossed Lucky's face. 'How do you mean?'

'You came to me originally because you'd received a threatening letter and phone call so you naturally thought you might be in some danger. That's right isn't it?'

'Yes, of course.'

'Since then, you've been shot, poisoned, kidnapped and attacked.'

'Which shows I had every reason to be afraid.'

'Exactly. Well the good news is, you're not in danger anymore.'

He didn't look as relieved as might have been expected. 'How do you work that out? Those Jenkinsons don't give up.'

'Maybe not, but the Jenkinsons had no quarrel with you personally, despite the earlier trouble with your ex-wife. They were working as hired muscle for a property company called Oates International.'

'I don't know them.'

'I think you do. They were the firm trying to buy the Pig and Hamster before you stepped in. You said the previous owner had been having trouble with vandals and that's why she wanted to get rid. Well, that's correct but the vandals were set up by Oates International to help persuade her to sell up.'

'Vandalism's one thing, shooting's another.'

'They missed, Lucky. That's the point. They were softening you up.'

'So why has it all stopped now?'

'They were forging contracts for people who wouldn't sell but two of the people who were going to be witnesses are dead.'

'What's that got to do with me?'

'You're the last witness, Lucky. The one person left alive who can swear that the contract between Oates and Molly Laffin is a fake, because she sold the pub to you not them.'

'So I *am* in danger. Is that what you're saying?'

'No. Now Oates International know who you are, you're in no danger at all.'

'Who I am?' He looked puzzled. 'Who am I?'

'You are the son of Victor Learoyd who is buying the whole plot from Oates International. Oates know you wouldn't risk jeopardising the deal for your old man by testifying against them.'

'Oh.' He was unsure what the point was but he was soon to find out.

'However, I don't think you'll be performing on a stage again for a very long time.'

His face clouded over. 'What do you mean?'

'I know everything, Lucky. I know that you and Jeanne McGhee stole £50,000 from Leprechaun Developments. I'm sure she was very impressed when she first saw your mansion. I bet you never took her to your cheap shagging pad. Quite the Bonnie and Clyde weren't you? When did you first hatch the plot to swindle Oates and Leprechaun?'

Lucky hesitated for a moment then sighed, crossed his legs and started to talk, almost conversationally.

'I met her at Aintree Races when I was there with the old man. She'd just ditched her boyfriend and was thinking of moving up this end. We hit it off and I took her number. A

few weeks went by and when I knew Liverpool was favourite
for this City of Culture thing, I thought it might be an idea to
get into property so I rang her and suggested she get a job
with one of the new companies coming up to Liverpool to
cash in on the boom.'

'What had you in mind?'

'At that point, I was just hoping for advance news of properties before the public got to hear of them.'

'Sort of insider dealing?'

'That's right. Anyway, she got the job with Oates and
moved up to Birkdale.'

'Why Birkdale and not Liverpool?'

'The area. Birkdale was posh and Jeanne liked posh. She
said they had a good library nearby and she used to read a lot.
Also, she didn't want to be on top of the job. This was just far
enough away from work and, at the same time, near enough to
her old mates in Preston.' He stopped. 'Where was I?'

'Insider dealing.'

'Oh yes. When I mentioned it to Jeanne, she had grander
ideas.'

'The blackmail scam?'

'You know about that? Right. But then she told me about
the deal Stewart Davis, her boss, was setting up with
Leprechaun Developments to buy this plot of land. I had the
idea of getting Jeanne to suggest he demand a deposit from
them and put it into her bank account, ostensibly to keep it
from his partners. Don't you think it was clever, Johnny?''

No wonder he was on the stage. It was if he was waiting
for applause after every revelation.'

'Very clever, Lucky.' I wasn't so sure Stewart Davis's
widow would regard it in quite the same way. 'So you persuad-
ed Jeanne to seduce Davis?'

'He didn't take much seducing. He was very gullible.'

'He was in love with her.'

'That's no excuse for being gullible. The stupid sod really believed all that guff she spun him about going away together.' For the first time, Lucky Learoyd showed his hard side.

'Why kill him?'

'I didn't kill him,' said Lucky surprisingly. 'Jeanne did.'

'What?'

'He wanted Jeanne to hand over the cash to him when she withdrew it from the bank. She wouldn't. He tried to get the money off her, there was a struggle, she grabbed a kitchen knife and stabbed him. She probably didn't mean to kill him but it went straight through his heart. I helped her dump the body in Kensington that night and we cut his head off as we thought it would appear more likely a man had done it. Women don't usually decapitate their victims.'

'Most women don't kill,' I pointed out acidly.

'She knew that the Irish outfit had been threatening Davis so they'd be the chief suspects.'

'It must have given the two of you a perverse pleasure hiring me to protect you both, knowing I knew nothing about what you were really doing.'

'No, come on Johnny. We knew we were both in danger. We needed you.' He sounded quite indignant. 'Oates had sent the Jenkinsons after me because of the pub and the Irish lot were after Jeanne.'

'So on that Friday night when you discharged yourself from hospital after being shot, both you and Jeanne were hidden away in your place at Hoylake?'

'Yes.'

'So when my partner was waiting for you getting back, you were already inside.'

'Yes.'

'With the fifty grand?'

'Yes.'

'Not, as you told me, seeing a man about a gig and getting

home in the early hours after Cameron had left.'

'Sorry, Johnny.'

'What happened next?'

'She stayed at mine all Saturday. I did the gig at the Old Swan Social Club as you know, and came to the Masquerade with you afterwards. But on Sunday morning we had a row and she stormed out.'

'I know. I saw her Honda Accord come out of your gateway on Sunday morning.'

'She went to Preston to stay with Sadie Farley. I was worried. I thought she might shop me. Even worse, I thought she might come back and kill me. After all, I'd kept hold of the fifty grand and you know what they say about killing?'

'No. What do they say?'

'After the first one's over, you get a taste for it. I didn't want to be the next victim.'

'So what did you do?'

'I couldn't do anything immediately. I had a gig in Accrington on Sunday night.'

'The show must go on. How noble,' I said sarcastically.

'Can't let the public down, Johnny,' declared Lucky. Ever the showman. 'Anyway, first thing Monday I rang Sadie's, because I guessed Jeanne would be there.'

'Why would she not just go home?'

'The Oates mob might have been waiting for her.'

'And she was at Sadie's?'

'Yes.'

So why had Sadie lied about not seeing Jeanne? Lucky had the answer.

'Sadie is my father's mistress. Her riding stables were going down the pan till the old man stepped in. She's not going to grass him up. Too much to lose.'

So I was right about Victor. Old men with money did attract young women. I just got the wrong young woman.

Lucky went on. 'I told Jeanne I was sorry and I'd bring her share of the money straight round. I think she'd somehow got the wind up by then because I found her in this phone box outside the stables and she quickly put the phone down when she saw me coming.'

'She was phoning me, Lucky, to say she'd meet me at her flat that night but she never made it.'

'No. I took her back to the house, gave her a nice meal, we watched a romantic movie on TV and then I killed her.'

Even Big Alec winced at the casual way he said it.

'Thoughtful of you to make her last day so pleasant, Lucky. I'm surprised you didn't give her a good shag as well.'

'Oh I did. Just thought it a trifle improper to mention it.'

'And then you stabbed her,'

'Several times. I didn't have a good aim like she did.'

I realised now that Lucky Learoyd was a psychopath. Never had I been more relieved to have Big Alec beside me.

'And you went out in the early hours to dump her on the railway line.'

'That's about it. After I'd had a sleep, that is. Got to look after yourself in show business.'

'Hang on, Alec here was supposed to be guarding you on that Monday.'

'I rang Tommy McKale on Sunday night and told him I was staying in Accrington after the gig. Alec caught up with me on Tuesday morning. Nothing had happened to me. I was alive and well so he was happy.'

I glanced across at Big Alec. He looked anything but happy now.

'Tell me, how much of this does your father know?'

This struck a nerve. He jumped up. 'None of it,' he snarled.

I wondered. It must have crossed the old man's mind but he couldn't allow himself to betray his own son.

Lucky continued angrily. 'Do you think I have to run to

him all the time. I can make millions just as well as he can.'

And out of his pocket he produced a gun. I froze.

'Sorry about this, Johnny, but you know too much now.'

He flicked off the safety catch. I turned to Alec. He was sitting unmoved, watching us.

Lucky was too far away from me to jump him. He stood with his back to the wall facing Alec on his left and me on his right. I figured the odds were 50-50. One of us could take him but not in time to stop him shooting the other.

A social club in Holyhead wasn't the place I would have chosen to die.

I waited. Tense. Lucky pointed the gun at Alec.

'You first. Sorry and all that. Nothing against you but...' and he pulled the trigger.

I jerked backwards instinctively, waiting for the explosion and expecting to see Alec collapse.

Instead, there was a click. Big Alec rose to his feet wearily, took the gun from Lucky's hand and, without breaking sweat broke his jaw with a right uppercut that took the singer a good foot off the floor. He fell awkwardly, banging his head on the sharp edge of the shelf, and lay unconscious on the floor.

'After your phone call earlier, I removed his bullets,' explained Alec evenly. He put the gun carefully into his pocket. 'I collect these.'

'I've got one at home you can have,' I said, remembering the weapon I'd taken at the Bamalama fracas.

'What now?'

'We take him back to Liverpool and hand him over to the police.'

'Can't we just dump him in the Irish Sea,' suggested Big Alec. 'With a bit of luck, he'll float across to Dublin and they can use him as target practice for the IRA.'

'Brownie points, Alec. DI Reubens will owe me one after this. You can't sing by any chance, can you?" Alec looked at me questioningly. 'Only, they're going to be short of an act here tonight.'

* * *

Sam Reubens, we were on first name terms now, took Lucky Learoyd into custody where he was transferred straight to the hospital for an emergency operation on his jaw.

'Was it really necessary for your friend to do a Lennox Lewis on him?' bemoaned the policeman. 'It's all extra paperwork.'

'Think of the man hours I've saved you by bringing him in,' I said.

'Let's hope we can make the charges stick. His old man will bring in a top brief with his money.'

'No problem there. Alec got him to sign a written confession before he lost consciousness again.'

'If that was Alec who carried him in, I think I'd have admitted to being the Boston Strangler rather than upset him. That'll never hold up in court.'

'You need to see a lady called Adrienne Farley.' I gave him the address. She sheltered Jeanne McGhee over that missing weekend. She'll talk when pressed. And, while you are at it, get hold of her boyfriend too. Victor Learoyd.'

'I've heard of him.'

'Lucky's father and one-time gangster. He has a huge spread out at Hesketh Bank.'

'I'll need a statement from you to tie up all the loose ends.'

'Fine. Why don't we do it now?'

'Because it's nearly midnight and I want some sleep. Come back in the morning at a civilised hour.'

'Coming down the club for a quick one?' Alec asked me as we left the police station.

'Might as well.'

For some reason, there seemed to be more gangsters than usual in the Masquerade.

'Tommy's having a Blues Brothers Night, so everyone's

dressing up,' explained Alec. 'Him and Denis are doing a turn for the cabaret.'

'This I must see.'

We were just in time to see the McKale Brothers take to the stage wearing black pork pie hats, dark suits and shades. They started off with Wilson Pickett's *In the midnight hour,* arms round each other, kicking their legs out and hollering along to backing tapes that sounded suspiciously like the Muscle Shoals originals.

'Never thought I'd see Tommy up there,' said Alec as we made our way to the bar. 'I tell you what, they look the part. They could almost be mistaken for the originals.'

'In this light, certainly,' I agreed. 'Could be a whole new career for him.'

Vince came over and I ordered the drinks. He was also wearing a black pork pie hat and shades but with a black leather suit.

A voice behind me made me turn round. 'Johnny, you're back. I thought you were in Anglesey.'

It was Hilary.

'We got back earlier than we thought.'

'Come and have a dance.'

We had a few dances. The McKale Brothers completed their set to riotous applause from the regulars. Tommy came over and I told him what had happened in Anglesey.

'Nicely wrapped up then,' he said.

'I hope you got your money off Lucky.'

Tommy smiled. 'A month in advance and I never paid him for the spot he did so we're quids in.'

Just as I might have expected. I'd had the grand off Jeanne so I wasn't complaining.

'Are you staying at the flat tonight, Johnny,' asked Hilary hopefully.

I hesitated but not for long. 'Sorry Hil. I've got to go

home tonight. I'm due at the police station first thing.'

And after that, one last piece of unfinished business.

Maria was asleep when I crept into the bedroom at 2a.m., but she woke when I climbed in beside her.

'I didn't expect you, love. Is it all solved then?' she asked.

'Almost. Just one more spectacular arrest to make tomorrow.' Or today as it was.

'You're enjoying this, aren't you?

'It beats playing the drums, that's for sure.'

'And the property business?'

'I suppose so.'

'As long as nothing happens to you, Johnny. Vikki would miss having her Dad around. This isn't going to be dangerous is it, this last arrest as you call it?'

'No. Just routine,' I said.

Yet another gigantic miscalculation.

*   *   *

Chapter Thirty-Two

I presented myself at the police station at eleven next morning, after I'd rung Ricky Creegan at the radio station to tell him I'd be back to do the show that evening.

Sam Reubens took me into his office with DS Monk in close attendance. The coffee machine was on the blink so we had to make do with the hot chocolate, albeit still in the awful polystyrene cups.

'Have you arrested the Jenkinsons yet?' I asked.

'Yep. Six of them in all. We've got four safely locked up, the other two turned up in hospital.' replied Sam. 'Did you come across a fellow with H A R D tattooed on his head?'

'Yes. He was one of the men who kidnapped Lucky Learoyd outside the Mersey Tunnel.' So Big Alec hadn't wasted him after all.

'He's called Tweedale. Larry Tweedale. A cousin of the Jenkinsons. A bad lot. They all piss in the same pot, that family. He's in the Spinal Unit. The story is, he fell down a lift shaft.'

'Easily done.'

'Oddly enough, his mate Bernie Gibbon, another of Jenkinson's cousins, fell down the same shaft. He's in the next bed.'

'They were probably playing "Follow my leader" at the time and didn't look where they were going.'

Reubens gritted his teeth but refrained from commenting. 'We're throwing the book at the lot of them. Arson, criminal damage to property, threatening to kill, you name it. Best of all, we're charging Jason Jenkinson and his brother Wayne with murder. Jason for the Greek up in Dunoon and Wayne for killing the Wavertree landlady.'

So the ex-Mrs Lucky Learoyd would be left on her own. Would Lucky derive a certain satisfaction from that as he reflected in his cell?   "Run with the ferrets and expect to be bitten", as my old headmaster used to say.

'Have they confessed?'

'Oh yes.   Couldn't stop them talking once we told them they'd left DNA evidence all over the show.'

'And had they?'

'Probably. The others are pleading not guilty which suits us because the evidence will come out in court. They've admitted they were working for Oates International, and we have the forged contracts to show the jury, so we should be able to stick a conspiracy to murder charge on Taggart and Dixon.'

'A good result then.'

'It gets better. Benjamin Learoyd has made a statement admitting he murdered Jeanne McGhee and confirming she killed Stewart Davis so that completes the set as it were.' He looked at me curiously. 'Is Learoyd mad, Johnny? They say he's been singing all night long; he kept everyone in the ward awake. A terrible racket, according to the sister.'

'People pay good money to hear that, Sam. Mind you, his broken jaw can't have helped. Did he split his trousers as well?' But the allusion was lost on the inspector.

I told him the full story including the part played by Lucky's father and Adrienne Farley.

'I might have something else for you later, Sam' I promised him before I left. 'Give me your mobile number and I'll be in touch.'

'What's this about?'

'Can't tell you till I'm 100% sure but it will finish everything off for you nicely.'

I met up with Cameron for lunch at the Everyman Bistro. The place was full of University people but we managed to find a table in the no smoking area.

'One more call to make and everything's complete,' I said after we'd finished the meal. I stood up. 'Are you coming?'

'Where are we going?'

'To Oliver Clarke's showroom.'

'Going mob-handed are we?

'I have a theory.'

'Another one.'

'I want to test it out on Ollie.'

'And I'm there as a witness?'

'Something like that.'

'Sounds mysterious. I thought he was all sorted. Sold out to the global moguls along with all the rest'

'That side of it is sorted. There's just a little loose end I want to clear up.'

'What's that?'

I explained about the woman I'd seen with Oliver Clarke in la Tasca and later at the Quarter.

'I recognised her at the Crematorium. It was Graham Wharton's widow.'

'So?'

'So, if Ollie was slipping her a length then he had a motive for getting rid of her old man.'

'You've always had a way with words, Johnny.'

'Until now, everyone assumed that the fallen ramp was an accident. Only Ollie tried to make out it was deliberately tampered with, that it was meant to kill him. This was to throw everyone off the scent. In fact, that ramp killed the very person it was intended to but because Graham Wharton was an ordinary bloke, popular with his mates and without an enemy in the world, it never crossed anyone's mind he was the true victim.'

Cameron took it up. 'But secretly, Ollie was hitting it with his old lady and they wanted Graham out of the way.'

'I'm sure of it and my hunches are never wrong. Well, not often,' I hastily added, remembering Victor Learoyd. ' In the end, of course, it all boils down to religion. I blame the Pope.'

'How do you make that out?'

'The Wharton's are strict Catholic. What's the betting she asked Graham for a divorce and he refused to give it her?'

'Could well be.'

'So in Ollie's mind, he's no other option. He's always been a man who gets what he wants and the opportunity was there. The fact he'd had the vandals played into his hands. He could blame it on them wrecking his equipment and threatening him. He had a ready made alibi and all of it officially documented.'

Ollie was standing at the door of his garage when we drove up. The showroom was still gutted with tangled metal and broken glass strewn amongst the burnt out wrecks of the cars.'

'Doesn't he possess a brush and shovel?' asked Cameron. 'How long is it since the fire?'

'He's moving isn't he? Probably thinks he might as well as leave it for the new owners to clear up but they're only going to sell it on anyway.'

'Interesting to see who ends up with this land when everything is sorted out,' mused Cameron. 'My bet's on Wimpy.'

'Hello Johnny, what are you doing here?'

'Came for a little chat, Ollie.'

'Oh yes?' A cloud of suspicion passed over his face. 'What about?'

I jumped out of the car, shut the door after me and started walking towards the garage. Cameron and Ollie followed behind.

'Sale still going through OK is it?' I asked him.

'Yes. Any reason it shouldn't?'

'No. When do you move to the new site?'

'Another six weeks. I've got the builders in there now, tarting the place up.'

I stopped by the pit. An rusting old Citroen AX was up on

the ramp. I went across and examined the controls.

'How did you get on with the Health and Safety? DI Reubens told me you'd had the report.'

'All clear. They couldn't find any sign of a mechanical fault.'

'That's good news for you then. You won't be liable for any damages.'

'That's right.'

'On the other hand,' I said carefully. 'It's bad news as well isn't it?'

'How do you work that out?'

'Well, something made that ramp fall so if it wasn't mechanical failure, then it must have been activated by a person.'

I walked away from him, alongside the edge of the pit.

'Well I said that all along, didn't I? Someone trying to kill me.'

'You did Ollie, and I believed you, even if the police didn't. But that was before I saw you in the Quartet.'

'What do you mean?'

'The café in Falkner Street. I saw you in there with a woman last week?'

'I never saw you.'

'You wouldn't. You were too engrossed in one another.'

'So? Am I not allowed to go out with a woman.'

'I saw you with her a week earlier too, at La Tasca in Queens Square.'

Ollie's expression darkened.

'Have you been following me, Johnny?'

'Don't be silly. Why would I do that?'

'That's what I'd like to know.'

'No, it was just coincidence. But the strange thing is, I saw your lady friend on another occasion too. At Springwood Crematorium last Friday, mourning the death of her husband,

Graham Wharton. You killed him didn't you, Ollie?'

Ollie's mouth opened but nothing came out. I carried on.

'You'd been having an affair with your chief mechanic's wife. You wanted to go away together but her husband wouldn't give her a divorce so you planned to get rid of him. It was so easy. Set the ramp to drop at the moment you walk out of the garage to greet me. Make out it was meant for you and you conveniently had all these attacks on your premises to give credence to your story. You'd had death threats. Someone wanted to kill you. Nobody had a motive to kill Graham Wharton. Nobody except you.'

'Go on.'

'That's it.'

'You can't prove it.'

'I think when I put the facts to our friend Detective Inspector Reubens, he'll be able to gather enough evidence.'

'You haven't told him yet then?'

'I thought we might go to the station together. Best get it off your chest, Ollie. I've never had you down as a killer at heart. In fact I wouldn't be surprised if your friend Mrs Wharton didn't put you up to it. Women can be the more evil of the species.' Look at Jeanne McGhee.

'That's where you're wrong.' Ollie moved away to the corner of the garage. Fenella wouldn't hurt a fly. She'd no idea Wharton's death was anything but an accident. She's a decent person.'

'But not decent enough to be faithful to her husband?'

'Fenella is a lively, intelligent woman. What was she doing married to a boring little runt like Graham Wharton.'

'She must have liked him once.'

'It was all over a long time ago but he wouldn't let her go.'

'How long had you been seeing her, Ollie?'

'Two years. Nobody here had any idea. We were very discreet. Wharton never knew she was seeing anyone, just that she wanted out of the marriage but he refused.'

'So you killed him.'

'Yes, I killed him. But you won't live to tell anybody,' and with a quick movement of his arm, he picked up a wheel brace and hurled it at me. As I ducked to avoid it, my foot slipped on a patch of oil and I fell into the same pit in which Graham Wharton had died.

Ollie ran to the ramp controls to reach for the switch that activated the mechanism. The Citroen was suspended just feet above me. I tried to stand but I'd twisted my angle. I dragged myself along the floor of the pit, painfully slowly. Any second now the car might come crashing down.

I heard Ollie scream 'This'll shut you up you interfering bastard,' and then came sounds of a struggle. I gripped the side of the pit and raised myself into a position where I could see Ollie wrestling with Cameron at the side of the pit beside the controls. As she broke from his grip, Ollie seized his opportunity and picked up tyre lever. He swung it at Cameron's head. She stepped back to avoid it then drop-kicked him in the stomach sending him tumbling into the pit beside me.

Cameron jumped down after him and, before he could regain his feet, silenced him with a pressure hold on his neck. He slid to the floor.

She turned to me. 'Does this mean promotion?'

'No, but I think it calls for champagne. If only I could walk.'

She helped me clamber out of the pit and I called Sam Reubens on my mobile.

'Another one for the rope, Sam.' I gave him the bare outline.

'They don't do the rope anymore, Johnny, more's the pity, but we'll take him in anyway. I'll send a car or will he need an ambulance like most of the people you bring us?'

I looked down into the pit. Ollie hadn't moved. 'Yeah,

you're right, Sam. Better make it an ambulance. He's had a nasty fall.'

'I thought something like that might have happened. Not a lift shaft by any chance was it?'

We waited outside the garage for Reubens to arrive. Within ten minutes, an orange and blue patrol car came screeching up the road, sirens blazing, blue light flashing.

'The only vehicle we had available,' he apologised.

'Get away, you love it.' I limped towards the pit. 'He's down there.'

'The ambulance is on its way. How is he?'

'He'll live'

'You don't look so clever yourself.'

'He's twisted his ankle,' explained Cameron.

'I thought it was his sympathy limp.'

'You've got Ronni here to thank for this one, Sam. It's her judo training. He was about to drop that battered old Citroen up there onto me. Imagine the ignominy of it. I wouldn't want to be crushed by anything less than a Bentley.'

'We picked up Victor Learoyd, by the way.' said Reubens.

'Are you able to pin anything on him?'

'Conspiring to pervert the course of justice, for starters. And that goes for his lady friend too, Mrs Farley. Did you know her husband was a doctor?'

'Is that a fact?'

'You realise I'll need you both to come and make a statement regarding the alleged murder of Mr Wharton?'

'Not another one,' I protested. 'Make it tomorrow can you, Sam? I've got a radio show to do in two hours time.'

'You can't drive with that ankle,' said Cameron. 'I'd better run you there.'

She stayed with me in the studio and, after the show, drove me home. Roly ran to the front door to greet her, jumping up and licking her face. Maria was right behind him. She took one look at me hobbling in and asked Cameron, 'What's he done?'

'I can still answer questions,' I objected.✱

'He can still answer questions,' said Cameron. 'But he's twisted his ankle. This fleabag tried to drop a car on him.'

'A Citroen AX.'

'Lucky it wasn't a Bentley,' said Maria, 'we'd never have heard the last of it. Jim Burroughs just rang, Johnny. He wants you to do him a big favour.'

'What's that?'

'He's got a last minute booking at the Floral Pavilion, New Brighton and the drummer's let them down. He wondered if you'd help him out. They're due on stage in an hour.'

'No chance.'

'Jim said it's a big show. Linda Gail Lewis is topping the bill.'

'Not Jerry Lee's sister?' Maria knew she was one of my favourite singers.

'That's the one. I'd better ring him and tell him you can't do it.'

'Hang on…'

'You can't do it with one leg.'

'I can't let Jim down, Maria, not on an important gig like this'

'Just as long as you don't think of reforming The Cruzads.'

'Never in a million years.' I looked at Cameron. 'You can drive me there, can't you, Ronni?'

'That's what you hired me for isn't it? Book it.'

Maria and I exchanged bemused glances.

'I think it means we're going,' I said.

Cameron grinned. 'Solid,' she said. 'You're getting there, guv'nor.'

'Ride on,' I replied. 'Let's hit it.'